THE
YELLOW STREAK

Valentine Williams

1st WORLD
LIBRARY
Literary Society

The Yellow Streak

Valentine Williams

© 1st World Library – Literary Society, 2005
PO Box 2211
Fairfield, IA 52556
www.1stworldlibrary.org
First Edition

LCCN: 2004195661

Softcover ISBN: 1-4218-0497-2
Hardcover ISBN: 1-4218-0397-6
eBook ISBN: 1-4218-0597-9

Purchase *"The Yellow Streak"*
as a traditional bound book at:
www.1stWorldLibrary.org/purchase.asp?ISBN=1-4218-0497-2

The Yellow Streak
contributed by Tim, Ed & Rodney
in support of
1st World Library Literary Society

CONTENTS

CHAPTER I

THE MASTER OF HARKINGS

Of all the luxuries of which Hartley Parrish's sudden rise to wealth gave him possession, Bude, his butler, was the acquisition in which he took the greatest delight and pride. Bude was a large and comfortable-looking person, triple-chinned like an archdeacon, bald-headed except for a respectable and saving edging of dark down, clean-shaven, benign of countenance, with a bold nose which to the psychologist bespoke both ambition and inborn cleverness. He had a thin, tight mouth which in itself alone was a symbol of discreet reticence, the hall-mark of the trusted family retainer.

Bude had spent his life in the service of the English aristocracy. The Earl of Tipperary, Major-General Lord Bannister, the Dowager Marchioness of Wiltshire, and Sir Herbert Marcobrunner, Bart., had in turn watched his gradual progress from pantry-boy to butler. Bude was a man whose maxim had been the French saying, "*Je prends mon bien où je le trouve.*"

In his thirty years' service he had always sought to discover and draw from those sources of knowledge which were at his disposal. From MacTavish, who had supervised Lord Tipperary's world-famous gardens, he had learnt a great deal about flowers, so that the arrangement of the floral decorations was always one of the features at Hartley Parrish's *soigné* dinner-parties. From Brun, the unsurpassed *chef*, whom Lord Bannister had picked up when serving with the Guards in Egypt, he had gathered sufficient knowledge of the higher branches of the cuisine to enable Hartley Parrish to leave the arrangement of the menu in his butler's hands.

Bude would have been the first to admit that, socially speaking, his present situation was not the equal of the positions he had held. There was none of the staid dignity about his present employer which was inborn in men like Lord Tipperary or Lord Bannister, and which Sir Herbert Marcobrunner, with the easy assimilative faculty of his race, had very successfully acquired. Below middle height, thick-set and power-fully built, with a big head, narrow eyes, and a massive chin, Hartley Parrish, in his absorbed concentration on his business, had no time for the acquisition or practice of the Eton manner.

It was characteristic of Parrish that, seeing Bude at a dinner-party at Marcobruaner's, he should have engaged him on the spot. It took Bude a week to get over his shock at the manner in which the offer was made. Parrish had approached him as he was super-vising the departure of the guests. Waving aside the footman who offered to help him into his overcoat, Parrish had asked Bude point-blank what wages he was getting. Bude mentioned the generous remune-ration he was receiving from Sir Herbert Marcob-runner, whereupon Parrish had remarked:

"Come to me and I'll double it. I'll give you a week to

Valentine Williams

think it over. Let my secretary know!"

After a few discreet enquiries, Bude, faithful to his maxim, had accepted Parrish's offer. Marcobrunner was furiously angry, but, being anxious to interest Parrish in a deal, sagely kept his feelings to himself. And Bude had never regretted the change. He found Parrish an exacting, but withal a just and a generous master, and he was not long in realizing that, as long as he kept Harkings, Parrish's country place where he spent the greater part of his time, running smoothly according to Parrish's schedule, he could count on a life situation.

The polish of manner, the sober dignity of dress, acquired from years of acute observation in the service of the nobility, were to be seen as, at the hour of five, in the twilight of this bleak autumn afternoon, Bude moved majestically into the lounge-hall of Harkings and leisurely pounded the gong for tea.

The muffled notes of the gong swelled out brazenly through the silent house. They echoed down the softly carpeted corridors to the library where the master of the house sat at his desk. For days he had been immersed in the figures of the new issue which Hornaway's, the vast engineering business of his creation, was about to put on the market. They reverberated up the fine old oak staircase to the luxurious Louis XV bedroom, where Lady Margaret Trevert lay on her bed idly smiling through an amusing novel. They crashed through the thickly padded baize doors leading to the servants' hall, where, at sixpence a hundred, Parrish's man, Jay, was partnering Lady Margaret's maid against Mrs. Heever, the housekeeper, and Robert, the chauffeur, at a friendly game of bridge. And they even boomed distantly into the far-away billiard-room and broke into the talk which Robin Greve was having with Mary Trevert.

"Damn!" exclaimed Greve savagely, as the distant gonging came to his ears.

"It's the gong for tea," said Mary demurely.

She was sitting on one of the big leather sofas lining the long room. Robin, as he gazed down at her from where he stood with his back against the edge of the billiard-table, thought what an attractive picture she made in the half-light.

The lamps over the table were lit, but the rest of the room was almost dark. In that lighting the thickly waving dark hair brought out the fine whiteness of the girl's skin. There was love, and a great desire for love, in her large dark eyes, but the clear-cut features, the well-shaped chin , and the firm mouth , the lips a little full, spoke of ambition and the love of power.

"I've been here three whole days," said Robin, "and I've not had two words with you alone, Mary. And hardly have I got you to myself for a quiet game of pills when that rotten gong goes ..."

"I'm sorry you're disappointed at missing your game," the girl replied mischievously, "but I expect you will be able to get a game with Horace or one of the others after tea ..."

Robin kicked the carpet savagely.

"You know perfectly well I don't want to play billiards ..."

He looked up and caught the girl's eye. For a fraction of a second he saw in it the expression which every man at least once in his life looks to see in the eyes of one particular woman. In the girl's dark-blue eyes fringed with long black lashes he saw the dumb appeal, the mute surrender, which, as surely as the white flag on the battlements in war, is the signal of capitulation in woman.

But the expression was gone on the instant. It passed so swiftly that, for a second, Robin, seeing the gently mocking glance that succeeded it, wondered whether he had been mistaken.

But he was a man of action - a glance at his long, well-moulded head, his quick, wide-open eye, and his square jaw would have told you that - and he spoke.

"It's no use beating about the bush," he said. "Mary, I've got so fond of you that I'm just miserable when you're away from me ..."

"Oh, Robin, please ..."

Mary Trevert stood up and remained standing, her head turned a little away from him, a charming silhouette in her heather-blue shooting-suit.

The young man took her listless hand.

"My dear," he said, "you and I have been pals all our lives. It was only at the front that I began to realize just how much you meant to me. And now I know I can't do without you. I've never met any one who has been to me just what you are. And, Mary, I must have you as my wife ..."

The girl remained motionless. She kept her face averted. The room seemed very still.

"Oh, Robin, please ..." she murmured again.

Resolutely the young man put an arm about her and drew her to him. Slowly, reluctantly, she let him have his way. But she would not look at him.

"Oh, my dear," he whispered, kissing her hair, "don't you care a little?"

She remained silent.

"Won't you look at me, Mary?"

There was a hint of huskiness in his voice. He raised her face to his.

"I saw in your eyes just now that you cared for me," he whispered; "oh, my Mary, say that you do!"

Then he bent down and kissed her. For a brief instant their lips met and he felt the caress of the girl's arm about his neck.

"Oh, Robin!" she said.

That was all.

But then she drew away.

Valentine Williams

Reluctantly the man let her go. The colour had faded from his cheeks when she looked at him again as he stood facing her in the twilight of the billiard-room.

"Robin, dear," she said, "I'm going to hurt you."

The young man seemed to have had a premonition of what was coming, for he betrayed no sign of surprise, but remained motionless, very erect, very pale.

"Dear," said the girl with a little despairing shrug, "it's hopeless! We can't afford to marry!"

"Not yet, I know," said Robin, "but I'm getting on well, Mary, and in another year or two ..."

The girl looked down at the point of her little brogue shoe.

"I don't know what you will think of me," she said, "but I can't accept ... I can't face ... I ..."

"You can't face the idea of being the wife of a man who has his way to make. Is that it?"

The voice was rather stern.

The girl looked up impulsively.

"I can't, Robin. I should never make you happy. Mother and I are as poor as church-mice. All the money in the family goes to keep Horace in the Army and pay for my clothes."

She looked disdainfully at her pretty suit.

"All this," she went on with a little hopeless gesture indicating her tailor-made, "is Mother's investment. No, no, it's true ... I can tell you as a friend, Robin, dear, we are living on our capital until I have caught a rich husband ..."

"Oh, my dear," said Robin softly, "don't say things like that ..."

The girl laughed a little defiantly.

"But it's true," she answered. "The war has halved Mother's income and there's nothing between us and bankruptcy but a year or so ... unless I get married!"

Her voice trembled a little and she turned away.

"Mary," said the young man hoarsely, "for God's sake, don't do that!"

He moved a step towards her, but she drew back.

"It's all right," she said with the tears glistening wet on her face, and dabbed at her eyes with her tiny handkerchief, "but, oh, Robin boy, why couldn't you have held your tongue?"

"I suppose I had no right to speak ..." the young man began.

The girl sighed.

"I oughtn't to say it ... now," she said slowly, and looked across at Robin with shining eyes, "but, Robin dear, I'm ... I'm glad you did!"

She paused a moment as though turning something over in her mind.

"I've...I've got something to tell you, Robin," she began. "No, stay where you are! We must be sensible now."

She paused and looked at him.

"Robin," she said slowly, "I've promised to marry somebody else ..."

There was a moment's silence.

"Who is it?" Robin asked in a hard voice.

The girl made no answer.

"Who is it? Do I know him?"

Still the girl was silent, but she gave a hardly perceptible nod.

"Not ...? No, no, Mary, it isn't true? It can't be true?"

The girl nodded, her eyes to the ground.

"It's a secret still," she said. "No one knows but Mother. Hartley doesn't want it announced yet!"

The sound of the Christian name suddenly seemed to infuriate Greve.

"By God!" he cried, "it shan't be! You must be mad, Mary, to think of marrying a man like Hartley Parrish. A fellow who's years older than you, who thinks of nothing but money, who stood out of the war and made a fortune while men of his own age were doing the fighting for him! It's unthinkable ... it's ... it's damnable to think of a gross, ill-bred creature like Parrish ..."

"Robin!" the girl cried, "you seem to forget that we're staying in his house. In spite of all you say he seems to be good enough for you to come and stay with ..."

"I only came because you were to be here. You know that perfectly well. I admit one oughtn't to blackguard one's host, but, Mary, you must see that this marriage is absolutely out of the question!"

The girl began to bridle up,

"Why?" she asked loftily.

"Because ... because Parrish is not the sort of man who will make you happy ..."

"And why not, may I ask? He's very kind and very generous, and I believe he likes me ..."

Robin Greve made a gesture of despair.

"My dear girl," he said, trying to control himself to speak quietly, "what do you know about this man? Nothing. But there are beastly stories circulating about his life ..."

Mary Trevert laughed cynically.

"My dear old Robin," she said, "they tell stories about every bachelor. And I hardly think you are an unbiassed judge ..."

Robin Greve was pacing up and down the floor.

"You're crazy, Mary," he said, stopping in front of her, "to dream you can ever be happy with a man like Hartley Parrish. The man's a ruthless egoist. He thinks of nothing but money and he's out to buy you just exactly as you ..."

"As I am ready to sell myself!" the girl echoed. "And I *am* ready, Robin. It's all very well for you to stand there and preach ideals at me, but I'm sick and disgusted at the life we've been leading for the past three years, hovering on the verge of ruin all the time, dunned by tradesmen and having to borrow even from servants ... yes, from old servants of the family ... to pay Mother's bridge debts. Mother's a good sort. Father spent all her money for her and she was brought up in exactly the same helpless way as she brought up me. I can do absolutely nothing except the sort of elementary nursing which we all learnt in the war, and if I don't marry well Mother will have to keep a boarding-house or do something ghastly like that. I'm not going to pretend that I'm thinking only of her, because I'm not. I can't face a long engagement with no prospects except castles in Spain. I don't mean to be callous, Robin, but I expect I am naturally hard. Hartley Parrish is a good sort. He's very fond of me, and he will see that Mother lives comfortably for the rest of her life. I've promised to marry him because I like him and he's a suitable match. And I don't see by what right you try and run him down to me behind his back! If it's jealousy, then it shows a very petty spirit!"

Robin Greve stepped close up to Mary Trevert. His eyes were very angry and his jaw was set very square.

"If you are determined to sell yourself to the highest bidder," he said, "I suppose there's no stopping you. But you're making a mistake. If Parrish were all you claim for him, you might not repent of his marriage so long as you did not care for somebody else. But I know you love me, and it breaks my heart to see you blundering into everlasting unhappiness ..."

"At least Hartley will be able to keep me," the girl flashed out. Directly she had spoken she regretted her words.

A red flush spread slowly over Robin Greve's face.

Then he laughed drily.

"You won't be the first woman he's kept!" be retorted, and stamped out of the billiard-room.

The girl gave a little gasp. Then she reddened with anger.

"How dare he?" she cried, stamping her foot; "how dare he?"

She sank on the lounge and, burying her face in her hands, burst into tears.

"Oh, Robin, Robin, dear!" she sobbed - incomprehensibly, for she was a woman.

CHAPTER II

AT TWILIGHT

There is a delicious snugness, a charming lack of formality, about the ceremony of afternoon tea in an English country-house - it is much too indefinite a rite to dignify it by the name of meal - which makes it the most pleasant reunion of the day. For English country-house parties consist, for the most part, of a succession of meals to which the guests flock the more congenially as, in the interval, they have contrived to avoid one another's companionship.

And so, scarcely had the last reverberation of Bude's measured gonging died away than the French window leading from the lounge-hall on to the terrace was pushed open and two of Hartley Parrish's guests emerged from the falling darkness without into the pleasant comfort of the firelit room.

They were an oddly matched pair. The one was a tubby little man with short bristly grey hair and a short bristly grey moustache to match. His stumpy legs looked ridiculous in his baggy golf knickers of rough tweed, which he wore with gaiters extending half-way up his short, stout calves. As he came in, he slung off the heavy tweed shooting-cloak he had been wearing and placed it with his Homburg hat on a chair.

This was Dr. Romain, whose name thus written seems indecently naked without the string of complementary initials indicative of the honours and degrees which years of bacteriological research had heaped upon him. His companion was a tall, slim, fair-haired young man, about as good a specimen of the young Englishman turned out by the English public school as one could find. He was extremely good-looking with a proud eye and finely chiselled features, but the suggestion of youth in his face and figure was countered by a certain poise, a kind of latent seriousness which contrasted strangely with the general cheery *insouciance* of his type.

A soldier would have spotted the symptoms at once, "Five years of war!" would have been his verdict - that long and strange entry into life of so many thousands of England's manhood which impressed the stamp of premature seriousness on all those who came through. And Captain Sir Horace Trevert, Bart., D.S.O., had gone from his famous school straight into a famous regiment, had won his decoration before he was twenty-one, and been twice wounded into the bargain.

"Where's everybody?" queried the doctor, rubbing his hands at the blazing log-fire.

"Robin and Mary went off to play billiards," said the young man, "and I left old Parrish after lunch settling down for an afternoon's work in the library ..."

He crossed the room to the fire and stood with his back to the flame.

"What a worker that man is!" ejaculated the doctor. "He had one of his secretaries down this morning with

Valentine Williams

a car full of portfolios, blue-prints, specifications, and God knows what else. Parrish polished the whole lot off and packed the fellow back to London before midday. Some of Hornaway's people who were waiting went in next, and he was through with them by lunchtime!"

Trevert wagged his head in admiration.

"And he told me he wanted to have a quiet week-end!" he said. "That's why he has no secretary living in the house."

"A quiet week-end!" repeated Romain drily. "Ye gods!"

"He's a marvel for work," said the young man.

"He certainly is," replied the doctor. "He's done wonders with Hornaway's. When he took the place over at the beginning of the war, they were telling me, it was a little potty concern making toy air guns or lead soldiers or something of the sort. And they never stop coining money now, it seems. Parrish must be worth millions ..."

"Lucky devil!" said Trevert genially.

"Ah!" observed the doctor sententiously, "but he's had to work for it, mark you! He's had the most extraordinary life, they tell me. He was at one period of his career a bartender on the Rand, a man was saying at the club the other day. But most of his life he's lived in Canada, I gather. He was telling us the other evening, before you and Mary came down, that he was once a brakeman on the Canadian Pacific Railway. He said he invested all his savings in books on engineering and read them in his brakeman's van on his trips across the Dominion. Ah! he's a fine fellow!"

He lowered his voice discreetly.

"And a devilish good match, eh, Horace?"

The young man flushed slightly.

"Yes," he said unwillingly.

"A dam' good match for somebody," urged the doctor with a malicious twinkle in his eye.

"Here, Doc," said Horace, suddenly turning on him, "you stick to your bugs and germs. What do you know about matchmaking, anyway?"

Dr. Romain chuckled.

"We bacteriologists are trained observers. One learns a lot watching the life and habits of the bacillus, Horace, my boy. And between ourselves, Parrish would be a lucky fellow if ..."

Trevert turned to him. His face was quite serious, and there was a little touch of hauteur in his voice. He was the 17th Baronet.

"My dear Doc," he said, "aren't you going a bit fast? Parrish is a very good chap, but one knows nothing about him ..."

Sagely the doctor nodded his grizzled head.

"That's true," he agreed. "He appears to have no relatives and nobody over here seems to have heard of him before the war. A man was saying at the Athenaeum the other day ..."

Trevert touched his elbow. Bude had appeared, portly, imperturbable, bearing a silver tray set out with the appliances for tea.

"Bude," cried Trevert, "don't tell me there are no tea-cakes again!"

"On the contrairey, sir," answered the butler in the richly sonorous voice pitched a little below the normal register which he employed abovestairs, "the cook has had her attention drawn to it. There are tea-cakes, sir!"

With a certain dramatic effect - for Bude was a trifle theatrical in everything he did - he whipped the cover off a dish and displayed a smoking pile of deliciously browned scones.

"Bude," said Trevert, "when I'm a Field Marshal, I'll see you get the O.B.E. for this!"

The butler smiled a nicely regulated three-by-one smile, a little deprecatory as was his wont. Then, like a tank taking a corner, he wheeled majestically and turned to cross the lounge. To reach the green baize door leading to the servants' quarters he had to cross the outer hall from which led corridors on the right and left. That on the right led to the billiard-room; that on the left to the big drawing-room with the library beyond.

As Bude reached the great screen of tooled Spanish

leather which separated a corner of the lounge from the outer hall, Robin Greve came hastily through the glass door of the corridor leading from the billiard-room. The butler with a pleasant smile drew back a little to allow the young man to pass, thinking he was going into the lounge for tea.

"Tea is ..." he began, but abruptly ended the sentence on catching sight of the young man's face. For Robin, habitually so self-possessed, looked positively haggard. His face was set and there was a weary look in his eyes. The young man appeared so utterly different from his wonted self that Bude fairly stared at him.

But Robin, without paying the least attention either to the butler or to the sound of voices in the lounge, strode across the outer hall and disappeared through the glass door of the corridor leading to the great drawing-room and the library.

Bude stood an instant gazing after him in perplexity, then moved across the hall to the servants' quarters.

In the meantime in the lounge the little doctor snapped the case of his watch and opined that he wanted his tea.

"Where on earth has everybody got to? What's become of Lady Margaret? I haven't seen her since lunch...."

That lady answered his question by appearing in person.

Lady Margaret was tall and hard and glittering. Like so many Englishwomen of good family, she was so saturated with the traditions of her class that her manner was almost indistinguishable from that of a man. Well-mannered, broadminded, wholly cynical, and absolutely fearless, she went through life exactly as though she were following a path carefully taped out for her by a suitably instructed Providence. Somewhere beneath the mask of smiling indifference she presented so bravely to a difficult world, she had a heart, but so carefully did she hide it that Horace had only discovered it on a certain grey November morning when he had started out for the first time on active service. For ever afterwards a certain weighing-machine at Waterloo Station, by which he had had a startling vision of his mother standing with heaving bosom and tear-stained face, possessed in his mind the attributes of some secret and sacred shrine.

But now she was cool and well-gowned and self-contained as ever.

"What a perfectly dreadful day!" she exclaimed in her pleasant, well-bred voice. "Horace, you must positively go and see Henry What's-his-name in the Foreign Office and get me a passport for Cannes. The weather in England in the winter is incredibly exaggerated!"

"At least," said the doctor, rubbing his back as he warmed himself at the fire, "we have fuel in England. Give me England, climate and all, but don't take away my fire. The sun doesn't shine on the Riviera at night, you know!"

Lady Margaret busied herself at the tea-table with its fine Queen Anne silver and dainty yellow cups. It was the custom at Harkings to serve tea in the winter without other illumination than the light of the great log-fire that spat and leaped in the open hearth.

Beyond the semi-circle of ruddy light the great lounge was all in darkness, and beyond that again was the absolute stillness of the English country on a winter's evening.

And so with a gentle clatter of teacups and the accompaniment of pleasantly modulated voices they sat and chatted - Lady Margaret, who was always surprising in what she said, the doctor who was incredibly opinionated, and young Trevert, who like all of the younger generation was daringly flippant. He was airing his views on what he called "Boche music" when he broke off and cried:

"Hullo, here's Mary! Mary, you owe me half a crown. Bude has come up to scratch and there are tea-cakes after ... but, I say, what on earth's the matter?"

The girl had come into the room and was standing in the centre of the lounge in the ruddy glow of the fire. Her face was deathly pale and she was shuddering violently. She held her little cambric handkerchief crushed up into a ball to her lips. Her eyes were fixed, almost glazed, like one who walks in a trance.

She stood like that for an instant surveying the group - Lady Margaret, a silver tea-pot in one hand, looking at her with uplifted brows. Horace, who in his amazement had taken a step forward, and the doctor at his side scrutinizing her beneath his shaggy eyebrows.

"My dear Mary " - it was Lady Margaret's smooth and pleasant voice which broke the silence - "whatever is the matter? Have you seen a ghost!"

The girl swayed a little and opened her lips as if to

Valentine Williams

speak. A log, crashing from the fire into the grate, fell upon the silence of the darkening room. It seemed to break the spell.

"Hartley!"

The name came hoarsely from the girl. Everybody, except Lady Margaret, sprang to his feet It was the doctor who spoke first.

"Miss Mary," he said, "you seem frightened, what ..."

His voice was very soothing.

Mary Trevert made a vague gesture towards the shadows about the staircase.

"There ... in the library ... he's got the door locked ... there was a shot ..."

Then she suddenly screamed aloud.

In a stride both the doctor and her brother were by her side. But she motioned them away.

"I'm frightened about Hartley," she said in a low voice, "please go at once and see what ... that shot ... and he doesn't answer!"

"Come on, Doctor!"

Horace Trevert was halfway to the big screen separating the lounge from the outer hall. As he passed the bell, he pressed it.

"Send Bude to us, Mother, when he comes, please!" he

called as he and the doctor hurried away.

Lady Margaret had risen and stood, one arm about her daughter, on the Persian rug spread out before the cheerful fire. So the women stood in the firelight in Hartley Parrish's house, surrounded by all the treasures which his wealth had bought, and listened to the footsteps clattering away through the silence.

CHAPTER III

A DISCOVERY

Harkings was not a large house. Some three hundred years ago it had been a farm, but in the intervening years successive owners had so altered it by pulling down and building on, that, when it passed into the possession of Hartley Parrish, little else than the open fireplace in the lounge remained to tell of the original farm. It was a queer, rambling house of only two stories whose elongated shape was accentuated by the additional wing which Hartley Parrish had built on.

For the decoration of his country-house, Parrish had placed himself unreservedly in the hands of the firm entrusted with the work. Their architect was given *carte blanche* to produce a house of character out of the rather dingy, out-of-date country villa which Harkings was when Hartley Parrish, attracted by the view from the gardens, first discovered it.

The architect had gone to his work with a zest. He had ripped up walls and ceilings and torn down irrational matchwood partitions, discovering some fine old oak wainscot and the blackened roof-beams of the original farmstead. In the upshot he transformed Harkings into a very fair semblance of a late Jacobean house, fitted with every modern convenience and extremely comfortable. Furnished throughout with genuine "period" furniture, with fine dark oak panelling and parquet floors, it was altogether picturesque. Neither within nor without, it is true, would a connoisseur have been able to give it a date.

But that did not worry Hartley Parrish. He loved a bargain and he had bought the house cheap. It was situated in beautiful country and was within easy reach by car of his town-house in St. James's Square where he lived for the greater part of the week. Last but not least Harkings was the casket enshrining a treasure, the realization of a lifelong wish. This was the library, Parrish's own room, designed by himself and furnished to his own individual taste.

It stood apart from the rest of the house at the end of the wing which Parrish had constructed. The wing consisted of a single ground floor and contained the drawing-room - which was scarcely ever used, as both Parrish and his guests preferred the more congenial surroundings of the lounge - and the library. A long corridor panelled in oak led off the hall to the new wing. On to this corridor both the drawing-room and the library gave. Halfway down the corridor a small passage ran off. It separated the drawing-room from the library and ended in a door leading into the gardens at the back of the house.

It was to the new wing that Horace Trevert and Dr. Komain now hastened. They hurried across the hall, where the big lamp of dulled glass threw a soft yellow light, and entered the corridor through the heavy oak door which shut it off from the hall. The corridor was wrapt in silence. Halfway down, where the small passage ran to the garden door, the electric light

Valentine Williams

was burning.

Horace Trevert ran down the corridor ahead of the doctor and was the first to reach the library door. He knocked sharply, then turned the handle. The door was locked.

"Hartley!" he cried and rapped again. "Ha-a-artley! Open the door! It's me, Horace!"

Again he knocked and rattled the handle. Not a sound came from the locked room. There was an instant's silence. Horace and the doctor exchanged an interrogatory look.

From behind the closed door came the steady ticking of a clock. The silence was so absolute that both men heard it.

Then the door at the end of the corridor was flung open and Bude appeared. He was running at a quick ambling trot, his heavy tread shaking the passage,

"Oh? sir," he cried, "whatever is it? What has happened?"

Horace spoke quickly, incisively.

"Something's happened to Mr. Parrish, Bude," he said. "The door's locked and he doesn't answer. We'll have to break the door down."

Bude shook his head.

"It's solid oak, sir," he began.

Then he raised his hand.

"Pardon me, gentlemen," he said, as though an idea had struck him. "If we were to go out by the garden door here, we might get in through the window. We could break the glass if needs be!"

"That's it!" exclaimed Horace. "Come on, Doctor!"

He dashed down the corridor towards the little passage. The doctor laid a hand on Bude's arm.

"One of us had better stay here," he said with a meaning glance at the closed door.

The butler raised an affrighted face to his.

"Go with Sir Horace, Bude," said the doctor. "I'll stay!"

Outside in the gardens of Harkings it was a raw, damp evening, pitch-black now, with little gusts of wind which shook the naked bushes of the rosery. The garden door led by a couple of shallow steps on to a gravel path which ran all along the back of the house. The path extended right up to the wall of the house. On the other side it flanked the rosery.

The glass door was banging to and fro in the night wind as Bude, his coat-collar turned up, hurried out into the darkness. The library, which formed the corner of the new wing, had two windows, the one immediately above the gravel path looking out over the rosery, the other round the corner of the house giving on the same path, beyond which ran a high hedge of clipped box surrounding the so-called Pleasure Ground, a plot of smooth grass with a sundial in

Valentine Williams

the centre.

A glow of light came from the library window, and in its radiance Bude saw silhouetted the tall, well-knit figure of young Trevert. As the butler came up, the boy raised something in his hand and there was a crash of broken glass.

The curtains were drawn, but with the breaking of the window they began to flap about. With the iron grating he had picked up from the drain below the window young Trevert smashed the rest of the glass away, then thrust an arm through the empty window-frame, fumbling for the window-catch.

"The catch is not fastened," he whispered, and with a resolute thrust he pushed the window up. The curtains leapt up wildly, revealing a glimpse of the pleasant, book-lined room. Both men from the darkness without saw Parrish's desk littered with his papers and his habitual chair beyond it, pushed back empty.

Trevert turned an instant, a hand on the window-sill.

"Bude," he said, "there's no one there!"

"Best look and see, sir," replied the butler, his coat-tails flapping in the wind.

Trevert hoisted himself easily on to the window-sill, knelt there for an instant, then thrust his legs over the sill and dropped into the room. As he did so he stumbled, cried aloud.

Then the heavy grey curtains were flung back and the butler saw the boy's face, rather white, at the open window.

"My God," he said slowly, "he's dead!"

A moment later Dr. Romain, waiting in the corridor, heard the key turn in the lock of the library door. The door was flung open. Horace Trevert stood there, silhouetted in a dull glow of light from the room. He was pointing to the open window, beneath which Hartley Parrish lay on his back motionless.

CHAPTER IV

BETWEEN THE DESK AND THE WINDOW

Hartley Parrish's library was a splendid room, square in shape, lofty and well proportioned. It was lined with books arranged in shelves of dark brown oak running round the four walls, but sunk level with them and reaching up to a broad band of perfectly plain white plasterwork.

It was a cheerful, comfortable, eminently modern room, half library, half office. The oak was solid, but uncompromisingly new. The great leather armchairs were designed on modern lines - for comfort rather than for appearance. There were no pictures; but vases of chrysanthemums stood here and there about the room. A dictaphone in a case was in a corner, but beside it was a little table on which were set out some rare bits of old Chelsea. There was also a gramophone, but it was enclosed in a superb case of genuine old black-and-gold lacquer. The very books in their shelves carried on this contrast of business with recreation. For while one set of shelves contained row upon row of technical works, company reports, and all manner of business reference books bound in leather, on another were to be found the vellum-bound volumes of the Kelmscott Press.

A sober note of grey or mole colour was the colour scheme of the room. The heavy pile carpet which stretched right up to the walls was of this quiet neutral shade: so were the easy-chairs, and the colour of the heavy curtains, which hung in front of the two high windows, was in harmony with the restful decorative scheme of the room.

The massive oaken door stood opposite the window overlooking the rosery - the window through which Horace Trevert had entered. Parrish's desk was in front of this window, between it and the door in consequence. By the other window, which, as has been stated, looked out on the clipped hedge surrounding the Pleasure Ground, was the little table with the Chelsea china, the dictaphone, and one of the easy-chairs. The centre of the room was clear so that nothing lay between the door and the carved mahogany chair at the desk. Here, as they all knew, Parrish was accustomed to sit when working, his back to the door, his face to the window overlooking the rosery.

The desk stood about ten feet from the window. On it was a large brass lamp which cast a brilliant circle of light upon the broad flat top of the desk with its orderly array of letter-trays, its handsome silver-edged blotter and silver and tortoise-shell writing appurtenances. By the light of this lamp Dr. Romain, looking from the doorway, saw that Hartley Parrish's chair was vacant, pushed back a little way from the desk. The rest of the room was wrapt in unrevealing half-light.

"He's there by the window!"

Horace was whispering to the doctor. Romain strode over to the desk and picked up the lamp. As he did so, his eyes fell upon the pale face of Hartley Parrish. He lay on his back in the space between the desk and the window. His head was flung back, his eyes, bluish-grey, - the narrow, rather expressionless eyes of the successful business man, - were wide open and fixed in a sightless stare, his rather full mouth, with its clean-shaven lips, was rigid and stern. With the broad forehead, the prominent brows, the bold, aggressive nose, and the square bony jaw, it was a fighter's face, a fine face save for the evil promise of that sensuous mouth. So thought the doctor with the swift psychological process of his trade.

From the face his gaze travelled to the body. And then Romain could not repress an involuntary start, albeit he saw what he had half expected to see. The fleshy right hand of Hartley Parrish grasped convulsively an automatic pistol. His clutching index finger was crooked about the trigger and the barrel was pressed into the yielding pile of the carpet. His other hand with clawing fingers was flung out away from the body on the other side. One leg was stretched out to its fullest extent and the foot just touched the hem of the grey window curtains. The other leg was slightly drawn up.

The doctor raised the lamp from the desk and, dropping on one knee, placed it on the ground beside the body. With gentle fingers he manipulated the eyes, opened the blue serge coat and waistcoat which Parrish was wearing. As he unbuttoned the waistcoat, he laid bare a dark red stain on the breast of the fine silk shirt. He opened shirt and under-vest, bent an ear to the still form, and then, with a little helpless gesture, rose to his feet.

"Dead?" queried Trevert.

Romain nodded shortly.

"Shot through the heart!" he said.

"He looked so ... so limp," the boy said, shrinking back a little, "I thought he was dead. But I never thought old Hartley would have done a thing like that ..."

The doctor pursed up his lips as if to speak. But he remained silent for a moment. Then he said:

"Horace, the police must be informed. We can do that on the telephone. This room must be left just as it is until they come. I can do nothing more for poor Hartley. And we shall have to tell the others. I'd better do that myself. I wonder where Greve is? I haven't seen him all the afternoon. As a barrister he should be able to advise us about - er, the technicalities: the police and all that ..."

Rapid footsteps reverberated down the corridor. Robin Greve appeared at the door. The fat and frightened face of Bude appeared over his shoulder.

"Good God, Doctor!" he cried, "what's this Bude tells me?"

The doctor cleared his throat.

"Our poor friend is dead, Greve," he said.

"But how? How?"

Greve stood opposite the doctor in the centre of the library. He had switched on the light at the door as he had come in, and the room was flooded with soft light thrown by concealed lamps set around the cornice of the ceiling.

"Look!" responded the doctor by way of answer and stepped aside to let the young man come up to the desk. "He has a pistol in his hand!"

Robin Greve took a step forward and stopped dead. He gazed for an instant without speaking on the dead face of his host and rival.

"Suicide!"

It was an affirmation rather than a question, and the little doctor took it up. He was not a young man and the shock and the excitement were beginning to tell on his nerves.

"I am not a police surgeon," he said with some asperity; "in fact, I may say I have not seen a dead body since my hospital days. I ... I ... know nothing about these things. This is a matter for the police. They must be summoned at once. Where's Bude?"

Robin Greve turned quickly.

"Get on to the police station at Stevenish at once, Bude," he ordered. "Do you know the Inspector?"

"Yessir," the butler answered in a hollow voice. His hands were trembling violently, and he seemed to control himself with difficulty. "Mr. Humphries, sir!"

"Well, ring him up and tell him that Mr. Parrish ... Hullo, what do all these people want?"

There was a commotion at the door. Frightened faces were framed in the doorway. Outside there was the sound of a woman whimpering. A tall, dark young man in a tail coat came in quickly. He stopped short when he saw the solemn faces of the group at the desk. It was Parrish's man, Jay. He stepped forward to the desk and in a frightened sort of way peered at the body as it lay on the floor.

"Oh, sir," he said breathlessly, addressing Greve, "what ever has happened to Mr. Parrish? It can't be true ..."

Greve put his hand on the young man's shoulder.

"I'm sorry to say it is true, Jay," he answered.

"He was very good to us all," the valet replied in a broken voice. He remained by the desk staring at the body in a dazed fashion.

"Who is that crying outside?" Greve demanded. "This is no place for women ..."

"It's Mrs. Heever, the housekeeper," Bude answered.

"Well, she must go back to her room. Send all those servants away. Jay, will you see to it? And take care that Lady Margaret and Miss Trevert don't come in here, either."

"Sir Horace is with them, sir, in the lounge," said Jay and went out.

"I'll go to them. I think I'd better," exclaimed the doctor. "I shall be in the lounge when they want me. A dreadful affair! Dreadful!"

The little doctor bustled out, leaving Greve and the butler alone in the room with the mortal remains of Hartley Parrish lying where he had fallen on the soft grey carpet.

"Now, Bude," said Greve incisively, "get on to the police at once. You'd better telephone from the servant's hall. I'll have a look round here in the meantime!"

Bude stood for an instant irresolute. He glanced shrewdly at the young man.

"Go on," said Robin quickly; "what are you waiting for, man? There's no time to lose."

Slowly the butler turned and tiptoed away, his ungainly body swaying about as he stole across the heavy pile carpet. He went out of the room, closing the door softly behind him. He left Greve sunk in a reverie at the desk, gazing with unseeing eyes upon the dead face of the master of Harkings.

That sprawling corpse, the startled realization of death stamped for ever in the wide, staring eyes, was indeed a subject for meditation. There, in the midst of all the evidences of Hartley Parrish's meteoric rise to afflu- ence and power, Greve pondered for an instant on the strange pranks which Fate plays us poor mortals.

Parrish had risen, as Greve and all the world knew, from the bottom rung of the ladder. He had had a bitter fight for existence, had made his money, as Greve had heard, with a blind and ruthless determination which spoke of the stern struggle of other days. And Robin, who, too, had had his own way to make in the world, knew how the memory of earlier struggles went to sweeten the flavour of ultimate success.

Yet here was Hartley Parrish, with his vast financial undertakings, his soaring political ambitions, his social aims which, Robin realized bitterly, had more than a little to do with his project for marrying Mary Trevert, stricken down suddenly, without warning, in the very heyday of success.

"Why should he have done it?" he whispered to himself, "why, my God, why?"

But the mask-like face at his feet, as he bent to scan it once more, gave no answer to the riddle. Determination, ambition, was portrayed on the keen, eager face even in death.

With a little hopeless gesture the young barrister glanced round the room. His eye fell upon the desk. He saw a neat array of letter-trays, costly silver and tortoise-shell writing appointments, a couple of heavy gold fountain pens, and an orderly collection of pencils. Lying flat on the great silver-edged blotter was a long brown envelope which had been opened. Propped up against the large crystal ink-well was a letter addressed simply "Miss Mary Trevert" in Hartley Parrish's big, vigorous, and sprawling handwriting.

The letter to Mary Trevert, Robin did not touch. But he picked up the long brown envelope. On the back it bore a printed seal. The envelope contained a document and a letter. At the sight of it the young man started. It was Hartley Parrish's will. The letter was merely a covering note from Mr. Bardy, of the firm of Jerringham, Bardy and Company, a well-known firm of solicitors, dated the previous evening. Robin replaced letter and document in their envelope without reading them.

"So that's it!" he murmured to himself. "Suicide? But why?"

All the letter-trays save one were empty. In this was a little heap of papers and letters. Robin glanced through them. There were two or three prospectuses, a notice of a golf match, a couple of notes from West End tradesmen enclosing receipts and an acknowledgement from the bank. There was only one personal letter - a business communication from a Rotterdam firm. Robin glanced at the letter. It was typewritten on paper of a dark slatey-blue shade. It was headed, "ELIAS VAN DER SPYCK & Co., GENERAL IMPORTERS, ROTTERDAM," and dealt with steel shipments.

Robin dropped the letter back into the tray and turned to survey the room. It was in perfect order. Except for the still form lying on the floor and the broken pane of glass in the window, there was nothing to tell of the tragedy which had been enacted there that afternoon. There were no papers to hint at a crisis save the prosaic-looking envelope containing the will, and Parrish's note for Mary. The waste-paper basket, a large and business-like affair in white wicker, had been cleared.

Robin walked across to the fireplace. The flames leapt eagerly about a great oak log which hissed fitfully on top of the glowing coals contained in the big iron fire-basket. The grate was bare and tidy. As the young man looked at the fire, a little whirl of blue smoke whisked out of the wide fireplace and eddied into the room.

Robin sniffed. The room smelt smoky. Now he remembered he had noticed it as he came in.

He stood an instant gazing thoughtfully at the blazing and leaping fire. He threw a quick glance at the window where the curtains tossed fitfully in the breeze coming through the broken pane. Suddenly he stepped quickly across the room and, lifting the reading-lamp from the table, bore it over to the window which he scrutinized narrowly by its light. Then he dropped on one knee beside the dead body, placing the lamp on the floor beside him.

He lifted the dead man's left hand and narrowly examined the nails. Without touching the right hand which clasped the revolver, he studied its nails too. He rose and took the gold-mounted reading-glass from the desk and scrutinized the nails of both hands through the glass.

Then he rose to his feet again and, having replaced lamp and reading-glass on the desk, stood there thoughtfully, his brown hands clasped before him. His eyes wandered from the desk to the window and from the window to the corpse. Then he noticed on the carpet between the dead body and the desk a little ball of slatey-blue paper. He bent down and picked it up. He had begun to unroll it when the library door was flung open. Robin thrust the scrap of paper in his pocket and turned to face the door.

CHAPTER V

IN WHICH BUDE LOOKS AT ROBIN GREVE

The library door opened. A large, square-built, florid man in the braided uniform of a police inspector stood on the threshold of the room. Beside him was Bude who, with an air of dignity and respectful mourning suitably blended, waved him into the room.

"The - ahem! - body is in here, Mr. Humphries, sir!"

Inspector Humphries stepped quickly into the room. A little countryfied in appearance and accent, he had the careful politeness, the measured restraint, and the shrewd eye of the typical police officer. In thirty years' service he had risen from village constable to be Inspector of county police. Slow to anger, rather stolid, and with an excellent heart, he had a vein of shrewd common sense not uncommonly found in that fast disappearing species, the English peasant.

He nodded shortly to Greve, and with a tread that shook the room strode across to where Hartley Parrish was lying dead. In the meantime a harassed-looking man with a short grey beard, wearing a shabby frock coat, had slipped into the room behind the Inspector. He approached Greve.

"Dr. Romain?" he queried, peering through his gold spectacles, "the butler said ..."

"No, my name is Greve," answered Robin. "I am staying in the house. This is Dr. Romain."

He motioned to the door. Dr. Romain came bustling into the room.

"Glad to see you here so promptly, Inspector," he said. "A shocking business, very. Is this the doctor? I am Dr. Romain ..."

Dr. Redstone bowed with alacrity.

"A great privilege, sir," he said staidly. "I have followed your work...."

But the other did not let him finish.

"Shot through the heart ... instantaneous death ... severe haemorrhage ... the pistol is there ... in his hand. A man with everything he wanted in the world ... I can't understand it. 'Pon my soul, I can't!"

The Inspector, who had been kneeling by the corpse, motioned with his head to the village doctor. Dr. Redstone went to him and began a cursory examination of the body. The Inspector rose.

"I understand from the butler, gentlemen," he said, "that it was Miss Trevert, a lady staying in the house, who heard the shot fired. I should like to see her, please. And you, sir, are you a relation of ..."

Greve, thus addressed, hastily replied.

"Only a friend, Inspector. I am staying in the house. I am a barrister. Perhaps I may be able to assist you ..."

Humphries shot a slow, shrewd glance at him from beneath his shaggy blond eyebrows.

"Thank you, sir, much obliged, I'm sure. Now" - he thrust a hand into his tunic and produced a large leather-bound notebook - "do you know anything as would throw a light on this business?"

Greve shook his head.

"He seemed perfectly cheerful at lunch. He left the dining-room directly after he had taken his coffee."

"Where did he go?"

"He came here to work. He told us at lunch that he was going to shut himself up in the library for the whole afternoon as he had a lot of work to get through."

The Inspector made a note or two in his book. Then he paused thoughtfully tapping the end of his pencil against his teeth.

"It was Miss Trevert, you say, who found the body?"

"No," Greve replied. "Her brother, Sir Horace Trevert. It was Miss Trevert who heard the shot fired."

"The door was locked, I think?"

"On the inside. But here is Sir Horace Trevert. He will tell you how he got through the window and discovered the body."

Horace Trevert gave a brief account of his entry into the library. Again the Inspector scribbled in his notebook.

"One or two more questions, gentlemen, please," he said, "and then I should wish to see Miss Trevert. Firstly, who saw Mr. Hartley Parrish last: and at what time?"

Horace Trevert looked at Greve.

"It would be when he left us after lunch, wouldn't it?" he said.

"Certainly, certainly," Dr. Romain broke in. "He left us all together in the dining-room, you, Horace and Robin and Lady Margaret and Mary ... Miss Trevert and her mother, you know," he added by way of explanation to the Inspector.

"And he went straight to the library?"

"Straight away, Mr. Humphries, sir," broke in Bude. "Mr. Parrish crossed me in the hall and gave me particular instructions that he was not to be disturbed."

"That was at what time?"

"About two-thirty, sir."

"Then you were the last person to see him before ..."

"Why, no ... that is, unless ..."

The butler hesitated, casting a quick glance round his audience.

"What do you mean?" rapped out the Inspector, looking up from his notebook. "Did anybody else see Mr. Parrish in spite of his orders?"

Bude was silent. He was looking at Greve.

"Come on," said Humphries sternly. "You heard my question? What makes you think anybody else had access to Mr. Parrish before the shot was heard?"

Bude made a little resigned gesture of the hands.

"Well, sir, I thought ... I made sure that Mr. Greve ..."

There was a moment's tense silence.

"Well?" snapped Humphries.

"I was going to say I made certain that Mr. Greve was going to Mr. Parrish in the library to tell him tea was ready. Mr. Greve passed me in the hall and went down the library corridor just after I had served the tea."

All eyes turned to Robin.

"It's perfectly true," he said. "I went out into the gardens for a mouthful of fresh air just before tea. I left the house by the side door off the corridor here. I didn't go to the library, though. It is an understood thing in this house that no one ever disturbs Mr. Parrish when he ..."

He broke off sharply.

"My God, Mary," he cried, "you mustn't come in here!"

All turned round at his loud exclamation. Mary Trevert stood in the doorway. Dr. Romain darted forward.

"My dear," he said soothingly, "you mustn't be here ..."

Passively she let him lead her into the corridor. The Inspector continued his examination.

"At what time did you come along this corridor, sir?" he asked Robin.

"It was not long after the tea gong went," answered Robin, "about ten minutes past five, I should say ..."

"And you heard nothing?"

Robin shook his head.

"Absolutely nothing," he replied. "The corridor was perfectly quiet. I stepped out into the grounds, went for a turn round the house, but it was raining, so I came in almost at once."

"At what time was that?"

"When I came in ... oh, about two or three minutes later, say about a quarter past five."

Humphries turned to Horace Trevert.

"What time was it when Miss Trevert heard the shot?"

Horace puckered up his brow.

"Well," he said, "I don't quite know. We were having tea. It wasn't much after five - I should say about a quarter past."

"Then the shot that Miss Trevert heard would have been fired just about the time that you, sir," he turned to Robin, "were coming in from your stroll."

"Somewhere about that time, I should say!" Robin answered rather thoughtfully.

"Did you hear it?" queried the Inspector.

"No," said Robin.

"But surely you must have been at or near the side door at the time as you were coming in ..."

"I came in by the front door," said Robin, "on the other side of the house ..."

Very carefully the Inspector closed his notebook, thrust the pencil back in its place along the back, fastened the elastic about the book, and turned to Horace Trevert.

"And now, sir, if I might speak to Miss Trevert alone for a minute ..."

"I say, though," expostulated Horace, "my sister's awfully upset, you know. Is it absolutely necessary?"

"Aye, sir, it is!" said the Inspector. "But there's no need for me to see her in here. Perhaps in some other room ..."

"The drawing-room is next to this," the butler put in; "they'd be nice and quiet in there, Sir Horace."

The Inspector acquiesced. Dr. Redstone drew him aside for a whispered colloquy.

The Inspector came back to Robin and Horace.

"The doctor would like to have the body taken upstairs to Mr. Parrish's room," he said. "He wishes to make a more detailed examination if Dr. Romain would help him. If one of you gentlemen could give orders about this ... I have two officers outside who would lend a hand. And this room must then be shut and locked. Sergeant Harris!" he called.

"Sir!"

A stout sergeant appeared at the library door.

"As soon as the body has been removed, you will lock the room and bring the key to me. And you will return here and see that no one attempts to get into the room. Understand?"

"Yessir!"

"Inspector!"

Robin Greve called Inspector Humphries as the latter was preparing to follow Bude to the drawing-room.

"Mr. Parrish seems to have written a note for Miss Trevert," he said, pointing at the desk. "And in that envelope you will find Mr. Parrish's will. I discovered it there on the desk just before you arrived!"

Again the Inspector shot one of his swift glances at the young man. He went over to the desk, shook the document and letter from their envelope, glanced at them, and replaced them.

"I don't rightly know that this concerns me, gentlemen," he said slowly. "I think I'll just take charge of it. And I'll give Miss Trevert her letter."

Taking the two envelopes, he tramped heavily out of the room.

Then in a little while Bude and Jay and two bucolic-looking policemen came to the library to move the body of the master of Harkings. Robin stood by and watched the little procession pass slowly with silent feet across the soft pile carpet and out into the corridor. But his thoughts were not with Parrish. He was haunted by the look which Mary Trevert had given him as she had stood for an instant at the library door, a look of fear, of suspicion. And it made his heart ache.

CHAPTER VI

THE LETTER

The great drawing-room of Harkings was ablaze with light. The cluster of lights in the heavy crystal chandelier and the green-shaded electric lamps in their gilt sconces on the plain white-panelled walls coldly lit up the formal, little-used room with its gilt furniture, painted piano, and huge marble fireplace.

This glittering Louis Seize environment seemed altogether too much for the homely Inspector. Whilst waiting for Mary Trevert to come to him, he tried several attitudes in turn. The empty hearth frightened him away from the mantelpiece, the fragile appearance of a gilt settee decided him against risking his sixteen stone weight on its silken cushions, and the vastness of the room overawed him when he took up his position in the centre of the Aubusson carpet. Finally he selected an ornate chair, rather more solid-looking than the rest, which he drew up to a small table on the far side of the room. There he sat down, his large red hands spread out upon his knees in an attitude of singular embarrassment.

But Mary Trevert set him quickly at his ease when presently she came to him. She was pale, but quite self-possessed. Indeed, the effort she had made to regain her self-control was so marked that it would have scarcely escaped the attention of the Inspector, even if he had not had a brief vision of her as she had stood for that instant at the library door, pale, distraught, and trembling. He was astonished to find her cool, collected, almost business-like in the way she sat down, motioned him to his seat, and expressed her readiness to tell him all she knew.

The phrases he had been laboriously preparing - "This has been a bad shock for you, ma'am"; "You will forgive me, I'm sure, ma'am, for calling upon you at a moment such as this" - died away on his lips as Mary Trevert said:

"Ask me any questions you wish, Inspector. I will tell you everything I can."

"That's very good of you, ma'am, I'm sure," answered the Inspector, unstrapping his notebook, "and I'll try and not detain you long. Now, then, tell me what you know of this sad affair ..."

Mary Trevert plucked an instant nervously at her little cambric handerchief in her lap. Then she said:

"I went to the library from the billiard-room ..."

"A moment," interposed the Inspector. "What time was that?"

"A little after five. The tea gong had gone some time. I was going to the library to tell Mr. Parrish that tea was ready ..."

Mr. Humphries made a note. He nodded to show he

was listening.

"I crossed the hall and went down the library corridor. I knocked on the library door. There was no reply. Then I heard a shot and a sort of thud."

Despite her effort to remain calm, the girl's voice shook a little. She made a little helpless gesture of her hands. A diamond ring she was wearing on her finger caught the light and blazed for an instant.

"Then I got frightened. I ran back along the corridor to the lounge where the others were and told them."

"When you knocked at the door, you say there was no reply. I suppose, now, you tried the handle first."

"Oh, yes ..."

"Then Mr. Parrish would have heard the two sounds? The turning of the handle and then the knocking on the door? That's so, isn't it?"

"Yes, I suppose so ..."

"Yet you say there was no reply?"

"No. None at all."

The Inspector jotted a word or two in his notebook as it lay open flat upon the table.

"The shot, then, was fired immediately after you had knocked? Not while you were knocking?"

"No. I knocked and waited, expecting Mr. Parrish to

answer. Instead of him answering, there came this shot ..."

"I see. And after the shot was fired there was a crash?"

"A sort of thud - like something heavy falling down."

"And you heard no groan or cry?"

The girl knit her brows for a moment.

"I ... I ... was frightened by the shot. I ... I ... don't seem able to remember what happened afterwards. Let me think ... let me think ..."

"There, there," said the Inspector paternally, "don't upset yourself like this. Just try and think what happened after you heard the shot fired ..."

Mary Trevert shuddered, one slim white hand pressed against her cheek.

"I do remember now," she said, "there *was* a cry. It was more like a sharp exclamation ..."

"And then you heard this crash?"

"Yes ..."

The girl had somewhat regained her self-possession. She dabbed her eyes with her handkerchief quickly as though ashamed of her weakness.

"Now," said Humphries, clearing his throat, as though to indicate that the conversation had changed, "you and Lady Margaret Trevert knew Mr. Parrish pretty well, I believe, Miss Trevert. Have you any idea why he should have done this thing?"

Mary Trevert shook her dark head rather wearily.

"It is inconceivable to me ... to all of us," she answered.

"Do you happen to know whether Mr. Parrish had any business worries?"

"He always had a great deal of business on hand and he has had a great deal to do lately over some big deal."

"What was it, do you know?"

"He was raising fresh capital for Hornaway's - that is the big engineering firm he controls ..."

"Do you know if he was pleased with the way things were shaping?"

"Oh, yes. He told me last night that everything would be finished this week. He seemed quite satisfied."

The Inspector paused to make a note.

Then he thrust a hand into the side-pocket of his tunic and produced Hartley Parrish's letter.

"This," he said, eyeing the girl as he handed her the letter, "may throw some light on the affair!"

Open-eyed, a little surprised, she took the plain white envelope from his hand and gazed an instant without

Valentine Williams

speaking, on the bold sprawling address -

"Miss Mary Trevert."

"Open it, please," said the Inspector gently.

The girl tore open the envelope. Humphries saw her eyes fill, watched the emotion grip her and shake her in her self-control so that she could not speak when, her reading done, she gave him back the letter.

Without asking her permission, he took the sheet of fine, expensive paper with its neat engraved heading and postal directions, and read Hartley Parrish's last message.

> My dear [it ran], I signed my will at Bardy's office yesterday, and he sent it back to me to-day. Just this line to let you know you are properly provided for should anything happen to me. I wanted to fix things so that you and Lady Margaret would not have to worry any more. I just had to *write*. I guess you understand why.
>
> H.

There was a long and impressive silence while the Inspector deliberately read the note. Then he looked interrogatively at the girl.

"We were engaged, Inspector," she said. "We were to have been married very soon."

A deep flush crept slowly over Mr. Humphries's florid face and spread into the roots of his tawny fair hair.

"But what does he mean by 'having to write'?" he asked.

The girl replied hastily, her eyes on the ground.

"Mr. Parrish was under the impression that ... that ... without his money I should not have cared for him. That is what he means ..."

"You knew he had provided for you in his will?"

"He told me several times that he intended to leave me everything. You see, he has no relatives!"

"I see!" said the Inspector in a reflective voice.

"Had he any enemies, do you know? Anybody who would drive him to a thing like this?"

The girl shook her head vehemently.

"No!"

The monosyllable came out emphatically. Again the Inspector darted one of his quick, shrewd glances at the girl. She met his scrutiny with her habitual serene and candid gaze. The Inspector dropped his eyes and scribbled in his book.

"Was his health good?"

"He smoked far too much," the girl said, "and it made him rather nervy. But otherwise he never had a day's illness in his life."

Humphries ran his eye over the notes he had made.

Valentine Williams

"There is just one more question I should like to ask you, Miss Trevert," he said, "rather a personal question."

Mary Trevert's hands twisted the cambric handkerchief into a little ball and slowly unwound it again. But her face remained quite calm.

"About your engagement to Mr. Parrish ... when did it take place?"

"Some days ago. It has not yet been announced."

The Inspector coughed.

"I was only wondering whether, perhaps, Mr. Parrish was not quite ... whether he was, maybe, a little disturbed in his mind about the engagement ..."

The girl hesitated. Then she said firmly:

"Mr. Parrish was perfectly happy about it. He was looking forward to our being married in the spring."

Mr. Humphries shut his notebook with a snap and rose to his feet.

"Thank you very much, ma'am," he said with a little formal bow. "If you will excuse me now. I have the doctor to see again and there's the Coroner to be warned ..."

He bowed again and tramped towards the door with a tread that made the chandelier tinkle melodiously.

The door closed behind him and his heavy footsteps

died away along the corridor. Mary Trevert had risen to her feet calm and impassive. But when he had gone, her bosom began to heave and a spasm of pain shot across her face. Again the tears welled up in her eyes, brimmed over and stole down her cheeks.

"If I only *knew!*" she sobbed, "if I only *knew!*"

CHAPTER VII

VOICES IN THE LIBRARY

The swift tragedy of the winter afternoon had convulsed the well-organized repose of Hartley Parrish's household. Nowhere had his master grasp of detail been seen to better advantage than in the management of his country home. Overwhelmed with work though he constantly was, accustomed to carry his business and often part of his business staff to Harkings with him for the week-ends, there was never the least confusion about the house. The methodical calm of Harkings was that of a convent.

Hartley Parrish was wont to say that he paid his butler and housekeeper well to save himself from worry. It was rather to ensure his orders being punctiliously and promptly carried out. His was the mind behind the method which ensured that meals were punctually served and trains at Stevenish Station never missed.

But it was into a house in turmoil that Mary Trevert stepped when she left the drawing-room and passed along the corridor to go to her room. Doors slammed and there was the heavy thud of footsteps on the floor above. The glass door leading into the gardens was open, as Mary passed it, swinging in the gusts of cold rain. In the gardens without there was a confused murmur of voices and the flash of lanterns.

In the hall a knot of servants were gossiping in frightened whispers with a couple of large, rather bovine country constables who, bareheaded, without their helmets, which they held under their arms, looked curiously undressed.

The whispers died away as Mary crossed the hall. All eyes followed her with interest as she went. It was as though an echo of her talk with the Inspector had by some occult means already spread through the little household. Through the half-open green baize door leading to the servants' quarters some unseen person was bawling down the telephone in a heated controversy with the exchange about a long-distance call to London. And but an hour since, the girl reflected sadly, as she mounted the oaken staircase, the house had been wrapt in its wonted evening silence in response to that firm and dominating personality who had passed out in the gloom of the winter twilight.

When, about six months before, Mary and her mother had begun to be regular visitors at Harkings, Hartley Parrish had insisted on giving Mary a boudoir to herself. This, in response to a chance remark of Mary's in admiration of a Chinese room she had seen at a friend's house, Parrish had had decorated in the Chinese style with black walls and black-and-gold lacquer furniture. The room had been transformed from a rather prosaic morning-room with old oak and chintz in the space of three days as a surprise for Mary. She remembered now how Parrish had left her to make the discovery of the change for herself. She loved colour and line, and the contrast between this quaint and delightful room with her rather shabby bedroom in her mother's small house in Brompton had made this surprise one of the most delightful she had ever experienced.

She rang the bell and sat down listlessly in a charmingly lacquered Louis Seize armchair in front of the log-fire blazing brightly in the fireplace. She was conscious that a great disaster had overtaken her, but only dimly conscious. For more poignantly than this dull sense of tragedy she was aware of a great aching at her heart, and her thoughts, after hovering over the events of the afternoon, settled down upon her talk that afternoon ... already how far off it seemed ... with Robin Greve in the library,

Robin had always been her hero. She could see him now in the glow of the fire as he had been when in the holidays he had come and snatched her away from a home already drab and difficult for a matinée and an orgy of cream cakes at Gunter's afterwards. He was then a long, slim, handsome boy of irrepressible spirits and impulsive generosity which usually left him, after the first few days of his holidays, in a state of lamentable impecuniosity. All their lives, it seemed to her, they had been friends, but with no stronger feeling between them until Robin, having joined the Army on the outbreak of war, had come to say good-bye on being ordered to France.

But by that time money troubles at home with which, as it seemed to her, she had been surrounded all her life, had grown so pressing that, apart from Lady Margaret's reiterated counsels, she herself had come to recognize that a suitable marriage was the only way out of their ever-increasing embarrassment.

She and Robin, she recalled with a feeling of relief, had never discussed the matter. He, too, had understood and had sailed for France without seeking to take advantage of the circumstance.

Outside in the black night a car throbbed. Footsteps crunched the gravel beneath her window. The sounds brought her back to the present with a sudden pang. She began to think of Hartley Parrish. All her life she had been so very poor that, until she had met this big, vigorous, intensely vital man, she had never known what a lavish command of money meant. Hartley Parrish did things in a big way. If he wanted a thing he bought it, as he had bought Bude, as he had bought a car he had seen standing outside a Pall Mall club and admired. He had rooted the owner out, bade him name his price, and had paid it, there and then, by cheque, and driven Mary off to a lawn tennis tournament at Queen's, hugely delighted by her bewilderment.

She did not love him. She could never have learnt to love him. There was a gleeful zest in his enjoyment of his money, an ostentatious parade of his riches which repelled her. And there was a look in his face, those narrow eyes, that hard mouth, which revealed to her womanly intuition a ruthlessness which she guessed he kept for his business. But she liked him, especially his reverent and chivalrous devotion to her, and the thought that his dominating and vital personality was extinguished for ever made her conscious of a great void in her life.

And now she was rich. Hartley Parrish's idea of "proper provision" for her, she knew, meant wealth for her beyond anything she had ever dreamed. The perpetual debasing struggle with poverty which she

Valentine Williams

and her mother had carried on for years was a thing of the past. Money meant freedom, freedom to live ... and to love.

She stretched her hands out to the blaze. Was she free to love? What had driven Hartley Parrish to suicide? Or who? She went over in her mind her interview with Robin Greve in the billiard-room. He had spoken of other women in connection with Hartley Parrish. Had he used that knowledge to threaten his rival? What had Robin done after he had left her that afternoon with his final taunt?

She felt the blood rise to her cheeks as she thought of it. Mary Trevert had all the pride of her ancient race. The recollection of that taunt galled her. Her loyalty to the man from whom she had received nothing but chivalry, whose fortune was to banish a hideous nightmare from her life, rose up in arms. What had Robin done? She must know the truth ...

A tap came at the door. Bude appeared.

"I think you rang, Miss," he said in his quiet, deep voice. "I was with the Inspector, Miss, and I couldn't come before. Was there anything?..."

The girl turned in her chair.

"Come in and shut the door, Bude," she said. "I want to speak to you."

The butler obeyed and came over to where she sat. He seemed ill at ease and rather apprehensive.

"Bude," said the girl, "I want you to tell me why you

were certain that Mr. Greve was going to Mr. Parrish in the library when he passed you in the hall this afternoon!"

The butler smoothed his hands down his trousers in embarrassment.

"I thought he ... Mr. Greve ... would be sure to be going to fetch Mr. Parrish in to tea, Miss ..." he replied, eyeing the girl anxiously.

Mary Trevert continued gazing into the fire.

"You know it is a rule in this house, Bude," she said, "that Mr. Parrish is never disturbed in the library ..."

The butler changed his position uneasily.

"Yes, Miss, but I thought ..."

Slowly Mary Trevert turned and looked at the man.

"Bude," - her voice was very calm, - "I want you to tell me the truth. You know that Mr. Greve went in to Mr. Parrish ..."

Bude looked uneasily about him.

"Oh, Miss," he answered, almost in a whisper, "whatever are you saying?"

"I want your answer, Bude," the girl said coldly.

Bude did not speak. He rubbed his hands up and down his trousers in desperation.

"I wish to know why Mr. Parrish did this thing, Bude. I mean to know. And I think you are keeping something back!"

The challenge resounded clearly, firmly.

"Miss Trevert, ma'am," the butler said in a low voice, "I wouldn't take it upon me to say anything as would get anybody in this house into trouble...."

"You saw Mr. Greve go into Mr. Parrish?"

The butler raised his hands in a quick gesture of denial.

"God forbid, Miss!" he ejaculated in horror.

"What, then, do you know that is likely to get anybody here into trouble?"

The butler hesitated an instant. Then he spoke.

"That Inspector Humphries has been asking me questions, Miss, in a nasty, suspicious sort o' way. I told him, what I told him already, that just after I'd done serving the tea Mr. Greve crossed the hall and went down the library corridor...."

"You didn't tell him everything, Bude?"

The butler took a step nearer.

"Oh, Miss," he said, lowering his voice, "if you'll pardon my frankness, but I know as how you and Mr. Greve are old friends, and I wouldn't take it upon me to tell the police anything as might ..."

Mary Trevert stood up and faced the man.

"Bude," said she, "Mr. Parrish was your master, a kind and generous master as he was kind and generous to every one in this house. We must clear up the mystery of his ... of his death. Neither you nor I nor Mr. Greve nor anybody must stand in the way. Now, tell me the truth!"

She dropped back into her chair. She gave the order imperiously like the mistress of the house. The butler, trained through life to receive orders, surrendered.

"There's nothing much to tell, Miss. When Mr. Humphries asked me if I were the last person to see Mr. Parrish alive, I made sure that Mr. Greve would say he had been in to tell him tea was ready. But Mr. Greve, who heard the Inspector's question and my answer, said nothing. So I thought, maybe, he had his reasons and I did not feel exactly as how it was my place ..."

Mary Trevert tapped with her foot impatiently.

"But what grounds have you for saying that Mr. Greve went in to Mr. Parrish? Mr. Greve declared quite positively that he went out by the side door and did not go into the library at all."

"But, Miss, I heard him speaking to Mr. Parrish ..."

The girl turned round and the man saw fear in her wide-open eyes.

The butler put his hand on the back of her chair and leaned forward.

"Better leave things where they are, Miss," he said in a low voice. "Mr. Parrish, I dare say, had his reasons. He's gone to his last account now. What does it matter why he done it ..."

The man was agitated, and in his emotion his carefully studied English was forsaking him.

But the girl broke in incisively.

"Please explain what you mean!" she commanded.

"Why, Miss," replied the butler, "we know that Mr. Greve had no call to like Mr. Parrish seeing how things were between you and the master ..."

"You mean the servants know that Mr. Parrish and I were engaged ..."

Bude made a deprecatory gesture.

"Know, Miss? I wouldn't go so far as to say 'know.' But there has been some talk in the servants' 'all, Miss. You know what young female servants are, Miss ..."

"And you think that Mr. Greve went to Mr. Parrish to talk about ... me?"

Mary Trevert's voice faltered a little. She looked eagerly at the other's fat, smooth face.

"I presoomed as much, Miss, I must confess!"

"But what did you hear Mr. Greve say?"

"I heard nothing, Miss, except just only the sound of

voices. After Mr. Greve had crossed me in the hall, I took the salver I was carrying into the butler's pantry. I stayed there a minute or two, and then I remembered I had not collected the letters from the box in the hall for the chauffeur to take to the post, the same as he does every evening. I went back to the hall, and just as I opened the green baize door I heard voices from the library ..."

"Was it Mr. Greve's voice?"

"I cannot say, Miss. It was just the sound of voices, rather loud-like. I caught the sound because the door leading from the hall to the library corridor was ajar. Mr. Greve must have forgotten to shut it."

"What did you do?"

"Well, Miss, I closed the corridor door ..."

"Why did you do that?"

"Well, Miss, seeing the voices sounded angry-like, I thought perhaps it would be better not to let any one else hear.... And Mr. Greve looked upset-like when he passed me. He gave me quite a turn, he did, when I saw his face under the hall lamp...."

"Did you stay there ... and listen?"

Bude drew himself up.

"That is not my 'abit, Miss, not 'ere nor in hany of the 'ouses where I 'ave seen service...."

The butler broke off. The *h*'s were too much for him in

his indignation.

"I didn't mean to suggest anything underhand," the girl said quickly. "I mean, did you hear any more?"

"No, Miss. I emptied the letter-box and took the letters to the servants' hall."

"But," said Mary in a puzzled way, "why do you say it was Mr. Greve if you didn't hear his voice?"

Bude spread out his hands in bewilderment.

"Who else should it have been, Miss? Sir Horace and the doctor were in the lounge at tea. Jay and Robert were in the servants' hall. It could have been nobody else...."

The girl's head sank slowly on her breast. She was silent. The butler shifted his position.

"Was there anything more, Miss?" he asked after a little while.

"There is nothing further, thank you, Bude," replied Mary. "About Mr. Greve, I am sure there must be some mistake. He cannot have understood Mr. Humphries's question. I'll ask him about it when I see him. I don't think I should say anything to the Inspector about it, at any rate, not until I've seen Mr. Greve. He'll probably speak to you about it himself...."

Bude made a motion as though he were going to say something. Then apparently he thought better of it, for he made a little formal bow and in his usual slow and dignified manner made his exit from the room.

CHAPTER VIII

ROBIN GOES TO MARY

The house telephone, standing on the long and grace-fully designed desk with its elaborately lacquered top, whirred. Mary started from her reverie in her chair by the fire. By the clock on the mantelshelf she saw that it was a quarter past eight. She remembered that once her mother had knocked at her door and bidden her come down to dinner. She had refused the invitation, declining to unlock the door.

She lifted the receiver.

"That you, Mary?"

Robin was speaking.

"May I come up and see you? Or would you rather be left alone?"

His firm, pleasant voice greatly comforted her. Only then she realized how greatly she craved sympathy. But the recollection of Bude's story suddenly interposed itself like a barrier between them.

"Yes, come up," she said, "I want to speak to you!"

Her voice was dispirited,

"I don't want to see him," she told herself as she replaced the receiver, got up, and unlocked the door, "but I must *know*!"

A gentle tap came at the door. Robin came in quickly and crossed to where she stood by the fire.

"My dear!" he said and put out his two hands.

Her hands were behind her back, the fingers nervously intertwining. She kept them there and made no sign that she had observed his gesture.

He looked at her in surprise.

"This has been terrible for you, Mary," he said. "I wish to God I could make you realize how very, very much I feel for you in what you must be going through...."

The phrase was formal and he brought it out irresolutely, chilled as he was by her reception. She was looking at him dispassionately, her forehead a little puckered, her eyes a trifle hard.

"Won't you sit down," she said. "There is something I wanted to say!"

He was looking at her now in a puzzled fashion. With rather feigned deliberation he chose a chair and sat down facing the fire. A lamp on the mantelpiece - the only light in the room - threw its rays on his face. His chin was set rather more squarely than his wont and his eyes were shining.

"Mary," - he leant forward towards her, - "please forget what I said this afternoon. It was beastly of me, but I hardly knew what I was doing...."

She made a little gesture as if to wave his apology aside. Then, with her hands clasped in front of her, scanning the nails, she asked, almost casually:

"What did you say to Hartley Parrish in the library this afternoon?"

Robin stared at her in amazement.

"But I was not in the library!" he answered.

The girl dropped her hands sharply to her side.

"Don't quibble with me, Robin," she said. "What did you say to Hartley Parrish after you left me this afternoon in the billiard-room?"

He was still staring at her, but now there was a deep furrow between his brows. He was breathing rather hard.

"I did not speak to Parrish at all after I left you."

His answer was curt and incisive.

"Do you mean to tell me," Mary said, "that, after you left me and went down the corridor towards the library, you neither went in to Hartley nor spoke to him!"

"I do!"

"Then how do you account for the fact that, almost

immediately after you had crossed Bude in the hall, he heard the sound of voices in the library?"

Robin Greve stood up abruptly.

"Bude, you say, makes this statement?"

"Certainly!"

"To whom, may I ask?"

He spoke sharply and there was a challenging ring in his voice. It nettled the girl.

"Only to me," she said quickly, and added: "You needn't think he has told the police!"

Very deliberately Robin plucked his handkerchief from his sleeve, wiped his lips, and replaced it. The girl saw that his hands were trembling.

"Why do you say that to me?" he demanded rather fiercely.

Mary Trevert shrugged her shoulders.

"This afternoon," she said, "when I told you of my engagement to Hartley, you began by abusing him to me, you rushed from the room making straight for the library where we all know that Hartley was working, and a few minutes after Bude hears voices raised in anger proceeding from there. The next thing we know is that Hartley has ..."

She broke off and looked away.

"Mary," - Robin's voice was grave, and he had mastered all signs of irritation, - "you and I have known one another all our lives. You ought to know me well enough by now to understand that I don't tell you lies. When I say I haven't seen or spoken to Hartley Parrish since lunch this afternoon, that is the truth!"

"How can it be the truth?" the girl insisted. "Horace and Dr. Romain were both in the lounge-hall, Bude was in the hall, the other menservants were in the servants' hall. You are the only man in the house not accounted for, and a minute before Bude heard these voices you go down the corridor towards the library. I can understand you wanting to keep it from the police, but why do you want to deceive *me*?"

"Mary," answered the young man sternly, "I know you're upset, but that's no justification for persisting in this stupid charge against me. I tell you I never saw Parrish or spoke to him, either, between lunch and when I saw him lying dead in the library. I am not going to repeat the denial. But you may as well understand now that I am not in the habit of allowing my friends to doubt my word!"

Mary flamed up at his tone.

"If you are my friend," she cried, "why can't you trust me? Why should I find this out from Bude? Why should I be humiliated by hearing from the butler that he kept this evidence from the police in order to please me because you and I are friends? I am only trying to help you, to shield you ..."

"That will do, Mary," he said. "No, you must hear what I have to say. If you insist on disbelieving me, you must. But I don't want you to help me. I don't want you to shield me. I shall make it my business to see that Bude's evidence is brought before the detective inspector from Scotland Yard who is being brought down here to handle the case ..."

"A detective from Scotland Yard?" the girl repeated.

"Yes, a detective. Humphries is puzzled by several points about this case and has asked for assistance from London. He is right. Neither the circumstances of Parrish's death nor the motive of his act are clear. Bude's evidence is sufficient proof that somebody did gain access to the library this afternoon. In that case...."

"Yes...."

"In that case," said Greve slowly, "it may not be suicide...."

Mary put one hand suddenly to her face as women do when they are frightened. She shrank back.

"You mean...."

He nodded.

"Murder!"

The girl gave a little gasp. Then she stretched out her hand and touched his arm.

"But, Robin," she spoke in quick gasps, - "you can't give the police this evidence of Bude's. Don't you see it incriminates *you?* Don't you realize that every scrap of evidence points to you as being the man that visited

Mr. Parrish in the library this afternoon? You're a lawyer, Robin. You understand these things. Don't you see what I mean?"

He nodded curtly.

"Perfectly," he replied coldly.

"Bude will do what I tell him," the girl hurried on. "There is no need for the police to know...."

"On the contrary," said the other imperturbably, "it is essential they should be told at once."

The girl grasped the lapels of his coat in her two hands. Her breath came quickly and she trembled all over.

"Are you mad, Robin?" she cried. "Who could have wanted to kill poor Hartley? Why should you put these ideas into the heads of the police? Bude may have imagined everything. Now, you'll be sensible, promise me...."

Very gently he detached the two slim hands that held his coat. His mouth was set in a firm line.

"We are going to sift this thing to the bottom, Mary," he said, "no matter what are the consequences. You owe it to Parrish and you owe it to me...."

The telephone trilled suddenly.

Robin picked up the receiver,

"Yes, Bude," he said.

There was a moment's silence in the room broken as the clock on the mantelpiece chimed nine times. Then Robin said into the telephone:

"Right! Tell him I'll be down immediately!"

He put down the receiver and turned to Mary.

"A detective inspector has arrived from London. He is asking to see me. I must go downstairs."

Mary, her elbows on the mantelpiece, was staring into the fire. At the sound of his voice she swung round quickly.

"Robin!" she cried.

But she spoke too late.

Robin Greve had left the room.

CHAPTER IX

MR. MANDERTON

A quality which had gone far to lay the foundations of the name which Robin Greve was rapidly making at the bar was his strong intuitive sense. He had the rare ability of correctly 'sensing' an atmosphere, an uncanny *flair* for driving instantly at the heart of a situation, which rendered him in the courts a dexterous advocate and a redoubtable opponent.

Now, as he came into the lounge from the big oak staircase, he instantly realized that he had entered an unfriendly atmosphere. The concealed lights which were set all round the cornice of the room were turned on, flooding the pleasantly snug room with soft reflected light. A little group stood about the fire, Bude, Jay, Hartley Parrish's man, and a stranger. Jay was engaged in earnest conversation with the stranger. But at the sound of Greve's foot upon the staircase, the conversation ceased and a silence fell on the group.

Greve's attention was immediately attracted towards the stranger, whom he surmised to be the detective from Scotland Yard. He was a big, burly man with a heavy dark moustache, straight and rather thin black hair, and coarse features. He looked a full-blooded, plethoric person with reddish-blue veins on his florid

Valentine Williams

face, and a heavy jowl which over-feeding, Robin surmised, had made fullish. He was very neatly dressed in his black overcoat with velvet collar carefully brushed, his natty black tie with its pearl pin, and well-polished boots. His black bowler hat, with a pair of heavy dogskin gloves, neatly folded, lay on the table.

"This Mr. Greve?"

Bude and Jay fell back as Robin joined the group. The detective bent his gaze on the young barrister as he put his question, and Robin for the first time noticed his eyes. Keen and clear, they were ill-suited, he thought, to the rather gross features of the man. By right he should have had either the small and roguish or the pale and expressionless eyes which are habitually found in individuals of the sanguine temperament.

The detective had a trick of dropping his eyes to his boots. When he raised them, the effect was to alter his whole expression. His eyes, well-open, keenly observant, in perpetual motion, lent an air of alertness, of shrewdness, to his heavy, florid countenance.

"That is my name," said Robin, answering his question. "I am a barrister. I have met some of your people at the Yard, but I don't think...."

"Detective-Inspector Manderton," interjected the big man, and paused as though to say, "Let that sink in!"

Robin knew him well by repute. His qualities were those of the bull-dog, slow-moving, obstinately brave, and desperately tenacious. His was a name to conjure with among the criminal classes, and his career was starred with various sensational tussles with desperate criminals, for Detective-Inspector Manderton, when engaged on a case, invariably "took a hand himself," as he phrased it, when an arrest was to be made. A bullet-hole in his right thigh and an imperfectly knitted right collar-bone remained to remind him of this propensity of his. His motto, as he was fond of saying, was, "What I have I hold!"

"Well, Mr. Greve," said the detective in a loud, hectoring voice, "perhaps you will be good enough to tell me what you know of this affair?"

Robin flushed angrily at the man's manner. But there was no trace of resentment in his voice as he replied. He told Manderton what he had already told Humphries: how he had gone from the billiard-room across the hall and down the library corridor to the side-door into the grounds, intending to have a stroll before tea, but, finding that it was threatening rain, had returned to the house by the front door.

The detective scanned the young man's face closely as he spoke. When Robin had finished, the other dropped his eyes and seemed to be examining the brilliant polish of his boots. He said nothing, and again Robin became aware of the atmosphere of hostility towards him which this man radiated.

"It is dark at five o'clock?"

Manderton turned to Bude.

"Getting on that way, sir," the butler agreed.

" Are you in the habit , sir," - the detective turned to

Robin now, - "of going out for walks in the dark?"

Greve shrugged his shoulders.

"I had been sitting in the billiard-room. It was rather stuffy, so I thought I'd like some air before tea!"

"You left Miss Trevert in the billiard-room?"

"Yes!"

"Why?"

Greve put a hand to his throat and eased his collar.

"The gong had sounded for tea," the detective went on imperturbably; "surely it would have been more natural for you to have brought Miss Trevert with you?"

"I didn't wish to!"

Mr. Manderton cleared his throat.

"Ah!" he grunted. "You didn't wish to. I should like you to be frank with me, Mr. Greve, please. Was it not a fact that you and Miss Trevert had words?"

He looked up sharply at him with contracted pupils.

"You took a certain interest in this young lady?"

"Mr. Manderton," - Robin spoke with a certain *hauteur*, - "don't you think we might leave Miss Trevert's name out of this?"

"Mr. Greve," replied the detective bluntly, "I don't!"

Robin made a little gesture of resignation.

"Before the servants...."

"Come, come, sir," the detective broke in, "with all respect to the young lady and yourself, it was a matter of common knowledge in the house that she and you were ... well, old friends. It was remarked, Mr. Greve, I may remind you, that you looked very upset-like when you left the billiard-room to" - he paused perceptibly - "to go for your stroll in the dark."

Robin glanced quickly round the group. Jay averted his eyes. As for Bude, he was the picture of embarrassment.

"You seem to be singularly well posted in the gossip of the servants' hall, Mr. Manderton!" said Robin hotly.

It was a foolish remark, and Robin regretted it the moment the words had left his mouth.

"Well, yes," commented the detective slowly, "I am. I shall be well posted on the whole of this case, presently, I hope, sir!"

His manner was perfectly respectful, but reserved almost to a tone of menace.

"In that case," said Robin, "I'll tell you something you don't know, Mr. Manderton. Has Bude told you what he heard after I had passed him in the hall?"

Interest flashed at once into the detective's face. He

turned quickly to the butler. Robin felt he had scored.

"What did you hear?" he said sharply.

Bude looked round wildly. His large, fish-like mouth twitched, and he made a few feeble gestures with his hands.

"It was only perhaps an idea of mine, sir," he stammered, - "just a sort of idea ... I dare say I was mistaken. My hearing ain't what it was, sir...."

"Don't you try to hoodwink me," said Manderton, with sudden ferocity, knitting his brows and frowning at the unfortunate butler. "Come on and tell us what you heard. Mr. Greve knows and I mean to. Out with it!"

Bude cast a reproachful glance at Robin. Then he said:

"Well, sir, a minute or two after Mr. Greve had passed me, I went back to the hall and through the open door of the corridor leading to the library, I heard voices!"

"Voices, eh? Did you recognize them?"

"No, sir. It was just the sound of talking!"

"You told Miss Trevert they were loud voices, Bude!" Robin interrupted.

"Yes, sir," replied the butler, "they were loudish in a manner o' speaking, else I shouldn't have heard them!"

"Why not?"

The detective rapped the question out sharply.

"Why, because the library door was locked, sir!"

"How do you know that?"

"Because Miss Trevert and Dr. Romain both tried the handle and couldn't get in!"

"Ah!" said Manderton, "you mean the door was locked *when the body was found!* Now, as to these voices. Were they men's voices?"

"Yes, sir, I should say so."

"Why?"

"Because they were deep-like!"

"Was Mr. Hartley Parrish's voice one of them?"

The butler spread out his hands.

"That I couldn't say! I just heard the murmur-like, then shut the passage door quickly ..."

"Why?"

"Well, sir, I thought ... I didn't want to listen...."

"You thought one of the voices was Mr. Greve's, eh? Having a row with Mr. Parrish, eh? About the lady, isn't that right?"

"Aren't you going rather too fast?" said Robin quietly.

But the detective ignored him.

"Come on and answer my question, my man," he said harshly. "Didn't you think it was Mr. Hartley Parrish and Mr. Greve here having a bit of a dust-up about the young lady being engaged to Mr. Parrish?"

"Well, perhaps I did, but...."

Like a flash the detective turned on Robin.

"What do you know about this?" he demanded fiercely.

"Nothing," said Greve. "As I have told you already, I did not see Mr. Parrish alive again after lunch, nor did I speak to him. What I would suggest to you now is that upon this evidence of Bude's depends the vitally important question of how Mr. Parrish met his death. Though he was found with a revolver in his hand, none of us in this house know of any good motive for his suicide. I put it to you that the man who can furnish us with this motive is the owner of the voice heard by Bude in conversation with Mr. Parrish, since obviously nobody other than Mr. Parrish and possibly this unknown person was in the library block at the time. And I would further remark, Mr. Manderton, that, until the bullet has been extracted, we do not know that Mr. Parrish killed *himself*..."

"No," said the detective significantly, "we don't!"

He had dropped his eyes to the ground now and was studying the pattern of the hearth-rug.

"You say you heard no shot?" he suddenly asked Robin.

"No!"

"No one other than Miss Trevert, I gather, heard the shot?"

"That is so!"

Mr. Manderton consulted a slip of paper which he drew from his pocket.

"Inspector Humphries," he said, "has drawn up a rough time-table of events leading up to Mr. Parrish's death, based on the evidence he has taken here this evening. You will tell me if it tallies."

He read from the slip:

> 5 P.M.   Bude sounds the gong for tea.
>
> 5.10   Mr. Greve passes Bude in the hall and goes down the corridor leading to the library. Mr. Greve states he went straight out by the side door into the gardens.

The detective looked up from his reading.

"At 5.12, let us say, Bude comes back from the servants' quarters to the hall and hears voices from the library. He closes the passage door. Is that right?"

Bude nodded.

"It would be about two minutes after I saw Mr. Greve the first time," he agreed.

"Very well!"

The detective resumed his reading.

| 5.15 P.M. | Miss Trevert goes to fetch Mr. Parrish in to tea. She finds the library door locked. Tries the handle and hears a shot. |

5.18 (say) Miss Trevert comes into the lounge hall and gives the alarm.

"Now, sir," said Mr. Manderton briskly, "I should like to ask you one or two further questions. Firstly, how long were you out on your stroll in the dark?"

"I should think about two or three minutes."

"That is to say, if you left the house by the side door at 5.10, you were back in the house by 5.13."

"Yes, that would be right," Robin agreed.

"And what did you do when you came in?"

"I went up to my room to fetch a letter for the post."

"Miss Trevert heard the shot fired at 5.15. Where were you at that time?"

"In my bedroom, I should say. I was there for a few minutes as I had to write a cheque...."

"And where is your bedroom?"

"In the other wing above the billiard-room."

"Hm! A pistol shot makes a great deal of noise. It seems strange that nobody in the house should have heard it."

Here Bude interposed.

"Mr. Parrish, sir, was very particular about noise. He had the library door and the door leading from the front hall to the library corridor specially felted so that he should not hear any sounds from the house when he was working in the library. That library wing was absolutely shut off from the rest of the house. It was always uncommon quiet...."

But the detective, ignoring him, turned to Robin again.

"I have been round the house," he said. "It does not seem to me it ought to take you three or even two minutes to walk from the side door to the front door. I should say it would be a matter of about thirty seconds!"

"Excuse me," Robin answered quickly, "I didn't say I went straight from the side to the front door. I went through the gardens following the path that leads to the main drive. There I turned and came back to the front door."

"And you assert that you heard nothing?"

"I heard nothing."

"Neither the 'loud voices' which the butler heard within two minutes of your leaving the house nor the shot fired five minutes later?"

"I heard nothing."

Mr. Manderton examined the toes of his boots carefully.

"You heard nothing!" he repeated.

The door opened suddenly and Dr. Romain appeared. With him was the village practitioner and Inspector Humphries.

Dr. Redstone carried in his hand a little pad of cotton wool. He bore it over to the fireplace and unwrapping the lint showed a twisted fragment of lead lying on the bloodstained dressing.

"Straight through the heart and lodged in the spine," he said. "Death was absolutely instantaneous."

The detective picked up the bullet and scrutinized it closely.

"Browning pistol ammunition," observed Humphries; "it fits the gun he used. There's half a dozen spare rounds in one of the drawers of his dressing-room upstairs."

Mr. Manderton drew Inspector Humphries and Dr. Redstone into a corner of the room where they conversed in undertones. Bude and Jay had vanished. Dr. Romain turned to Robin Greve, who stood lost in a reverie, staring into the fire.

"A clear case of suicide," he said. "The medical evidence is conclusive on that point. A most amazing affair. I can't conceive what drove him to it. Why *did* he do it?"

"Ah! why?" said Robin.

CHAPTER X

A SMOKING CHIMNEY

A Red sun glowed dully through a thin mist when, on the following morning, Robin Greve emerged from the side door into the gardens of Harkings. It was a still, mild day. Moisture from the night's rain yet hung translucent on the black limbs of the bare trees and glistened like diamonds on the closely cropped turf of the lawn. In the air was a pleasant smell of damp earth.

Robin paused an instant outside the door in the library corridor and inhaled the morning air greedily. He had spent a restless, fitful night. His sleep had been haunted by the riddle which, since the previous evening, had cast its shadow over the pleasant house. The mystery of Hartley Parrish's death obsessed him. If it was suicide, - and the doctors were both positive on the point - the motive eluded him utterly.

His mind, trained to logical processes of reasoning by his practice of the law, baulked at the theory. When he thought of Hartley Parrish as he had seen him at luncheon on the day before, striding with his quick, vigorous step into the room, boyishly curious to know what the *chef* was giving them to eat, devouring his lunch with obvious animal enjoyment, brimful of energy , dominating the table with his forceful, eager personality....

The sound of voices in the library broke in upon his thoughts. Robin raised his head and listened. Some one appeared to be talking in a loud voice ... no, not talking ... rather declaiming.

Stepping quietly on the hard gravel path, Robin turned the corner of the house and came into view of the library window. The window-pane gaped, shattered where Horace Trevert had broken the glass on the previous evening when effecting an entrance into the room. Framed in the ragged outline of the splintered glass, bulked the large form of Sergeant Harris. He stood half turned from the window so as to catch the light on a copy of *The Times* which he held in his red and freckled hands. He was reading aloud in stentorian tones from a leading article.

"While this country," he bawled sonorously, "cannot ... in h'our belief ... hevade ... er ... responsibility ... er ... h'm disquieting sitwation ..."

"Dear me!" thought Robin to himself, "what a very extraordinary morning pursuit for our police!"

Suddenly the reading was interrupted.

Robin heard the library door open. Then Manderton's voice cried:

"That'll do, thank you, Sergeant!"

"Did you 'ear me, sir?" asked the sergeant, who seemed very much relieved to be quit of his task.

"Not a word!" was the reply. "But we'll try with the library door open! I'll go back to the hall and you start again!"

A thoughtful look on his face, Robin turned quickly and, hurrying round the side of the house, entered by the front door. Standing by the door leading to the library corridor he found Manderton.

The detective did not seem particularly glad to see him.

"Good-morning, Inspector," said Robin affably, "you're early to work, I see. Having a little experiment, eh?"

Manderton nodded without replying. Then the stentorian tones of Sergeant Harris proclaiming the views of "The Thunderer" on the Silesian situation rolled down the corridor and struck distinctly on the ears of the listeners in the hall.

Presently Manderton closed the corridor door, shutting off the sound abruptly.

"I think you said you could not hear the sergeant with the library door shut?" queried Robin suavely.

"With the door shut - no," answered the detective shortly. "But with the door open ..."

He broke off significantly and dropped his eyes to his boots.

"Would it be troubling you," Robin struck in, "if we pushed your experiment one step farther?"

Manderton lifted his eyes and looked at the young man, Robin met his gaze unflinchingly.

"Well?"

There was no invitation in his voice, but Robin affected to disregard the other's coldness.

"Let the library door be shut," said Robin, "but leave the glass door leading into the garden open. Then give Sergeant Harris another trial at his reading...."

The detective smiled rather condescendingly.

"With the library door shut, you'll hear nothing," he remarked.

"The library window is open," Robin retorted, "or rather it is as good as open, as one of the two big panes is smashed...."

His voice vibrated with eagerness. The detective looked at him curiously.

"Oh, try if you like," he said carelessly.

Without waiting for his assent, Robin had already plucked open the corridor door and was halfway down the passage as the other replied. He was back again almost at once and, motioning the detective to silence, took his place at his side by the open door. Then the sound of the policeman's voice was heard from the corridor. It was muffled and indistinct so that the sense of his words could not be made out. But the voice was audible enough.

Robin turned to the detective.

"Bude could make out no words," he said.

"But how do we know that the glass door was open?" queried the detective sceptically.

"Because I left it open myself," Robin countered promptly, "when I went out for my walk before tea. Sir Horace told me that he found the door banging about in the wind when he went out lo get into the library by the window."

Mr. Manderton allowed his fat, serious face to expand very slowly into a broad, superior smile.

"Doesn't it seem a little curious," he said, "that Mr. Hartley Parrish should choose to sit and work in the library on a gusty and dark winter evening with the window wide open? You'll allow, I think, that the window was not broken until after his death ..."

Robin's nerves were ragged. The man's tone nettled him exceedingly. But he confined himself to making a little gesture of impatience.

"No, no, sir," said Mr. Manderton, very decidedly, "I prefer to think that the library door was open, left open by the party who went in to speak to Mr. Parrish yesterday afternoon ... and who knows more about the gentleman's suicide than he would have people think ..."

Robin boiled over fairly at this.

" Good God, man!" he exclaimed, "do you accept this

theory of suicide as blandly as all that? Have you examined the body? Don't you use your eyes? I tell you ... bah, what's the use? I'm not here to do your work for you!..."

"No, sir," said the detective, quite unruffled, "you are not. And I think I'll continue to see about it myself!"

With that he opened the corridor door and vanished down the passage.

With great deliberation Robin selected a cigarette from his case, lit it, and walked out through the front door into the fresh air again. More than ever he felt the riddle of Hartley Parrish's death weighing upon his mind.

His intuitive sense rebelled against the theory of suicide, despite the medical evidence, despite the revolver in the dead man's hand, despite the detective's assurance. And floating about in his brain, like the gossamer on the glistening bushes in the gardens, were broken threads of vague suspicions, of half-formed theories, leading from his hasty observations in the death chamber ...

In itself the death of Hartley Parrish left him cold. Yes, he must admit that. But the look in Mary Trevert's eyes, as she had urged him to shield himself from the suspicion of having driven Hartley Parrish to his death, haunted him. Already dimly he was beginning to realize that Hartley Parrish in death might prove as insuperable a bar between him and Mary Trevert as ever he had been in life ...

She was now a wealthy woman. Hartley Parrish's will

had ensured that, he knew. But it was not the barrier of riches that Robin Greve feared. He had asked Mary Trevert to be his wife before there was any thought of her inheriting Parrish's fortune. He derived a little consolation from that reflection. At least he could not appear as a fortune-hunter in her eyes. But, until he could clear himself of the suspicion lurking in Mary Trevert's mind that he, Robin Greve, was in some way implicated in Hartley Parrish's death, the dead man, he felt, would always stand between them. And so ...

Robin pitched the stump of his cigarette into a rose bush with a little gesture of resignation. Almost without knowing it, he had strolled into the rosery up a shallow flight of steps cut into the bank of green turf, which ran along the side of the house facing the library window to the corner of the house where it met the clipped box-hedge of the Pleasure Ground.

The rosery was a pleasant rectangle framed in a sort of rustic bower which in the summer was covered with superb roses of every hue and variety. Gravel paths intersected rose-beds cut into all manner of fantastic shapes where stood the slender shoots of the young rose-trees each with its tag setting forth its kind, for Hartley Parrish had been an enthusiastic amateur in this direction.

Robin turned round and faced the house. From his elevation he could look down into the library through the window with its shattered pane. He could see the gleaming polish on Hartley Parrish's big desk and the great arm-chair pushed back as Hartley Parrish had pushed it from him just before his death.

The bare poles of the woodwork festooned with the

black arms of the creeping roses, standing out dark in the fast falling winter evening, must, he reflected, have been the last view that Hartley Parrish had had before ...

But then he broke off his meditations abruptly. His eye had fallen on a narrow white patch standing out on one of the uprights supporting the clambering roses.

It was a stout young tree, the light brown bark left adhering to its surface. It was a long blaze on the bark on the side of the trunk which had caught his eye. Robin walked round the gravel path until he was within a foot of the pole to get a better view.

The pole stood almost exactly opposite the library window. The scar in the bark was high up and diagonal and quite freshly made, for the wood was dead white and much splintered.

The young man put a hand on the upright for support and leant forward, carefully refraining from putting his foot on the soft brown mould of the flower-bed which fringed the path between it and the rustic woodwork. Then he ran lightly down the steps until he stood with his back to the library window. From here he carefully surveyed the upright again, then, returning to the rosery, began a careful scrutiny of the gravel paths and the beds.

Apparently his search gave little result, for he presently abandoned it and turned his attention to the wooden framework on the other side of the rectangular rose-garden. He plunged boldly in among the rose-bushes and examined each upright in turn. He spent about half an hour in this meticulous investigation, and then, his boots covered with mould, his rough shooting-coat glistening with moisture, he walked slowly down the steps and reentered the house.

As he was wiping the mud off his boots on the great mat in the front hall, Bude came out of the lounge hall with a pile of dishes on a tray.

"Bude," said Robin, "can you tell me if the fire in the library has been smoking of late?"

"Well, sir," replied the butler, "we've always had trouble with that chimdy when the wind's in the southwest."

"Has it been smoking lately?" The young man reiterated his question impatiently.

The man looked up in surprise.

"Well, sir, now you come to mention it, it has. As a matter o'fact, sir, the sweep was ordered for to-day ..."

"Why?"

"Well, sir, Mr. Parrish had mentioned it to me ..."

"When?"

The question came out like a pistol shot.

"Yesterday, sir," answered the butler blandly. "Just before luncheon, it was, sir. Mr. Parrish told me to have that chimdy seen to at once. And I telephoned for the sweep immediately after luncheon, sir ..."

"Did Mr. Parrish say anything else, Bude?"

Robin eagerly scanned the butler's fat, unimpressive countenance. Bude, his tray held out stiffly in front of him, contracted his bushy eyebrows in thought.

"I don't know as he did, sir ..."

"Think, man, think!" Robin urged.

"Well, sir," said Bude, unmoved, "I believe, now I come to think of it, that Mr. Parrish did say something about the wind blowing his papers about ..."

"That is to say, he had been working with the window open?"

Robin Greve's question rang out sharply. It was an affirmation more than a question.

"Yes, sir, leastways I suppose so, sir ..."

"Which window?"

"Why, the one Mr. Parrish always liked to have open in the warm weather, sir, ... the one opposite the desk. The other window was never opened, sir, because of the dictaphone as stands in front of it. The damp affects the mechanism ..."

"Thank you, Bude," said the young man.

With his accustomed majesty the butler wheeled to go. In the turn of his head as he moved there was a faint suggestion of a shake ... a shake of uncomprehending pity.

CHAPTER XI

"... SPEED THE PARTING GUEST!"

Dr. Romain was just finishing his breakfast as Robin Greve entered the dining-room, a cosy oak-panelled room with a bow window fitted with cushioned window-seats. Horace Trevert stood with his back to the fire. There was no sign of either Lady Margaret or of Mary. Silence seemed to fall on both the doctor and his companion as Robin came in. They wore that rather abashed look which people unconsciously assume when they break off a conversation on an unexpected entry.

"Morning, Horace! Morning, Doctor!" said Robin, crossing to the sideboard. "Any sign of Lady Margaret or Mary yet?"

The doctor had risen hastily to his feet.

"I rather think Dr. Redstone is expecting me," he said rapidly; "I half promised to go over to Stevenish ... think I'll just run over. The walk'll do me good ..."

He looked rather wildly about him, then fairly bolted from the room.

Robin, the cover of the porridge dish in his hand,

turned and stared at him.

"Why, whatever's the matter with Romain?" he began.

But Horace, who had not spoken a word, was himself halfway to the door.

"Horace!" called out Robin sharply.

The boy stopped with his back towards the other. But he did not turn round.

Robin put the cover back on the porridge dish and crossed the room.

"You all seem in the deuce of a hurry this morning ..." he said.

Still the boy made no reply.

"Why, Horace, what's the matter?"

Robin put his hand on young Trevert's shoulder. Horace shook him roughly off.

"I don't care to discuss it with you, Robin!" he said.

Robin deliberately swung the boy round until he faced him.

"My dear old thing," he expostulated. "What does it all mean? *What* won't you discuss with me?"

Horace Trevert looked straight at the speaker. His upper lip was pouted and trembled a little.

"What's the use of talking?" he said. "You know what I mean. Or would you like me to be plainer ..."

Robin met his gaze unflinchingly.

"I certainly would," he said, "if it's going to enlighten me as to why you should suddenly choose to behave like a lunatic ..."

Horace Trevert leant back and thrust his hands into his pockets.

"After what happened here yesterday," he said, speaking very clearly and deliberately, "I wonder you have the nerve to stay ..."

"My dear Horace," said Kobin quite impassively, "would you mind being a little more explicit? What precisely are you accusing me of? What have I done?"

"Done?" exclaimed the young man heatedly. "Done? Good God! Don't you realize that you have dragged my sister into this wretched business? Don't you understand that her name will be bandied about before a lot of rotten yokels at the inquest?"

Robin Greve's eyes glittered dangerously.

"I confess," he said, with elaborate politeness, "I scarcely understand what it has to do with me that Hartley Parrish should apparently commit suicide within a few days of becoming engaged to your sister ..."

"Ha!"

Horace Trevert snorted indignantly.

"You don't understand, don't you? We don't understand either. But, I must say, we thought *you* did!"

With that he turned to go. But Robin caught him by the arm.

"Listen to me, Horace," he said. "I'm not going to quarrel with you in this house of death. But you're going to tell here and now what you meant by that remark. Do you understand? I'm going to know!"

Horace Trevert shook himself free.

"Certainly you shall know," he answered with *hauteur*, "but I must say I should have thought that, as a lawyer and so on, you would have guessed my meaning without my having to explain. What I mean is that, now that Hartley Parrish is dead, there is only one man who knows what drove him to his death. And that's yourself! Do you want it plainer than that?"

Robin took a step back and looked at his friend. But he did not speak.

"And now," the boy continued, "perhaps you will realize that your presence here is disagreeable to Mary ..."

"Did Mary ask you to tell me this?" Robin broke in.

His voice had lost its hardness. It was almost wistful. The change of tone was so marked that it struck Horace. He hesitated an instant.

"Yes," he blurted out. "She doesn't want to see you again. I don't want to be offensive, Robin.."

"Please don't apologize," said Greve. "I quite understand that this is your sister's house now and, of course, I shall leave at once. I'll ask Jay to pack my things if you could order the car ..."

The boy moved towards the door. Before he reached it Robin called him back.

"Horace," he said pleasantly, "before you go I want you to answer me a question. Think before you speak, because it's very important. When you got into the library yesterday evening through the window, you smashed the glass, didn't you?"

Horace Trevert nodded.

"Yes," he replied, looking hard at Robin.

"Why?"

"To get into the room, of course!"

"Was the window bolted?"

The boy stopped and thought.

"No," he said slowly, "now I come to think of it, I don't believe it was. No, of course, it wasn't. I just put my arm through the broken pane and shoved the window up. But why do you ask?"

"Oh, nothing," answered Robin nonchalantly. "I just was curious to know, that's all!"

Horace stood and looked at him for an instant. Then he went out.

A quarter of an hour later, Hartley Parrish's Rolls-Royce glided through the straggling main street of Stevenish. A chapel bell tinkled unmusically, and on the pavements, gleaming with wet, went a procession of neatly dressed townsfolk bound, prayer-book in hand, for their respective places of worship. A news-boy, sorting out the Sunday newspapers which had just come down by train from London, was the only figure visible on the little station platform. Kobin bought a selection.

"There's all about Mr. Parrish," said the boy, "'im as they found dead up at 'Arkings las' night. And the noospapers 'asn't 'arf been sendin' down to-day ... reporters and photographers ... you oughter seen the crowd as come by the mornin' train ..."

"I wonder what they'll get out of Manderton," commented Robin rather grimly to himself as his train puffed leisurely, after the habit of Sunday trains, into the quiet little station.

In the solitude of his first-class smoker he unfolded the newspapers. None had more than the brief fact that Hartley Parrish had been found dead with a pistol in his hand, but they made up for the briefness of their reports by long accounts of the dead man's "meteoric career." And, Robin noted with relief, hitherto Mary Trevert's name was out of the picture.

He dropped the papers on to the seat, and, as the train steamed serenely through the Sunday calm of the country towards London's outer suburbs, he reviewed in his mind such facts as he had gleaned regarding the circumstances of his late host's death.

He would, he told himself, accept for the time being as *facts* what, he admitted to himself, so far only seemed to be such. Hartley Parrish, then, had been seated in his library at his desk with the door locked. The fire was smoking, and therefore he had opened the window. According to Horace Trevert, the window had not been bolted when he had entered the library, for, after smashing the pane in the assumption that the bolt was shot, he had had no difficulty in pushing up the window. Hartley Parrish had opened the window himself, for on the nail of the middle finger of his left hand Robin had seen, with the aid of the magnifying-glass, a tiny fragment of white paint.

Who had closed it? He had no answer ready to *that* question.

Now, as to the circumstances of the shooting. The suicide theory invited one to believe that Hartley Parrish had got up from his desk, pushing back his chair, had gone round it until he stood between the desk and the window, and had there shot himself through the heart. Why should he have done this?

Robin had no answer ready to this question either. He passed on again. Bude had heard loud voices a very few minutes before Mary had heard the shot. That morning's experiments had shown that Bude could have heard these sounds only by way of the open window of the library and the open doors of the garden and the library corridor. Additional proof, if Bude had heard aright, that the library window was open.

Leaning back in his seat, his finger-tips pressed together, Robin Greve resolutely faced the situation to which his deductions were leading him.

"The voice heard at the open window," he told himself, "was the voice of the man who murdered Parrish and who closed the window, that is, of course, if the murder theory proves more conclusive than that of suicide."

This brought him back to his investigations in the rosery. The abrasure he had discovered on the timber upright was the mark of a bullet and a mark freshly made at that. Moreover, it had almost certainly been fired from the library window - from the window which Parrish had opened; the angle at which it had struck and marked the tree showed that almost conclusively.

Yet there had been but one shot! If only he had been able to find that bullet in the rosery! Robin thought ruefully of his long hunt among the sopping rose-bushes.

Yes, there had been only one shot. Mary Trevert had stated it definitely. Besides, the bullet that had killed Hartley Parrish had been fired from his own revolver and had been found in the body. Robin Greve felt the murder theory collapsing about him. But the suicide theory did not stand up, either. What possible, probable motive had Hartley Parrish for taking his own life?

"He wasn't the man to do it!"

The wheels of the train took up the rhythm of the phrase and dinned it into his ears.

"He wasn't the man to do it!"

The riddle seemed more baffling than ever.

Robin thrust one hand into his right-hand pocket to get his pipe, his other hand into his left-hand pocket to find his pouch. His left hand came into contact with a little ball of paper.

He drew it out. It was the little ball of slatey-blue paper he had found on the floor of the library beside Hartley Parrish's dead body.

CHAPTER XII

MR. MANDERTON IS NONPLUSSED

Horace Trevert walked abruptly into Mary's Chinese boudoir. Lady Margaret and the girl were standing by the fire.

"Well," said Horace, dropping into a chair, "he's gone!"

"Who?" said Lady Margaret.

"Robin," answered the boy, "and I must say he took it very well ..."

"You don't mean to tell me, Horace," said his mother, "that you have actually sent Robin Greve away ...?"

Mary Trevert put her hand on her mother's arm.

" I wished it, Mother. I asked Horace to send him away ..."

"But, my dear," protested Lady Margaret.

Mary interrupted her impatiently.

"Robin Greve was impossible here. I had to ask him to

go. I suppose he can come back if ... if they want him for the inquest ..."

Lady Margaret was looking at her daughter in a puzzled way. She was a woman of the world and had brought her daughter up to be a woman of the world. She knew that Mary was not impulsive by nature. She knew that there was a wealth of good sense behind those steady eyes.

In response to a look from his mother, Horace got up and left the room.

"Mary, dear," said the older woman, "don't you think you are making a mistake?"

The girl turned away, one slim shoe tapping restlessly against the brass rail of the fireplace.

"My dear," her mother went on, "remember I have known Robin Greve all his life. His father, the Admiral, was a very old friend of mine. He was the very personification of honour. Robin is very fond of you ... no, he has told me nothing, but I *know*. Don't you think it is rather hard on an old friend to turn him away just when you most want him?"

There was a heightened colour in the girl's face as she turned and looked her mother in the face.

"Robin has not behaved like a friend, Mother," she answered. "He knows more than he pretends about ... about this. And he lets me find out things from the servants when he ought to have told me himself. If he is suspected of having said something to Hartley which made him do this dreadful thing, he has only himself to thank. I *did* try to shield him - before I knew. But I'm not going to do so any more. If he stays I shall have the police suspecting me all the time. And I owe something to Hartley ..."

Her mother sighed a soft little sigh. She said nothing. She was a very wise woman.

" Robin left me to go to the library ... I am sure of that ..." Mary went on breathlessly.

"Why?" her mother asked.

The girl hesitated.

Then she said slowly:

"You and I have always been good pals, Mother, so I may as well tell you. Robin had just asked me to marry him. So I told him I was engaged to Hartley. He went on in the most awful way, and said that I was selling myself and that I would not be the first girl that Hartley had kept ..."

She broke off and raised her hands to her face. Then she put her elbows on the mantel-shelf and burst into tears.

"Oh, it was hateful," she sobbed.

Her mother put her arm round her soothingly.

"Well, my dear," she said, "Robin was always fond of you, and I dare say it was a shock to him. When men feel like that about a girl they generally say things they don't mean ..."

Mary Trevert straightened herself up and dropped her hands to her side. She faced her mother, the tear-drops glistening on her long lashes.

"He meant it, every word of it. And he was perfectly right. I *was* selling myself, and you know I was, Mother. Do you think we can go on for ever like this, living on credit and dodging tradesmen? I meant to marry Hartley and stick to him. But I never thought ... I never guessed ... that Robin ..."

"I know, my dear," her mother interposed, "I know. Perhaps it doesn't sound a very proper thing to say in the circumstances, but now that poor Hartley is gone, there is no reason whatsoever why you and Robin ..."

The Treverts were a hot-tempered race. Lady Margaret's unfinished sentence seemed to infuriate the girl.

"Do you think I'd marry Robin Greve as long as I thought he knew the mystery of Hartley's death!" she cried passionately. "I was willing to give up my self-respect once to save us from ruin, but I won't do it again. I'm not surprised to find you thinking I am ready to marry Robin and live happy ever after on poor Hartley's money. But I've not sunk so low as that! If you ever mention this to me again, Mother, I promise you I'll go away and never come back!"

"My dear child," temporized Lady Margaret, eyebrows raised in protest at this outburst, "of course, it shall be as you wish. I only thought ..."

But Mary Trevert was not listening. She leant on the mantel-shelf, her dark head in her hands, and she murmured:

"The tragedy of it! My God, the tragedy of it!"

Lady Margaret twisted the rings on her long white fingers.

"The tragedy of it, my dear," she said, "is that you have sent away the man you love at a time when you will never need him so badly again ..."

There was a discreet tapping at the door.

"Come in!" said Lady Margaret.

Bude appeared.

"Mr. Manderton, the detective, my lady, was wishing to know whether he might see Miss Trevert ..."

"Yes. Ask him to come up here," commanded Lady Margaret.

"He is without - in the corridor, my lady!"

He stepped back and in a moment Mr. Manderton stepped into the room, big, burly, and determined.

He made a little stiff bow to the two ladies and halted irresolute near the door.

"You wished to see my daughter, Mr. Manderton," said Lady Margaret.

The detective bowed again.

"And you, too, my lady," he said. "Allow me!"

He closed the door, then crossed to the fireplace.

"After I had seen you and Miss Trevert last night, my lady," he began, "I had a talk with Mr. Jeekes, Mr. Parrish's principal secretary, who came down by car from London as soon as he heard the news. My lady, I think this is a fairly simple case!"

He paused and scanned the carpet.

"Mr. Jeekes tells me, my lady," he went on presently, "that Mrs Fairish had been suffering from neurasthenia and a weak heart brought on by too much smoking. It appears that he had consulted, within the last two months, two leading specialists of Harley Street about his health. One of these gentlemen, Sir Winterton Maire, ordered him to knock off all work and all smoking for at least three months. He will give evidence to this effect at the inquest. Mr. Parrish disregarded these orders as he was wishful to put through his scheme for Hornaway's before taking a rest. Mr. Jeekes can prove that. In these circumstances, my lady...."

"Well?"

Lady Margaret, in her black crêpe de chine dress, setting off the silvery whiteness of her hair, was a calm, unemotional figure as she sat in her lacquer chair.

"Well?" she asked again.

"Well," said the detective, "the verdict will be one of 'Suicide whilst of unsound mind,' and in my opinion the medical evidence will be sufficient to bring that in.

There will not be occasion, I fancy, my lady, to probe any farther into the motives of Mr. Parrish's action...."

"And are you personally satisfied" - Mary's voice broke in clear and unimpassioned - "are you personally satisfied, Mr. Manderton, that Mr. Parrish shot himself?"

The detective cast an appealing glance at the tips of his well-burnished boots.

"Yes, Miss, I think I may say I am...."

"And what about the evidence of Bude, who said he heard voices in the library...."

Mr. Manderton gave his shoulders the merest suspicion of a shrug, raised his hands, and dropped them to his sides.

"I had hoped, my lady," he said, throwing a glance at Lady Margaret, "and you, Miss, that I had made it clear that in the circumstances we need not pursue that matter any further...."

Lady Margaret rose. Her dominating personality seemed to fill the room.

"We are extremely obliged to you, Mr. Manderton," she said, "for the able and discreet way in which you have handled this case. I sometimes meet the Chief Commissioner at dinner. I shall write to Sir Maurice and tell him my opinion."

Mr. Manderton reddened a little.

"Your ladyship is too good," he said.

Lady Margaret bowed to signify that the interview was at an end. But Mary Trevert left her side and walked to the door.

"Will you come downstairs with me, Mr. Manderton," she said. "I should like to speak to you alone for a minute!"

She led the way downstairs through the hall and out into the drive. A pale sun shone down from a grey and rainy sky, and the damp breeze blowing from the sodden trees played among the ringlets of her dark hair.

"We will walk down the drive," she said to the detective, who, rather astonished, had followed her. "We can talk freely out of doors."

They took a dozen steps in silence. Then she said:

"Who was it speaking to Mr. Parrish in the library?"

"Undoubtedly Mr. Greve," replied the man without hesitation.

"Why undoubtedly?" asked the girl.

"It could have been no one else. We know that he left you hot to get at Mr. Parrish and have words with him. Bude heard them talking with voices raised aloud...."

"But if the door were locked?"

" Mr. Parrish may have opened it and locked it again,

Mr. Greve getting out by the window. But there are no traces of that ... one would look to find marks on the paint on the inside. Besides, a little test we made this morning suggests that Mr. Greve spoke to Mr. Parrish through the window...."

"Was the window open?"

"Yes, Miss, it probably was. The fire had been smoking in the library. Mr. Parrish had complained to Bude about it. Besides, we have found Mr. Parrish's finger-prints on the inside of the window-frame. Outside we found other finger-prints ... Sir Horace's. Sir Horace was good enough to allow his to be taken."

The girl looked at the detective quickly.

"Were there any other finger-prints except Horace's on the outside?" she asked.

Mr. Manderton shook his head.

"No, Miss," he answered.

They had reached the lodge-gates at the beginning of the drive and turned to retrace their steps to the house.

"Then we shall never know exactly why Mr. Parrish did this thing?" hazarded Mary.

Mr. Manderton darted her a surreptitious glance.

"We shall see about that," he said.

There was menace in his voice.

Mary Trevert stopped. She put her hand on the detective's arm.

"Mr. Manderton," she said, "if you are satisfied, then, believe me, I am!"

The detective bowed.

"Miss Trevert," he said, - and he spoke perfectly respectfully though his words were blunt, - "I can well believe that!"

The girl looked up quickly. She scanned his face rather apprehensively.

"What do you mean?" she asked, "I don't understand...."

"I mean," was the detective's answer, given in his quiet, level voice, "that when you attempted to mislead Inspector Humphries you did nobody any good!"

The girl bent her head without replying, and in silence they regained the house. At the house door they parted, Mary going indoors while the detective remained standing on the drive. Very deliberately he produced a short briar pipe, cut a stub of dark plug tobacco from a flat piece he carried in his pocket, crammed the tobacco into his pipe, and lit it. Reflectively he blew a thin spiral of smoke into the still air.

"*He* told me about that fat butler's evidence," he said to himself; "*he* put me wise about that window being open; *he* gave me the office about the paint on the finger-nails of Mr. H.P."

He ticked off each point on his fingers with the stem of his pipe.

"Why?" said Mr. Manderton aloud, addressing a laurel-bush.

CHAPTER XIII

JEEKES

Mr. Albert Edward Jeekes, Hartley Parrish's principal private secretary, lunched with Lady Margaret, Mary and Horace. Dr. Romain seemed not to have got over his embarrassment of the morning, for he did not put in an appearance.

Mr. Jeekes was an old young man who supported bravely the weight of his Christian names, a reminder of his mother having occupied some small post in the household of Queen Victoria the Good. He might have been any age between 35 and 50 with his thin sandy hair, his myopic gaze, and his habitual expression of worried perplexity.

He was a shorthand-writer and typist of incredible dexterity and speed which, combined with an unquenchable energy, had recommended him to Hartley Parrish. Accordingly, in consideration of a salary which he would have been the first to describe as "princely," he had during the past four years devoted some fifteen hours a day to the service of Mr. Hartley Parrish.

He was unmarried. When not on duty, either at St. James's Square, Harkings, or Hartley Parrish's palatial offices in Broad Street, he was to be found at one of those immense and gloomy clubs of indiscriminate membership which are dotted about the parish of St. James's, S.W., and to which Mr. Jeekes was in the habit of referring in Early-Victorian accents of respect.

"When I heard the news at the club, Miss Trevert," said Jeekes, "you could have knocked me down with a feather. Mr. Parrish, as all of us knew, worked himself a great deal too hard, sometimes not knocking off for his tea, even, and wore his nerves all to pieces. But I never dreamed it would come to this. Ah! he's a great loss, and what we shall do without him I don't know. There was a piece in one of the papers about him to-day - perhaps you saw it? - it called him 'one of the captains of industry of modern England.'"

"You were always a great help to him, Mr. Jeekes," said Mary, who was touched by the little man's hero-worship; "I am sure you realized that he appreciated you."

"Well," replied Mr. Jeekes, rubbing the palms of his hands together, "he did a great deal for *me*. Took me out of a City office where I was getting two pound five a week. That's what he did. It was a shipping firm. I tell you this because it has a bearing, Miss Trevert, on what is to follow. Why did he pick me? I'll tell you.

"He was passing through the front office with one of our principals when he asked him, just casually, what Union Pacific stood at. The boss didn't know.

"'A hundred and eighty-seven London parity,' says I. He turned round and looked at me. 'How do you know that?' says he, rather surprised, this being in a shipping office, you understand.

"'I take an interest in the markets,' I replied. 'Do you?' he says. 'Then you might do for me,' and tells me to come and see him."

" I went. He made me an offer. When I heard the figure ... my word!"

Mr. Jeekes paused. Then added sadly:

"And I had meant to work for him to my dying day!"

They were in the billiard-room seated on the selfsame settee, Mary reflected, on which she and Robin had sat - how long ago it seemed, though only yesterday! Mary had carried the secretary off after luncheon in order to unfold to him a plan which she had been turning over in her mind ever since her conversation with the detective.

"And what are you going to do now, Mr. Jeekes?" she asked.

The little man pursed up his lips.

"Well," he said, "I'll have to get something else, I expect. I'm not expecting to find anything so good as I had with Mr. Parrish. And things are pretty crowded in the City, Miss Trevert, what with all the boys back from the war, God bless 'em, and glad we are to see 'em, I'm sure. I hope you'll realize, Miss Trevert, that anything I can do to help to put Mr. Parrish's affairs straight...."

"I was just about to say," Mary broke in, "that I hope

you will not contemplate any change, Mr. Jeekes. You know more about Mr. Parrish's affairs than anybody else, and I shall be very glad if you will stay on and help me. You know I have been left sole executrix...."

"Miss Trevert," - the little man stammered in his embarrassment, - "this is handsome of you. I surely thought you would have wished to make your own arrangements, appoint your own secretaries...."

Mr. Jeekes broke off and looked at her, blinking hard.

"Not at all," said Mary. "Everything shall be as it was. I am sure that Mr. Bardy will approve. Besides, Mr. Jeekes, I want your assistance in something else...."

"Anything in my power...." began Jeekes.

"Listen," said Mary.

She was all her old self-composed self now, a charming figure in her plain blue serge suit with a white silken shirt and black tie - the best approach to mourning her wardrobe could afford. Already the short winter afternoon was drawing in. Mysterious shadows lurked in the corners of the long and narrow room.

"Listen," said Mary, leaning forward. "I want to know why Mr. Parrish killed himself. I mean to know. And I want you, Mr. Jeekes, to help me to find out,"

Something stirred ever so faintly in the remote recesses of the billiard-room. A loose board or something creaked softly and was silent.

" What was that ? " the girl called out sharply.

"Who's there?"

Mr. Jeekes got up and walked over to the door. It was ajar. He closed it.

"Just a board creaking," he said as he resumed his seat.

"I want your aid in finding out the motive for this terrible deed," - Mary Trevert was speaking again, - "I can't understand.... I don't see clear...."

"Miss Trevert," said Mr. Jeekes, clearing his throat fussily, "I fear we must look for the motive in the state of poor Mr. Parrish's nerves. An uncommonly high-strung man he always was, and he smoked those long black strong cigars of his from morning till night. Sir Winterton Maire told him flatly - Mr. Parrish, I recollect, repeated his very words to me after Sir Winterton had examined him - that, if he did not take a complete rest and give up smoking, he would not be answerable for the consequences. Therefore, Miss Trevert...."

"Mr. Jeekes," answered the girl, "I knew Mr. Parrish pretty well. A woman, you know, gets to the heart of a man's character very often quicker than his daily associates in business. And I know that Mr. Parrish was the last man in the world to have done a thing like that. He was so ... so undaunted. He made nothing of difficulties. He relied wholly on himself. That was the secret of his success. For him to have killed himself like this makes me feel convinced that there was some hidden reason, far stronger, far more terrible, than any question of nerves...."

Leaning forward, her hands clasped tightly in front of

her, Mary Trevert raised her dark eyes to the little secretary's face.

"Many men have a secret in their lives," she said in a low voice. "Do you know of anything in Mr. Parrish's life which an enemy might have made use of to drive him to his death?"

Her manner was so intense that Mr. Jeekes quite lost his self-composure. He clutched at his *pince-nez* and readjusted them upon his nose to cover his embarrassment. The secretary was not used to gazing at beautiful women whose expressive features showed as clearly as this the play of the emotions.

"Miss Trevert," he said presently, "I know of no such secret. But then what do I - what does any one - know of Mr. Parrish's former life?"

"We might make enquiries in South Africa?" ventured the girl.

"I doubt if we should learn anything much through that," said the secretary. "Of course, Mr. Parrish had great responsibilities and responsibility means worry...."

A silence fell on them both. From somewhere in the dark shadows above the fire glowing red through the falling twilight a clock chimed once. There was a faint rustling from the neighborhood of the door. Mr. Jeekes started violently. A coal dropped noisily into the fireplace.

"There was something else," said Mary, ignoring the interruption, and paused. She did not look up when she spoke again.

"There is often a woman in cases like this," she began reluctantly.

Mr. Jeekes looked extremely uncomfortable.

"Miss Trevert," he said, "I beg you will not press me on that score...."

"Why?" asked the girl bluntly.

"Because ... because" - Mr. Jeekes stumbled sadly over his words - "because, dear me, there are some things which really I couldn't possibly discuss ... if you'll excuse me...."

"Oh, but you can discuss everything, Mr. Jeekes," replied Mary Trevert composedly. "I am not a child, you know. I am perfectly well aware that there's a woman somewhere in the life of every man, very often two or three. I haven't got any illusions on the subject, I assure you. I never supposed for a moment that I was the first woman in Mr. Parrish's life...."

This candour seemed to administer a knock-out blow to the little secretary's Victorian mind. He was speechless. He took off his *pince-nez*, blindly polished them with his pocket-handkerchief and replaced them upon his nose. His fingers trembled violently.

"I have no wish to appear vulgarly curious," the girl went on, - Mr. Jeekes made a quick gesture of dissent, - "but I am anxious to know whether Mr. Parrish was being blackmailed ... or anything like that...."

"Oh, no, Miss Trevert, I do assure you," the little man expostulated in hasty denial, "nothing like that, I am convinced. At least, that is to say ..."

He rose to his feet, clutching the little *attaché* case which he invariably carried with him as a kind of emblem of office.

"And now, if you'll excuse me, Miss Trevert," he muttered, "I should really be going. I am due at Mr. Bardy's office at five o'clock. He is coming up from the country specially to meet me. There is so much to discuss with regard to this terrible affair."

He glanced at his watch.

"With the roads as greasy as they are," he added, "it will take me all my time in the car to ..."

He cast a panic-striken glance around him. But Mary Trevert held him fast.

"You didn't finish what you were saying about Mr. Parrish, Mr. Jeekes," she said impassively. The secretary made no sign. But he looked a trifle sullen.

"I don't think you realize, Mr. Jeekes," she said, "that other people besides myself are keenly interested in the motives for Mr. Parrish's suicide. The police profess to be willing to accept the testimony of the specialists as satisfactory medical evidence about his state of mind. But I distrust that man, Manderton. He is not satisfied, Mr. Jeekes. He won't rest until he knows the truth."

The secretary cast her a frightened glance.

"But Mr. Manderton told me himself, Miss Trevert," he affirmed, "that the verdict would be, 'Suicide while temporarily insane,' on Sir Winterton Maire's evidence alone ..."

Mary Trevert tapped the ground impatiently with her foot.

"Manderton will get at the truth, I tell you," she said. "He's that kind of man. Do you want me to find out from them? At the inquest, perhaps?"

The secretary put his *attaché* case down on the lounge again.

"Of course, that would be most improper, Miss Trevert," he said. "But your question embarrasses me. It embarrasses me very much ..."

"What are you keeping back from me, Mr. Jeekes?" the girl demanded imperiously.

The secretary mopped his forehead with his handkerchief. Then, as though with an effort, he spoke.

"There is a lady, a French lady, who draws an income from Mr. Parrish ..."

The girl remained impassive, but her eyes grew rather hard.

"These payments are still going on?" she asked.

Jeekes hesitated. Then he nodded,

"Yes," he said.

"Well? Was she blackmailing ... him?"

"No, no," Mr. Jeekes averred hastily. "But there was some unpleasantness some months ago ... er ... a county court action, to be precise, about some bills she owed. Mr. Parrish was very angry about it and settled to prevent it coming into court. But there was some talk about it ... in legal circles ..."

He threw a rather scared glance at the girl.

"Please explain yourself, Mr. Jeekes," she said coldly. "I don't understand ..."

" Her lawyer was Le Hagen - it's a shady firm with a big criminal practice. They sometimes brief Mr. Greve ..."

Mary Trevert clasped and unclasped her hands quickly.

"I quite understand, Mr. Jeekes," she said. "You needn't say any more ..."

She turned away in a manner that implied dismissal. It was as though she had forgotten the secretary's existence. He picked up his *attaché* case and walked slowly to the door.

A sharp exclamation broke from his lips.

"Miss Trevert," he cried, "the door ... I shut it a little while back ... look, it's ajar!"

The girl who stood at the fire switched on the electric light by the mantelpiece.

"Is ... is ... the door defective? Doesn't it shut properly?"

The little secretary forced out the questions in an agitated voice.

The girl walked across the room and shut the door. It closed perfectly, a piece of solid, well-fitting oak.

"What does it mean?" said Mr. Jeekes in a whisper. "You understand, I should not wish what I told you just now about Mr. Parrish to be overheard ..."

They opened the door again. The dusky corridor was empty.

CHAPTER XIV

A SHEET OF BLUE PAPER

The sight of that crumpled ball of slatey-blue paper brought back to Robin's mind with astonishing vividness every detail of the scene in the library. Once more he looked into Hartley Parrish's staring, unseeing eyes, saw the firelight gleam again on the heavy gold signet ring on the dead man's hand, the tag of the dead man's bootlace as it trailed from one sprawling foot across the carpet. Once more he felt the dark cloud of the mystery envelop him as a mist and with a little sigh he smoothed out the crumpled paper.

It was an ordinary quarto sheet of stoutish paper, with a glazed surface, of an unusual shade of blue, darker than what the stationers call "azure," yet lighter than legal blue. At the top right-hand corner was typewritten a date: "Nov. 25." Otherwise the sheet was blank.

The curious thing about it was that a number of rectangular slits had been cut in the paper. Robin counted them. There were seven. They were of varying sizes, the largest a little over an inch, the smallest not more than a quarter of an inch, in length. In depth they measured about an eighth of an inch.

Robin stared at the paper uncomprehendingly. He remembered perfectly where he had found it on the floor of the library at Harkings, between the dead body and the waste-paper basket. The basket, he recalled, stood out in the open just clear of the desk on the left-hand side. From the position in which it was lying the ball of paper might have been aimed for the waste-paper basket and, missing it, have fallen on the carpet.

Robin turned the sheet over. The back was blank. Then he held the paper up to the light. Yes, there was a water-mark. Now it was easily discernible. "EGMONT FF. QU." he made out.

The train was slowing down. Robin glanced out of the window and saw that they were crossing the river in the mirky gloom of a London winter Sunday. He balanced the sheet of paper in his hands for a moment. Then he folded it carefully into four and stowed it away in his cigarette-case. The next moment the train thumped its way into Charing Cross.

A taxi deposited him at the Middle Temple Gate. He walked the short distance to the set of chambers he occupied. On his front door a piece of paper was pinned. By the rambling calligraphy and the phonetic English he recognized the hand of his "laundress."

> Dere sir [it ran], mr rite call he want to see u pertikler i tole im as you was in country & give im ur adress hope i dun rite mrs bragg

Robin had scarcely got his key in the door of his "oak" when there was a step on the stair. A nice-looking young man with close-cropped fair hair appeared round the turn of the staircase.

Valentine Williams

"Hullo, Robin," he exclaimed impetuously, "I *am* glad to have caught you like this. Your woman gave me your address, so I rang up Harkings at once and they told me you had just gone back to town. So I came straight here. You remember me, don't you? Bruce Wright ... But perhaps I'm butting in. If you'd rather see me some other time...."

"My dear boy," said Robin, motioning him into the flat, "of course I remember you. Only I didn't recognize you just for the minute. Shove your hat down here in the hall. And as for butting in," - he threw open the door of the living-room, - "why! I think there is no other man in England I would so gladly see at this very moment as yourself."

The living-room was a bright and cheery place, tastefully furnished in old oak with gay chintz curtains. It looked out on an old-world paved court in the centre of which stood a solitary soot-laden plane-tree.

"What's this rot about Parrish having committed suicide?" demanded the boy abruptly.

Robin gave him in the briefest terms an outline of the tragedy.

"Poor old H.P., eh?" mused young Wright; "who'd have thought it?"

"But the idea of suicide is preposterous," he broke out suddenly. "I knew Parrish probably better than anybody. He would never have done a thing like that. It must have been an accident...."

Robin shook his head.

"That possibility is ruled out by the medical evidence," he said, and stopped short.

Bruce Wright, who had been pacing up and down the room, halted in front of the barrister.

"I tell you that Parrish was not the man to commit suicide. Nothing would have even forced him to take his own life. You know, I was working with him as his personal secretary every day for more than two years, and I am sure!"

He resumed his pacing up and down the room.

"Has it ever occurred to you, Robin," he said presently, "that practically nothing is known of H.P.'s antecedents? For instance, do you know where he was born?"

"I understand he was a Canadian," replied Robin with a shrewd glance at the flushed face of the boy.

"He's lived in Canada," said Wright, "but originally he was a Cockney, from the London slums. And I believe I am the only person who knows that...."

Robin pushed an armchair at his companion.

"Sit down and tell me about it," he commanded.

The boy dropped into the chair.

"It was after I had been only a few months with him," he began, "shortly after I was discharged from the army with that lung wound of mine. We were driving back in the car from some munition works near Baling, and the chauffeur took a wrong turning near

Wormwood Scrubs and got into a maze of dirty streets round there...."

"I know," commented Robin, "Notting Dale, they call it...."

"H.P. wasn't noticing much," Wright went on, "as he was dictating letters to me, - we used to do a lot of work in the Rolls-Royce in those rush days, - but, directly he noticed that the chauffeur was uncertain of the road, he shoved his head out of the window and put him right at once. I suppose I seemed surprised at his knowing his way about those parts, for he laughed at me and said: 'I was born and brought up down here, Bruce, in a little greengrocer's shop just off the Latimer Road.' I said nothing because I didn't want to interrupt his train of thought. He had never talked to me or Jeekes or any of us like that before.

"'By Gad,' he went on, 'how the smell of the place brings back those days to me - the smell of decayed fruit, of stale fish, of dirt! Why, it seems like yesterday that Victor Marbran and I used to drive round uncle's cart with vegetables and coal. What a life to escape from, Bruce, my boy! Gad, you can count yourself lucky!'

"He was like a man talking to himself. I asked him how he had broken away from it all. At that he laughed, a bitter, hard sort of laugh. 'By having the guts to break away from it, boy,' he said. 'It was I who made Victor Marbran come away with me. We worked our passages out to the Cape and made our way up-country to Matabeleland. That was in the early days of Rhodes and Barney Barnato - long before I went to Canada. I made Victor's fortune for him and mine as well. But I made more than Victor and he never forgave me. He'd do me a bad turn if he could ...'

" Then he broke off short and went on with his dictating ..."

"Did he ever come back to this phase of his life?"

"Only when we got out of the car that morning. He said to me: 'Forget what I told you to-day, young fellow. Never rake up a man's past!' And he never mentioned the subject again. Of course, I didn't either ..."

Stretched full length in his chair, his eyes fixed on the ceiling, Robin remained lost in thought.

"The conversation came back to me to-day," said the boy, "when I read of Parrish's death. And I wondered ..."

"Well?"

"Whether the secret of his death may not be found somewhere in his adventurous past. You see he said that Victor Marbran was an enemy. Then there was something else. I never told you - when you took all that trouble to get me another job after Parrish had sacked me - the exact reason for my dismissal. You never asked me either. That was decent of you, Robin ..."

"I liked you, Bruce," said Robin shortly.

"Well, I'll tell you now," he said. "When I joined H.P.'s staff after I got out of the Army, I was put under old

Jeekes, of course, to learn the work. One of the first injunctions he gave me was with regard to Mr. Parrish's letters. I suppose you know more or less how secretaries of a big business man like Hartley Parrish work. They open all letters, lay the important ones before the big man for him to deal with personally, make a digest of the others or deal with them direct ..."

Robin nodded.

"Well," the boy resumed, "the first thing old Jeekes told me was that letters arriving in a blue envelope and marked 'Personal' were never to be opened ..."

"In a blue envelope?" echoed Robin quickly.

"Yes, a particular kind of blue - a sort of slatey-blue - Jeekes showed me one as a guide. Well, these letters were to be handed to Mr. Parrish unopened."

Robin had stood up.

"That's odd," he said, diving in his pocket.

"I say, hold on a bit," protested the boy, "this is really rather important what I am telling you. I'll never finish if you keep on interrupting."

"Sorry, Bruce," said Robin, and sat down again.

But he began to play restlessly with his cigarette case which he had drawn from his pocket.

"Well, of course," Bruce resumed, "I wasn't much of a private secretary really, and one day I forgot all about this injunction. Some days old H.P. got as many as three hundred letters. I was alone at Harkings with him, I remember, Jeekes was up at Sheffield and the other secretaries were away ill or something, and in the rush of dealing with this enormous mail I slit one of these blue envelopes open with the rest. I discovered what I had done only after I had got all the letters sorted out, this one with the rest. So I went straight to old H.P. and told him. By Jove!"

"What happened?" said Robin.

"He got into the most paralytic rage," said Bruce. "I have never seen a man in such an absolute frenzy of passion. He went right off the hooks, just like that! He fairly put the wind up me. For a minute I thought he was going to kill me. He snatched the letter out of my hand, called me every name under the sun, and finally shouted: 'You're fired, d'ye hear? I won't employ men who disobey my orders! Get out of this before I do you a mischief! I went straight off. And I never saw him again ..."

Robin Greve looked very serious. But his face displayed no emotion as he asked:

"And what was in the letter for him to make such a fuss about?"

The boy shrugged his shoulders.

"That was the extraordinary part of it. The letter was perfectly harmless. It was an ordinary business letter from a firm in Holland ..."

"In Holland?" cried Greve. "Did you say in Holland? Tell me the name! No , wait, see if I can remember.

'Van' something - 'Speck' or 'Spike' ..."

"I remember the name perfectly," answered Bruce, rather puzzled by the other's sudden outburst; "it was Van der Spyck and Co. of Rotterdam. We had a good deal of correspondence with them ..."

Robin Greve had opened his cigarette-case and drawn from it a creased square of blue paper folded twice across. Unfolding it, he held up the sheet he had found in the library at Harkings.

"Is that the paper those letters were written on?" he asked.

Bruce took the sheet from him. He held it up to the light.

"Why, yes," came the prompt answer. "I'd know it in a minute. Look, it's the same water-mark. 'Egmont.' Where did you get hold of it?"

"Bruce," said Robin gravely, without answering the question, "we're getting into deep water, boy!"

CHAPTER XV

SHADOWS

Robert Greve stood for an instant in silence by the window of his rooms. His fingers hammered out a tattoo on the pane. His eyes were fixed on the windows of the chambers across the court. But they did not take in the pleasant prospect of the tall, ivy-framed casements in their mellow setting of warm red brick. He was trying to fix a mental photograph of a letter - typewritten on paper of dark slatey blue - which he had seen on Hartley Parrish's desk in the library at Harkings on the previous afternoon.

Prompted by Bruce Wright, he could now recall the heading clearly. "ELIAS VAN DER SPYCK & Co., GENERAL IMPORTERS, ROTTERDAM," stood printed before his eyes as plainly as though he still held the typewritten sheet in front of him. But the mind plays curious tricks. Robin's brain had registered the name; yet it recorded no impression of the contents of the letter. Beyond the fact that it dealt in plain commercial fashion with some shipments or other, he could recall no particular whatever of it.

"But where did you get hold of this sheet of paper?" Bruce Wright's voice broke in impatiently behind him. "I'm most frightfully interested to know ..."

Valentine Williams

"Found it on the floor beside Parrish's body," answered Robin briefly. "There was a letter, too, on the same paper ..."

"By Gad!" exclaimed the boy eagerly, "have you got that too?"

Robin shook his head.

"It was only your story that made me think of it. I had the letter. But I left it where I found it - on Parrish's desk in the library ..."

"But you read it ... you know what was in it?"

Robin shrugged his shoulders.

"It was a perfectly straightforward business letter ... something about steel shipments ... I don't remember any more ..."

"A straightforward business letter," commented the boy. "Like the letter I read, eh?..."

"Tell me, Bruce," said Robin, after a moment's silence, "during the time you were with Hartley Parrish, I suppose these blue letters came pretty often?"

Young Wright wrinkled his brow in thought.

"It's rather difficult to say. You see, there were three of us besides old Jeekes, and, of course, these letters might have come without my knowledge anything about it. But during the seven months I worked with H.P. I suppose about half a dozen of these letters passed through my hands. They used to worry H.P., you know, Robin ..."

"Worry him?" exclaimed Robin sharply; "how do you mean?"

"Well," said Bruce, "Parrish was a very easygoing fellow, you know. He worked every one - himself included - like the devil, of course. But he was hardly ever nervy or grumpy. And so I was a bit surprised to find - after I had been with him for a time - that every now and then he sort of shrivelled up. He used to look ... well, careworn and ... and haggard. And at these times he was pretty short with all of us. It was such an extraordinary change from his usual cheery, optimistic self that sometimes I suspected him of dope or some horror like that ..."

Robin shook his head. He had a sudden vision of Hartley Parrish, one of his long, black Partagas thrust at an aggressive angle from a corner of his mouth, virile, battling, strong.

"Oh, no," he said, "not dope ..."

"No, no, I know," the boy went on quickly. "It wasn't dope. It was fear ..."

Robin swung round from the window.

"Fear? Fear of what?"

The boy cast a frightened glance over his shoulder rather as if he fancied he might be overheard.

"Of those letters," he replied. "I am sure it was that. I watched him and ... and I *know*. Every time he got one of those letters in the bluish envelopes, these curious fits of gloom came over him. Robin ..."

"What, Bruce?"

"I think he was being blackmailed!"

The barrister nodded thoughtfully.

"Don't you agree?"

The boy awaited his answer eagerly.

"Something very like that," replied the other.

Then suddenly he smashed his fist into the open palm of his other hand.

"But he wouldn't have taken it lying down!" he cried. "Hartley Parrish was a fighter, Bruce. Did you ever know a man who could best him? No, no, it won't fit! Besides ..."

He broke off and thought for an instant.

"We must get that letter from Harkings," he said presently. "Jeekes will have it. We can do nothing until ..."

His voice died away. Bruce, sunk in one of the big leather armchairs, was astonished to see him slip quickly away from the window and ensconce himself behind one of the chintz curtains.

"Here, Bruce," Robin called softly across the room. "Just come here. But take care not to show yourself.

Look out, keep behind the curtain and here ... peep out through this chink!"

Young Wright peered through a narrow slit between the curtain and the window-frame. In the far corner of the courtyard beneath the windows, where a short round iron post marked a narrow passage leading to the adjoining court, a man was standing. He wore a shabby suit and a blue handkerchief knotted about his neck served him as a substitute for the more conventional collar and tie. His body was more than half concealed by the side of the house along which the passage ran. But his face was clearly distinguishable - a peaky, thin face, the upper part in the shadow of the peak of a discoloured tweed cap.

"He's been there on and off all the time we've been talking," said Robin. "I wasn't sure at first. But now I'm certain. He's watching these windows! Look!"

Briskly the watcher's head was withdrawn to emerge again, slowly and cautiously, in a little while.

"But who is he? What does he want?" asked Bruce.

"I haven't an idea," retorted Robin Greve. "But I could guess. Tell me, Bruce," he went on, stepping back from the window and motioning the boy to do the same, "did you notice anybody following you when you came here?"

Bruce shook his head.

"I'm pretty sure nobody did. You see, I came in from the Strand, down Middle Temple Lane. Once service has started at Temple Church there's not a mouse stirring in the Inn till the church is out. I think I should have noticed if any one had followed me up to your chambers ..."

Robin set his chin squarely.

"Then he came after me," he said. "Bruce, you'll have to go to Harkings and get that letter!"

"By all means," answered the boy. "But, I say, they won't much like me butting in, will they?"

"You'll have to say you came down to offer your sympathy, ... volunteer your services ... oh, anything. But you *must* get that letter! Do you understand, Bruce? *You must get that letter* - if you have to steal it!"

The boy gave a long whistle.

"That's rather a tall order, isn't it?" he said.

Robin nodded. His face was very grave.

"Yes," he said presently, "I suppose it is. But there is something ... something horrible behind this case, Bruce, something dark and..and mysterious. And I mean to get to the bottom of it. With your help. Or alone!"

Bruce put his hand impulsively on the other's arm.

"You can count on me, you know," he said. "But don't you think ..."

He broke off shyly.

"What?"

"Don't you think you'd better tell me what you know. And what you suspect!"

Robin hesitated.

"Yes," he said, "that's fair. I suppose I ought. But there's not much to tell, Bruce. Just before Hartley Parrish was found dead, I asked Miss Trevert to marry me. I was too late. She was already engaged to Hartley Parrish. I was horrified ... I know some things about Parrish ... we had words and I went off. Five minutes later Miss Trevert went to fetch Parrish in to tea and heard a shot behind the locked door of the library. Horace Trevert got in through the window and found Parrish dead. Every one down at Harkings believes that I went in and threatened Parrish so that he committed suicide ..."

"Whom do you mean by every one?"

Robin laughed drily. "Mary Trevert, her mother, Horace Trevert ..."

"The police, too?"

"Certainly. The police more than anybody!"

"By Jove!" commented the boy.

"You ask me what I suspect," Robin continued. "I admit I have no positive proof. But I suspect that Hartley Parrish did not die by his own hand!"

Bruce Wright looked up with a startled expression on

his face.

"You mean that he was murdered?"

"I do!"

"But how? Why?"

Then Robin told him of the experiment in the library, of the open window and of the bullet mark he had discovered in the rosery.

"What I want to know," he said, "and what I am determined to find out beyond any possible doubt, is whether the bullet found in Hartley Parrish's body was fired from *his* pistol. But before we reach that point we have to explain how it happened that only one shot was heard and how a bullet which *apparently* came from Parrish's pistol was found in his body ..."

"If Mr. Parrish was murdered, the murderer might have turned the gun round in Parrish's hand and forced him to shoot himself ..."

"Hardly," said Robin. "Remember, Mary Trevert was at the door when the shot was fired. Your theory presupposes the employment of force, in other words, a struggle. Miss Trevert heard no scuffling. No, I've thought of that.. it won't do ..."

"Have you any suspicion of who the murderer might be?"

Robin shook his head decidedly.

"Not a shadow of an idea," he affirmed positively. "But

I have a notion that we shall find a clue in this letter which, like a blithering fool, I left on Parrish's desk. It's the first glimmer of hope I've seen yet ..."

Bruce Wright squared his shoulders and threw his head back.

"I'll get it for you," he said.

"Good boy," said Robin. "But, Bruce," he went on, "you'll have to go carefully. My name is mud in that house. You mustn't say you come from me. And if you ask boldly for the letter, they won't give it to you. Jeekes might, if he's there and you approach him cautiously. But, for Heaven's sake, don't try any diplomacy on Manderton ... that's the Scotland Yard man. He's as wary as a fox and sharp as needles."

Bruce Wright buttoned up his coat with an air of finality.

"Leave it to me," he said, "I know Harkings like my pocket. Besides I've got a friend there ..."

"Who might that be?" queried the barrister.

"Bude," answered the boy and laid a finger on his lips.

"But," he pursued, jerking his head in the direction of the window, "what are we going to do about him out there?"

Robin laughed.

"Him?" he said. "Oh, I'm going to take him out for an airing!"

Robin stepped out into the hall. He returned wearing his hat and overcoat. In his hand were two yale keys strung on a wisp of pink tape.

"Listen, Bruce," he said. "Give me ten minutes' start to get rid of this jackal. Then clear out. There's a train to Stevenish at 3.23. If you get on the Underground at the Temple you ought to be able to make it easily. Here are the keys of the chambers. I can put you up here to-night if you like. I'll expect you when I see you ... with that letter. Savvy?"

The boy stood up.

"You'll have that letter to-night," he answered. "But in the meantime," - he waved the blue sheet with its mysterious slots at Robin, - "what do you make of this?"

Robin took the sheet of paper from him and replaced it in his cigarette-case.

"Perhaps, when we have the letter," he replied, "I shall be able to answer that question!"

Then he lit a cigarette, gave the boy his hand, and a minute later Bruce Wright, watching through the chink of the curtain from the window of Robin Greve's chambers, saw a lanky form shuffle across the court and follow Robin round the angle of the house.

Robin strode quickly through the maze of narrow passages and tranquil, echoing courts into the Sabbath stillness of the Strand. An occasional halt at a shop-window was sufficient to assure him that the watcher of the Temple was still on his heels. The man, he was interested to see, played his part very unobtrusively, shambling along in nonchalant fashion, mostly hugging the sides of the houses, ready to dart out of sight into a doorway or down a side turning, should he by any mischance arrive too close on the heels of his quarry.

As he walked along, Robin turned over in his mind the best means for getting rid of his shadow. Should he dive into a Tube station and plunge headlong down the steps? He rejected this idea as calculated to let the tracker know that his presence was suspected. Then he reviewed in his mind the various establishments he knew of in London with double entrances, thinking that he might slip in by the one entrance and emerge by the other.

In Pall Mall he came upon Tony Grandell, whom he had last seen playing bridge in the company dugout on the Flesquieres Kidge. Then he had been in "battle order," camouflaged as a private soldier, as officers were ordered to go over the top in the latter phases of the war. Now he was resplendent in what the invitation cards call "Morning Dress" crowned by what must certainly have been the most reluctent top-hat in London.

"Hullo, hullo, hullo!" cried Tony, on catching sight of him; "stand to your kits and so forth! And how is my merry company commander? Robin, dear, come and relieve the medieval gloom of lunch with my aunt at Mart's!"

He linked his arm affectionately in Robin's.

Mart's ! Robin's brain snatched at the word. Mart's!

most respectable of "family hotels," wedged in between two quiet streets off Piccadilly with an entrance from both. If ever a man wanted to dodge a sleuth, especially a grimy tatterdemalion like the one sidling up Pall Mall behind them ...

"Tony, old son," said Robin, "I won't lunch with you even to set the board in a roar at your aunt's luncheon-party. But I'll walk up to Mart's with you, for I'm going there myself ..."

They entered Mart's together and parted in the vestibule, where Tony gravely informed his "dear old scream" that he must fly to his "avuncular luncheon." Robin walked quickly through the hotel and left by the other entrance. The street was almost deserted. Of the man with the dingy neckerchief there was no sign. Robin hurried into Piccadilly and hopped on a 'bus which put him down at his club facing the Green Park.

He had a late lunch there and afterwards took a taxi back to the Temple. The daylight was failing as he crossed the courtyard in front of his chambers. In the centre the smoke-blackened plane-tree throned it in unchallenged solitude. But, as Robin's footsteps echoed across the flags, something more substantial than a shadow seemed to melt into the gathering dusk in the corner where the narrow passage ran.

Robin stopped to listen at the entrance to his chambers. As he stood there he heard a heavy tread on the stone steps within. He turned to face a solidly built swarthy-looking man who emerged from the building.

He favoured Robin with a leisurely, searching stare, then strode heavily across the courtyard to the little passage where he disappeared from view.

Robin looked after him. The man was a stranger: the occupants of the other chambers were all known to him. With a thoughtful expression on his face Robin entered the house and mounted to his rooms.

Valentine Williams

CHAPTER XVI

THE INTRUDER

"D - !" exclaimed Bruce Wright.

He stood in the great porch at Harkings, his finger on the electric bell. No sound came in response to the pressure, nor any one to open the door. Thus he had stood for fully ten minutes listening in vain for any sound within the house. All was still as death. He began to think that the bell was out of order. He had forgotten Hartley Parrish's insistence on quiet. All bells at Harkings rang, discreetly muted, in the servants' hall.

He stepped out of the porch on to the drive. The weather had improved and, under a freshening wind, the country was drying up. As he reached the hard gravel, he heard footsteps, Bude appeared, his collar turned up, his swallow-tails floating in the wind.

"Now, be off with you!" he cried as soon as he caught sight of the trim figure in the grey overcoat; "how many more of ye have I to tell there's nothing for you to get here! Go on, get out before I put the dog on you!"

He waved an imperious hand at Bruce.

"Hullo, Bude," said the boy, "you've grown very inhospitable all of a sudden!"

"God bless my soul if it isn't young Mr. Wright!" exclaimed the butler. "And I thought it was another of those dratted reporters. It's been ring, ring, ring the whole blessed morning, sir, you can believe me, as if they owned the place, wanting to interview me and Mr. Jeekes and Miss Trevert and the Lord knows who else. Lot of interfering busybodies, *I* call 'em! I'd shut up all noospapers by law if I had my way ..."

"Is Mr. Jeekes here, Bude?" asked Bruce.

"He's gone off to London in the car, sir ... But won't you come in, Mr. Wright? If you wouldn't mind coming in by the side door. I have to keep the front door closed to shut them scribbling fellows out. One of them had the face to ask me to let him into the library to take a photograph ..."

He led the way round the side of the house to the glass door in the library corridor.

"This is a sad business, Bude!" said Bruce.

"Ah, indeed, it is, sir," he sighed. "He had his faults had Mr. Parrish, as well *you* know, Mr. Wright. But he was an open-handed gentleman, that I will say, and we'll all miss him at Harkings ..."

They were now in the corridor. Bude jerked a thumb over his shoulder.

"It was in there they found him," he said in a low voice, "with a hole plumb over the heart."

His voice sank to a whisper. "There's blood on the carpet!" he added impressively.

"I should like just to take a peep at the room, Bude," ventured the boy, casting a sidelong glance at the butler.

"Can't be done, sir," said Bude, shaking his head; "orders of Detective-Inspector Manderton. The police is very strict, Mr. Wright, sir!"

"There seems to be no one around just now, Bude," the young man wheedled. "There can't be any harm in my just going in for a second?..."

"Go in you should, Mr. Wright, sir," said the butler genially, "if I had my way. But the door's locked. And, what's more, the police have the key."

"Is the detective anywhere about?" asked Bruce.

"No, sir," answered Bude. "He's gone off to town, too! And he don't expect to be back before the inquest. That's for Toosday!"

"But isn't there another key anywhere?" persisted the boy.

"No, sir," said Bude positively, "there isn't but the one. And that's in Mr. Manderton's vest pocket!"

Young Wright wrinkled his brow in perplexity. He was very young, but he had a fine strain of perseverance in him. He was not nearly at the end of his resources, he told himself.

"Well, then," he said suddenly, "I'm going outside to have a look through the window. I remember you can see into the library from the path round the house!"

He darted out, the butler, protesting, lumbering along behind him.

"Mr. Wright," he panted as he ran, "you didn't reelly ought ... If any one should come ..."

But Bruce Wright was already at the window. The butler found him leaning on the sill, peering with an air of frightened curiosity into the empty room.

"The glazier from Stevenish" - Bude's voice breathed the words hoarsely in Wright's ear - "is coming to-morrow morning to put the window in. He wouldn't come to-day, him being a chapel-goer and religious. It was there we found poor Mr. Parrish - d'you see, sir, just between the window and the desk!"

But Bruce Wright did not heed him. His eyes were fixed on the big writing-desk, on the line of black japanned letter-trays set out in orderly array. Outside, the short winter afternoon was drawing in fast, and the light was failing. Dusky shadows within the library made it difficult to distinguish objects clearly.

A voice close at hand cried out sharply:

"Mr. Bude! Mr. Bu-u-ude!"

"They're calling me!" whispered the butler in his ear with a tug at his sleeve; "come away, sir!"

But Bruce shook him off. He heard the man's heavy

tread on the gravel, then a door slam.

How dark the room was growing, to be sure! Strain his eyes as he might, he could not get a clear view of the contents of the letter-trays on the desk. But their high backs hid their contents from his eyes. Even when he hoisted himself on to the window-sill he could not get a better view.

He dropped back on to the gravel path and listened. The wind soughed sadly in the bare tree-tops, somewhere in the distance a dog barked hoarsely, insistently; otherwise not a sound was to be heard. He cast a cautious glance round the side of the house. The glass door was shut; the lamp in the corridor had not been lit.

Hoisting himself up to the window-sill again, he crooked one knee on the rough edge and thrusting one arm through the broken pane of glass, unbolted the window. Then, steadying himself with one hand, with the other he very gently pushed up the window, threw his legs across the sill, and dropped into the library. Very deliberately, he turned and pushed the window softly down behind him.

Some unconscious prompting, perhaps an unfamiliar surface beneath his feet, made him look down. Where his feet rested on the mole-grey carpet a wide dark patch stood out from the delicate shade of the rug. For a moment a spasm of physical nausea caught him.

"How beastly!" he whispered to himself and took a step towards the desk.

Hartley Parrish's desk was arranged just as he always

remembered it to have been. All the letter-trays save one were empty. In that was a little pile of papers held down by a massive marble paper-weight. Quickly he stepped round the desk.

He had put out his hand to lift the weight when there was a gentle rattle at the door.

Bruce Wright wheeled instantly round, back to the desk, to face the door, which, in the gathering dusk, was now but a squarer patch of darkness among the shadows at the far end of the library. He stood absolutely still, rooted to the spot, his heart thumping so fast that, in that silent room, he could hear the rapid beats.

Some one was unlocking the library door. As realization came to the boy, he tiptoed rapidly round the desk, the sound of his feet muffled by the heavy pile carpet, and reached the window. There was a click as the lock of the door was shot back. Without further hesitation Bruce stepped behind the long curtains which fell from the top of the window to the floor.

The curtains, of some heavy grey material, were quite opaque. Bruce realized, with a sinking heart, that he must depend on his ears to discover the identity of this mysterious interloper. He dared not look out from his hiding-place - at least not until he could be sure that the newcomer had his back to the window. He remained, rigid and vigilant, straining his ears to catch the slightest sound, scarcely daring to breathe.

He heard the door open, heard it softly close again. Then ... silence. Not another sound. The boy remembered the heavy pile carpet and cursed his luck. He would have to risk a peep round the curtains. But not yet! He must wait ...

A very slight rustling, a faint prolonged rustling, caught his ear. It came nearer, then stopped. There was a little rattling noise from somewhere close at hand, a small clinking sound.

Then silence fell again.

The wind whooshed sadly round the house, the window clattered dismally in its frame, the curtains tugged fretfully before the cold breeze which blew in at the broken pane. But the silence in the room was absolute.

It began to oppress the boy. It frightened him. He felt an uncontrollable desire to look out into the room and establish the identity of the mysterious entrant. He glided his hand towards the window-frame in the hope that he might find a chink between curtain and wall through which he might risk a peep into the room. But the curtain was fastened to the wall.

The room was almost entirely dark now. Only behind him was a patch of grey light where the lowering evening sky was framed in the window. He began to draw the curtain very slowly towards him, at the same time leaning to the right. Very cautiously he applied one eye to the edge of the curtain.

As he did so a bright light struck him full in the face. It streamed full from a lamp on the desk and almost blinded him. It was a reading-lamp and the bulb had been turned up so as to throw a beam on the curtain behind which the boy was sheltering.

Behind the desk, straining back in terror, stood a slim, girlish figure. The details of her dress were lost in the gathering shadows, but her face stood out in the gloom, a pale oval. Bruce could see the dark line made by the lashes on her cheek.

At the sight of her, he stepped boldly forth from his hiding-place, shielding his eyes from the light with his hand.

"It's Bruce Wright, Miss Trevert," he said, "don't you remember me?"

CHAPTER XVII

A FRESH CLUE

"Oh!" cried the girl, "you frightened me! You frightened me! What do you want here ... in this horrible room?"

She was trembling. One slim hand plucked nervously at her dress. Her breath came and went quickly.

"I saw the curtain move. I thought it was the wind at first. But then I saw the outline of your fingers. And I imagined it was he ... come back ..."

"Miss Trevert," said the boy abashed, "I must have frightened you terribly. I had no idea it was you!"

"But why are you hiding here? How did you get in? What do you want in this house?"

She spoke quickly, nervously. Some papers she held in her hand shook with her emotion. Bruce Wright stepped to the desk and turned the bulb of the reading-lamp down into its normal position.

"I must apologize most sincerely for the fright I gave you," he said. "But, believe me, Miss Trevert, I had no idea that anybody could gain access to this room. I climbed in through the window. Bude told me that the police had taken away the key ..."

The girl made an impatient gesture.

"But why have you come here?" she said. "What do you want?"

The boy measured her with a narrow glance. He was young, but he was shrewd. He saw her frank eyes, her candid, open mien, and he took a rapid decision.

"I think I have come," he answered slowly, "for the same purpose as yourself!"

And he looked at the papers in her hand.

"I used to be Mr. Parrish's secretary, you know," he said.

The girl sighed - a little fluttering sigh - and looked earnestly at him.

"I remember," she said. "Hartley liked you. He was sorry that he sent you away. He often spoke of you to me. But why have you come back? What do you mean by saying you have come for the same purpose as myself?"

Bruce Wright looked at the array of letter-trays. The marble paper-weight had been displaced. The tray in which it had lain was empty. He looked at the sheaf of papers in the girl's hand.

"I wanted to see," he replied, "whether there was anything here ... on his desk ... which would explain the mystery of his death ..."

The girl spread out the papers in her hand on the big blotter.

She laid the papers out in a row and leant forward, her white arms resting on the desk. From the other side of the desk the boy leant eagerly forward and scanned the line of papers.

At the first glimpse his face fell. The girl, eyeing him closely, marked the change which came over his features.

There were seven papers of various kinds, both printed and written, and they were all on white paper.

The boy shook his head and swept the papers together into a heap.

"It's not there?" queried the girl eagerly.

"No!" said Bruce absent-mindedly, glancing round the desk.

"What isn't?" flashed back the girl.

Bruce Wright felt his face redden with vexation. What sort of a confidential emissary was he to fall into a simple trap like this?

The girl smiled rather wanly.

"Now I know what you meant by saying you had come for the same purpose as myself," she said. "I suppose we both thought we might find something, a letter, perhaps, which would explain why Mr. Parrish did this dreadful thing, something to relieve this awful uncertainty about ... about his motive. Well, I've searched the desk ... and there's nothing! Nothing but just these prospectuses and receipts which were in the letter-tray here. They must have come by the post yesterday morning. And there's nothing of any importance in the drawers ... only household receipts and the wages book and a few odd things like that! You can see for yourself ..."

The lower part of the desk consisted of three drawers flanked on either side by cupboards. Mary Trevert pulled out the drawers and opened the cupboards. Two of the drawers were entirely empty and one of the cupboards contained nothing but a stack of cigar boxes. One drawer held various papers appertaining to the house. There was no sign of any letter written on the slatey-blue paper.

The boy looked very hard at Mary.

"You say there was nothing in the letter-tray but these papers here?" he asked.

"Nothing but these," replied the girl.

"You didn't notice any official-looking letter on bluish paper?" he ventured to ask.

"No," answered the girl. "I found nothing but these."

The boy thought for a moment.

"Do you know," he asked, "whether the police or anybody have been through the desk?"

"I don't know at all," said Mary, smoothing back a lock of hair from her temple; "I daresay Mr. Jeekes had a look round, as he had a meeting with Mr. Parrish's lawyer in town this afternoon!"

She had lost all trace of her fright and was now quite calm and collected.

"Do you know for certain whether Mr. Jeekes was in here?" asked Bruce.

"Oh, yes. The first thing he did on arriving last night was to go to the library."

"I suppose Jeekes is coming back here to-night?"

No, she told him. Mr. Jeekes did not expect to return to Harkings until the inquest on Tuesday.

Bruce Wright picked up his hat.

"I must apologize again, Miss Trevert," he said, "for making such an unconventional entrance and giving you such a fright. But I felt I could not rest until I had investigated matters for myself. I would have presented myself in the ordinary way, but, as I told you, Bude told me the police had locked up the room and taken away the key ..."

Mary Trevert smiled forgivingly.

"So they did," she said. "But Jay - Mr. Parrish's man, you know - had another key. He brought it to me."

She looked at Bruce with a whimsical little smile.

"You must have been very uncomfortable behind those curtains," she said. "I believe you were just as frightened as I was."

She walked round the desk to the window.

"It was a good hiding-place," she remarked, "but not much good as an observation post. Why! you could see nothing of the room. The curtains are much too thick!"

"Not a thing," Bruce agreed rather ruefully. "I thought you were the detective!"

He held out his hand to take his leave with a smile. He was a charming-looking boy with a remarkably serene expression which went well with close-cropped golden hair.

Mary Trevert did not take his hand for an instant. Looking down at the point of her small black suede shoe she said shyly:

"Mr. Wright, you are a friend of Mr. Greve, aren't you?"

"Rather!" was the enthusiastic answer.

"Do you see him often?"

The boy's eyes narrowed suddenly. Was this a cross-examination?

"Oh, yes," he replied, "every now and then!"

Mary Trevert raised her eyes to his.

"Will you do something for me?" she said. "Tell Mr. Greve not to trust Manderton. He will know whom I mean. Tell him to be on his guard against that man. Say he means mischief. Tell him, above all things, to be careful. Make him go away ... go abroad until this thing has blown over ..."

She spoke with intense earnestness, her dark eyes fixed on Bruce Wright's face.

"But promise me you won't say this comes from me! Do you understand? There are reasons, very strong reasons, for this. Will you promise?"

"Of course!"

She took Bruce's outstretched hand.

"I promise," he said.

"You mustn't go without tea," said the girl. "Besides," - she glanced at a little platinum watch on her wrist, - "there's not another train until six. There is no need for you to start yet. I don't like being left alone. Mother has one of her headaches, and Horace and Dr. Romain have gone to Stevenish. Come up to my sitting-room!"

She led the way out of the library, locking the door behind them, and together they went up to the Chinese boudoir where tea was laid on a low table before a bright fire. In the dainty room with its bright colours they seemed far removed from the tragedy which had darkened Harkings.

They had finished tea when a tap came at the door. Bude appeared. He cast a reproachful look at Bruce.

"Jay would be glad to have a word with you, Miss," he said.

The girl excused herself and left the room. She was absent for about ten minutes. When she returned, she had a little furrow of perplexity between her brows. She walked over to the open fireplace and stood silent for an instant, her foot tapping the hearth-rug.

"Mr. Wright," she said presently, "I'm going to tell you something that Jay has just told me. I want your advice ..."

The boy looked at her interrogatively. But he did not speak.

"I think this is rather important," the girl went on, "but I don't quite understand in what way it is. Jay tells me that Mr. Parrish had on his pistol a sort of steel fitting attached to the end ... you know, the part you shoot out of. Mr. Parrish used to keep his automatic in a drawer in his dressing-room, and Jay has often seen it there with this attachment fitted on. Well, when Mr. Parrish was discovered in the library yesterday, this thing was no longer on the pistol. And Jay says it's not to be found!..."

"That's rather strange!" commented Bruce. "But what was this steel contraption for, do you know? Was it a patent sight or something?"

"Jay doesn't know," answered the girl.

"Would you mind if I spoke to Jay myself?" asked the young man.

In reply the girl touched the bell beside the fireplace. Bude answered the summons and was despatched to find Jay. He appeared in due course, a tall, dark, sleek young man wearing a swallow-tail coat and striped trousers.

"How are you, Jay?" said Bruce affably.

"Very well, thank you, sir," replied the valet.

"Miss Trevert was telling me about this appliance which you say Mr. Parrish had on his automatic. Could you describe it to me?"

"Well, sir," answered the man rather haltingly, "it was a little sort of cup made of steel or gun-metal fitting closely over the barrel ..."

"And you don't know what it was for?"

"No, sir!"

"Was it a sight, do you think?"

"I can't say, I'm sure, sir!"

"You know what a sight looks like, I suppose. Was there a bead on it or anything like it?"

"I can't say, I'm sure, sir. I never gave any particular heed to it. I used to see the automatic lying in the drawer of the wardrobe in Mr. Parrish's room in a wash-leather case. I noticed this steel appliance, sir, because the case wouldn't shut over the pistol with it on and the butt used to stick out."

"When did you last notice Mr. Parrish's automatic?"

"It would be Thursday or Friday, sir. I went to that drawer to get Mr. Parrish an old stock to go riding in as some new ones he had bought were stiff and hurt him."

"And this steel cup was on the pistol then?"

"Oh, yes, sir!"

"And you say it was not on the pistol when Mr. Parrish's body was found?"

"No, sir!"

"Are you sure of this?"

"Yes, sir. I was one of the first in the room, and I saw the pistol in Mr. Parrish's hand, and there was no sign of the cup, sir. So I've had a good look among his things and I can't find it anywhere!"

Bruce Wright pondered a minute.

"Try and think, Jay," he said, "if you can't remember anything more about this steel cup, as you call it. Where did Mr. Parrish buy it?"

"Can't say, I'm sure, sir. He had it before ever I took service with him!"

Jay put his hand to his forehead for an instant.

"Now I come to think of it," he said, "there was the name of the shop or maker on it, stamped on the steel. 'Maxim,' that was the name, now I put my mind back, with a number ..."

"Maxim?" echoed Bruce Wright. "Did you say Maxim?"

"Yes, sir! That was the name!" replied the valet impassively.

"By Jove!" said the boy half to himself. Then he said aloud to Jay:

"Did you tell the police about this?"

Jay looked somewhat uncomfortable.

"No, sir."

"Why not?"

Jay looked at Mary Trevert.

"Well, sir, I thought perhaps I'd better tell Miss Trevert first. Bude thought so, too. That there Manderton has made so much unpleasantness in the house with his prying ways that I said to myself, sir ..."

Bruce Wright looked at Mary.

"Would you mind if I asked Jay not to say anything about this to anybody just for the present?" he asked.

"You hear what Mr. Wright says, Jay," said Mary. "I don't want you to say anything about this matter just yet. Do you understand?"

"Yes, Miss. Will that be all, Miss?"

"Yes, thank you, Jay!"

"Thanks very much, Jay," said the boy. "This may be important. Mum's the word, though!"

"I *quite* understand, sir," answered the valet and left the room.

Hardly had the door closed on him than the girl turned eagerly to Bruce.

"It *is* important?" she asked.

"It may be," was the guarded reply.

"Don't leave me in the dark like this," the girl pleaded. "This horrible affair goes on growing and growing, and at every step it seems more bewildering ... more ghastly. Tell me where it is leading, Mr. Wright! I can't stand the suspense much more!"

Her voice broke, and she turned her face away.

"You must be brave, Miss Trevert," said the boy, putting his hand on her shoulder. "Don't ask me to tell you more now. Your friends are working to get at the truth ..."

"The truth!" cried the girl. "God knows where the truth will lead us!"

Bruce Wright hesitated a moment.

"I don't think you have any need to fear the truth!" he said presently.

The girl took her handkerchief from her face and looked at him with brimming eyes.

"You know more than you let me think you did," she said brokenly. "But you are a friend of mine, aren't you?"

"Yes," said Bruce, and added boldly:

"And of his too!"

She did not speak again, but gave him her hand. He clasped it and went out hurriedly to catch his train back to London.

CHAPTER XVIII

THE SILENT SHOT

That faithful servitor of Fleet Street, the Law Courts clock, had just finished striking seven. It boomed out the hour, stroke by stroke, solemnly, inexorably, like a grim old judge summing up and driving home, point by point, an irrefutable charge. The heavy strokes broke in upon the fitful doze into which Robin Greve, stretched out in an armchair in his living-room, had dropped.

He roused up with a start. There was the click of a key in the lock of his front door. Bruce Wright burst into the room.

The boy shut the door quickly and locked it. He was rather pale and seemed perturbed. On seeing Robin he jerked his head in the direction of the courtyard.

"I suppose you know they're still outside?" he said.

Robin nodded nonchalantly.

"There are three of them now," the boy went on. "Robin, I don't like it. Something's going to happen. You'll want to mind yourself ... if it's not too late already!"

He stepped across to the window and bending down, peered cautiously round the curtain.

Robin Greve laughed.

"Bah!" he said, "they can't touch me!"

"You're wrong," Bruce retorted without changing his position. "They can and they will. Don't think Manderton is a fool, Robin. He means mischief ..."

Robin raised his eyebrows.

" Does he?" he said. "Now I wonder who told you that ..."

" Friends of yours at Harkings asked me to warn you ..." began Bruce awkwardly.

"My friends are scarcely in the majority there," retorted Robin. "Whom do you mean exactly?"

But the boy ignored the question.

"Three men watching the house!" he exclaimed; "don't you think that *this* looks as though Manderton meant business?"

He returned to his post of observation at the curtain.

Robin laughed cynically.

"Manderton doesn't worry me any," he said cheerfully. "The man's the victim of an *idée fixe*. He believes Parrish killed himself just as firmly as he believes that I frightened or bullied Parrish into doing it ..."

"Don't be too sure about that, Robin," said the boy, dropping the curtain and coming back to Robin's chair. "He may want you to think that. But how can we tell how much he knows?"

Robin flicked the ash off his cigarette disdainfully.

"These promoted policemen make me tired," he said.

Bruce Wright shook his head quickly with a little gesture of exasperation.

"You don't understand," he said. "There's fresh evidence ..."

Robin Greve looked up with real interest in his eyes. His bantering manner had vanished.

"You've got that letter?" he asked eagerly.

Bruce shook his head.

"No, not that," he said. Then leaning forward he added in a low voice:

"Have you ever heard of the Maxim silencer?"

"I believe I have, vaguely," replied Robin. "Isn't it something to do with a motor engine?"

"No," said Bruce. "It's an extraordinary invention which absolutely suppresses the noise of the discharge of a gun."

Robin shot a quick glance at the speaker.

"Go on," he said.

"It's a marvelous thing, really," the boy continued, warming to his theme. "A man at Havre had one when I was at the base there, during the war. It's a little cup-shaped steel fitting that goes over the barrel. You can fire a rifle fitted with one of these silencers in a small room and it makes no more noise than a fairly loud sneeze ..."

"Ah!"

Robin was listening intently now.

"Parrish had a Maxim silencer," Bruce went on impressively.

"*Parrish* had?"

"It was fitted on his automatic pistol, the one he had in his hand when they found him ..."

"There was no attachment of any kind on the gun Parrish was holding when he was discovered yesterday afternoon," declared Robin positively; "I can vouch for that. I was there almost immediately after they found him. And if there had been anything of the kind Horace Trevert would certainly have mentioned it ..."

"I know. Jay, who came in soon after you, was surprised to see that the silencer was not on the pistol. And he made a point of looking for it ..."

"But how do you know that Parrish had it on the pistol?..."

"Well, we don't know for certain. But we do know that it was permanently fitted to his automatic. Jay has often seen it. And if Parrish did remove it, he didn't leave it lying around any where. Jay has looked all through his things without finding it ..."

"When did Jay see it last?"

"On Thursday!"

"But are you sure that this is the same pistol as the one which Jay has been in the habit of seeing?"

"Jay is absolutely sure. He says that Parrish only had the one automatic which he always kept in the same drawer in his dressing-room ..."

Robin was silent for a moment. Very deliberately he filled his pipe, lit it, and drew until it burned comfortably. Then he said slowly:

"This means that Hartley Parrish was murdered, Bruce, old man. All through I have been puzzling my mind to reconcile the unquestionable circumstance that two bullets were fired - I told you of the bullet mark I found on the upright in the rosery - with the undoubted fact that only one report was heard. We can therefore presume, either that Hartley Parrish first fired one shot from his pistol with the silencer fitted and then removed the silencer and fired another shot without it, thereby killing himself, or that the second shot was fired by the person whose interest it was to get rid of the silencer. There is no possible or plausible reason why Parrish should have fired first one shot with the silencer and then one without. Therefore, I find myself irresistibly compelled to the conclusion that the shot heard by Mary Trevert was fired by the person who killed Parrish. Do I make myself clear?"

"Perfectly," answered Bruce.

"Now, then," the barrister proceeded, thoughtfully puffing at his pipe, "one weak point about my deductions is that they all hang on the question as to whether, at the time of the tragedy, Parrish actually had the silencer on his pistol or not. That is really the acid test of Manderton's suicide theory. You said, I think, that a rifle fired with the silencer attachment makes no more noise than the sound of a loud sneeze!"

"That's right," agreed Bruce; "a sort of harsh, spluttering noise. Not so loud either, Robin. Ph ... t-t-t! Like that!"

"Loud enough to be heard through a door, would you say?"

"Oh, I think so!"

Robin thought intently for a moment.

"Then Mary is the only one who can put us right on that point. Assuming that two shots were fired - and that bullet mark in the rosery is, I think, conclusive on that head - and knowing that she heard the loud report of the one, presumably, if Parrish had the silencer on his automatic, Mary must have heard the *muffled* report of the other. What it comes to is this, Mary heard the shot fired that killed Parrish. Did she hear the shot he fired at his murderer?"

"By Gad!" exclaimed Bruce Wright impressively, "I

believe you've got it, Robin! Parrish fired at somebody at the window - a silent shot - and the other fellow fired back the shot that Mary Trevert heard, the shot that killed Parrish. Isn't that the way you figure it out?"

"Not so fast, young man," remarked Robin. "Let's first find out whether Mary actually heard the muffled shot and, if so, *when ... before* or *after* the loud report."

He glanced across at the window and then at Bruce,

"I suppose this discovery about the silencer is responsible for the deputation waiting in the courtyard," he said drily.

"The police don't know about it yet," replied Bruce; "at least they didn't when I left."

Robin shook his head dubiously.

"If the servants know it, Manderton will worm it out of them. Hasn't he cross-examined Jay?"

"Yes," said Bruce. "But he got nothing out of him about this. Manderton seems to have put everybody's back up. He gets nothing out of the servants ..."

"If Parrish had had this silencer for some time, you may be sure that other people know about it. These silencers must be pretty rare in England. You see, an average person like myself didn't know what it was. By the way, another point which we haven't yet cleared up is this: supposing we are right in believing Parrish to have been murdered, how do you explain the fact that the bullet removed from his body fitted his pistol?"

"That's a puzzler, I must say!" said Bruce.

"There's only one possible explanation, I think," Robin went on, "and that is that Parrish was shot by a pistol of exactly the same calibre as his own. For the murderer to have killed Parrish with his own weapon would have been difficult without a struggle. But Miss Trevert heard no struggle. For murderer and his victim to have pistols of the same calibre argues a rather remarkable coincidence, I grant you. But then life is full of coincidences! We meet them every day in the law. Though, I admit, this is a coincidence which requires some explaining ..."

He fell into a brown study which Bruce interrupted by suddenly remembering that he had had no lunch.

For answer Robin pointed at the sideboard.

"There's a cloth in there," he said, "also the whisky, if my laundress has left any, and a siphon and there should be some claret - Mrs. Bragg doesn't care about red wine. Set the table, and I'll take a root round in the kitchen and dig up some tinned stuff."

They supped off a tinned tongue and some *pâté de foie gras*. Over their meal Bruce told Robin of his adventure in the library at Harkings.

"Jeekes must have collected that letter," Bruce said. "Before I came to you, I went to Lincoln's Inn Fields to see if he was still at Bardy's - Parrish's solicitor, you know. But the office was closed, and the place in darkness. I went on to the Junior Pantheon, that's Jeekes's club, but he wasn't in. He hadn't been there all day, the porter told me. So I left a note asking him to ring you up here ..."

"The case reeks of blackmail," said Robin thoughtfully, "but I am wondering how much we shall glean
from this precious letter when we do see it. I am glad
you asked Jeekes to ring me up, though. He should be
able to tell us something about these mysterious letters
on the blue paper that used to put Parrish in such a
stew ... Hullo, who can that be?"

An electric bell trilled through the flat. It rang once ...
twice ... and then a third time, a long, insistent peal.

"See who's there, will you, Bruce?" said Robin.

"Suppose it's the police ..." began the boy.

Robin shrugged his shoulders.

"You can say I'm at home and ask them in," he said.

He heard the heavy oaken door swing open, a murmur
of voices in the hall. The next moment Detective-
Inspector Manderton entered the sitting-room,

CHAPTER XIX

MR. MANDERTON LAYS HIS CARDS
ON THE TABLE

The detective's manner had undergone some subtle change which Robin, watching him closely as he came into the room, was quick to note. Mr. Manderton made an effort to retain his old air of rather patronizing swagger; but he seemed less sure of himself than was his wont. In fact, he appeared to be a little anxious.

He walked briskly into the sitting-room and looked quickly from Bruce to Robin.

"Mr. Greve," he said, "you can help me if you will by answering a few questions ..."

With another glance at Bruce Wright he added:

"... in private."

Bruce, obedient to a sign from Robin, said he would ring up in the morning and prepared to take his leave. Robin turned to the detective.

"There are some of your men, I believe," he said coldly, "watching thisb house. Would it be asking too much to request that my friend here might be permitted to return home unescorted?"

"He needn't worry," replied Manderton with a significant smile. "There's no one outside now!..."

They watched Bruce Wright pass into the hall and collect his hat and coat. As the front door slammed behind him, the detective added:

"I took 'em off myself soon after seven o'clock!"

"Why?" asked Robin bluntly.

Mr. Manderton dropped his heavy form into a chair.

"I'm a plain man, Mr. Greve," he said, "and I'm not above owning to it, I hope, when I'm wrong. For some little time now it has struck me that our lines of investigation run parallel ..."

"Instead of crossing!"

"Instead of crossing - exactly!"

"It's a pity you did not grasp that very obvious fact earlier," observed Robin pointedly.

Mr. Manderton crossed one leg over the other and, his finger-tips pressed together, looked at Robin.

"Will you help me?" he asked simply.

"Do you want my help?"

Mr. Manderton nodded.

Valentine Williams

"Allies, then?"

"Allies it is!"

Robin pointed to the table.

"It's dry work talking," he said. "Won't you take a drink?"

"Thanks, I don't drink. But I'll have a cigar if I may. Thank you!"

The detective helped himself to a cheroot from a box on the table and lit up. Then, affecting to scan the end of his cigar with great attention, he asked abruptly:

"What do you know of the woman calling herself Madame de Malpas?"

Robin pursed up his lips rather disdainfully.

"One of the late Mr. Parrish's lady friends," he replied. "I expect you know that!"

"Do you know where she lives?" pursued the detective, ignoring the implied question.

"She's dead."

A flicker of interest appeared for an instant in Mr. Manderton's keen eyes.

"You're sure of that?"

"Certainly," answered Robin.

"Who told you?"

"Le Hagen - the solicitor, you know. He acted for this Malpas woman on one or two occasions."

"When did she die?"

"Six or seven months ago ..."

"Did Jeekes know about it?"

"Jeekes? Do you mean Parrish's secretary?

"It's funny your asking that. As a matter of fact, it was through Jeekes that I heard the lady was dead. I was in Le Hagen's office one day when Jeekes came in, and Le Hagen told me Jeekes had come to pay in a cheque for the cost of the funeral and the transport of the body to France."

"This was six or seven months ago, you say? I take it, then, that any allowance that Parrish was in the habit of making to this woman has ceased?"

"I tell you the lady is dead!"

"Then what would you say if I informed you that Mr. Jeekes had declared that these payments were still going on ..."

Robin shrugged his shoulders.

"I should say he was lying ..."

"I agree. But why?"

"Whom did he tell this to?"

"Miss Trevert!"

"Miss Trevert?"

Robin repeated the name in amazement.

"I don't understand," he said. "Why on earth should Jeekes blacken his employer's character to Miss Trevert? What conceivable motive could he have had? Did she tell you this?"

"No," said Manderton; "I heard him tell her myself."

"Do you mean to tell me," protested Robin, growing more and more puzzled, "that Jeekes told Miss Trevert this offensive and deliberate lie in your presence!"

"Well," remarked Mr. Manderton slowly, "I don't know about his saying this in my presence exactly. But I heard him tell her for all that. Walls have ears, you know - particularly if the door is ajar!"

He looked shrewdly at Robin, then dropped his eyes to the floor.

"He also told her that Le Hagen and you were in business relations ..."

Robin sat up at this.

"Ah!" he said shortly. "I see what you're getting at now. Our friend has been trying to set Miss Trevert against me, eh? But why? I don't even know this man Jeekes except to have nodded 'Good-morning' to him a few times. Why on earth should he of all men go out of his way to slander me to Miss Trevert, to throw suspicion ..."

He broke off short and looked at the detective.

Mr. Manderton caressed his big black moustache.

"Yes," he repeated suavely, "you were saying 'to cast suspicion' ..."

The eyes of the two men met. Then the detective leaned back in his chair and, blowing a cloud of smoke from his lips, said:

"Mr. Greve, you've been thinking ahead of me on this case. What you've told me so far I've checked. And you're right. Dead right. And since you're, in a manner of speaking, one of the parties interested in getting things cleared up, I'd like you to tell me just simply what idea you've formed about it ..."

"Gladly," answered the barrister. "And to start with let me tell you that the case stinks of blackmail ..."

"Steady on," interposed the detective. "I thought so, too, at first. I've been into all that. Mr. Parrish made a clean break with the last of his lady friends about two months since; and, as far as our investigations go, there has been no blackmail in connection with any of his women pals. Vine Street knows all about Master Parrish. There were complaints about some of his little parties up in town. But I don't believe there's a woman in this case ..."

" I didn't say there was ," retorted Robin. " The

blackmail is probably being levied from Holland. A threat of violence was finally carried into effect on Saturday evening between 5 and 5.15 P.M. by some one conversant with the lie of the land at Harkings. This individual, armed with an automatic Browning of the same calibre as Mr. Parrish's, shot at Parrish through the open window of the library and killed him - probably in self-defence, after Parrish had had a shot at him ..."

"Steady there, whoa!" said Mr. Manderton in a jocular way clearly expressive of his incredulity; "there was only one shot ..."

"There were *two*," was Robin's dispassionate reply. "Though maybe only one was heard. Parrish had a Maxim silencer on his gun ..."

Mr. Manderton was now thoroughly alert.

"How did you find that out?" he asked.

"Jay, Parrish's man, came forward and volunteered this evidence ..."

"He said nothing about it when I questioned him," grumbled the detective.

Robin laughed.

"You're a terror to the confirmed criminal, they tell me, Manderton," he said, "but you obviously don't understand that complicated mechanism known as the domestic servant. No servant at Harkings will voluntarily tell *you* anything ..."

Mr. Manderton, who had stood up, shook his big frame impatiently.

"Explain the rest of your theories," he said harshly. "What's all this about blackmail being levied from Holland?"

Then Robin Greve told him of the letters written on the slatey-blue paper and of their effect upon Parrish, and of the letter headed, "Elias van der Spyck & Co., General Importers, Rotterdam," which had lain on the desk in the library when Parrish's dead body had been found.

Manderton nodded gloomily.

"It was there right enough," he remarked. "I saw it. A letter about steel shipments and the dockers' strike, wasn't it? As there seemed nothing to it, I left it with the other papers for Jeekes, the secretary chap. But what evidence is there that this was blackmail?"

"This," said Robin, and showed the detective the sheet of blue paper with its series of slits. "Manderton," he said, "these letters written on this blue paper were in code, I feel sure. Why should not this be the key? You see it bears a date - 'Nov. 25.' May it not refer to that letter? I found it by Parrish's body on the carpet in the library. I would have given it to you at Harkings, but I shoved it in my pocket and forgot all about it until I was in the train coming up to town this morning."

Mr. Manderton took the sheet of paper, turned it over, and held it up to the light. Then, without comment, he put it away in the pocket of his jacket.

"If Parrish killed himself," Robin went on earnestly, "that letter drove him to it. If, on the other hand, he was murdered, may not that letter have contained a warning?"

"I should prefer to suspend judgment until we've seen the letter, Mr. Greve," said the detective bluntly. "We must get it from Jeekes. In the meantime, what makes you think that the murderer (to follow up your theory) was conversant with the lay of the land at Harkings?"

"Because," answered Robin, "the murderer left no tracks on the grass or flower-beds. He stuck to the hard gravel path throughout. That path, which runs from the drive through the rosery to the gravel path round the house just under the library window, is precious hard to find in the dark, especially where it leaves the drive, as at the outset it is a mere thread between the rhododendron bushes. And, as I know from experience, unless you are acquainted with the turns in the path, it is very easy to get off it in the dark, especially in the rosery, and go blundering on to the flower-beds. And I'll tell you something else about the murderer. He - or she - was of small stature - not much above five foot six in height. The upward diagonal course of the bullet through Parrish's heart shows that ..."

Mr. Manderton shook his head dubiously.

"Very ingenious," he commented. "But you go rather fast, Mr. Greve. We must test your theory link by link. There may be an explanation for Jeekes's apparently inexplicable lie to the young lady. Let's see him and hear what he says. The grounds at Harkings must be searched for this second bullet, if second bullet there is, the mark on the tree examined by an expert. And since two bullets argue two pistols in this case, let us see what result we get from our enquiries as to where Mr. Parrish bought his pistol. He may have had two pistols ..."

"If Parrish used a silencer," remarked Robin, quite undisconcerted by the other's lack of enthusiasm, "and my theory that two shots were fired is correct, there must have been two reports, a loud one and a muffled one. Miss Trevert heard one report, as we know. Did she hear a second?"

"She said nothing about it," remarked the detective.

"She was probably asked nothing about it. But we can get this point cleared up at once. There's the telephone. Ring up Harkings and ask her now."

"Why not?" said Mr. Manderton and moved to the telephone.

There is little delay on the long-distance lines on a Sunday evening, and the call to Harkins came through almost at once. Bude answered the telephone at Harkings. Manderton asked for Miss Trevert. The butler replied that Miss Trevert was no longer at Harkings. She had gone to the Continent for a few days.

This plain statement, retailed in the fortissimo voice which Bude reserved for use on the telephone, produced a remarkable effect on the detective. He grew red in the face.

"What's that?" he cried assertively. "Gone to the Continent? I should have been told about this. Why wasn't I informed? What part of the Continent has she gone to?"

Mr. Manderton's questions, rapped out with a rasping vigour that recalled a machine-gun firing, brought Robin to his feet in an instant. He crossed over to the desk on which the telephone stood.

Manderton placed one big palm over the transmitter and turned to Robin.

"She's gone to the Continent and left no address," he said quickly.

"Ask him if Lady Margaret is there," suggested Robin.

Mr. Manderton spoke into the telephone again. Lady Margaret had gone to bed, Bude answered, and her ladyship was much put out by Miss Trevert gallivanting off like that by herself with only a scribbled note left to say that she had gone.

Had Bude got the note?

No, Mr. Manderton, sir, he had not. But Lady Margaret had shown it to him. It had simply stated that Miss Trevert had gone off to the Continent and would be back in a few days.

Again the detective turned to Robin at his elbow.

"These country bumpkins!" he said savagely. "I must go to the Yard and get Humphries on the 'phone. He may have telegraphed me about it. You stay here and I'll ring you later if there's any news. What do you make of it, Mr. Greve?"

"It beats me," was Robin's rueful comment. "And what about the inquest? It's for Tuesday, isn't it? Miss Trevert will have to give evidence, I take it?..."

"Oh," said Mr. Manderton, picking up his hat and speaking in an offhand way, "I'm getting *that* adjourned for a week!"

"The inquest adjourned! Why?"

There was a twinkle in the detective's eye as he replied.

"I thought, maybe, I might get further evidence ..."

Robin caught the expression and smiled.

"And when did you come to this decision, may I ask?"

"After our little experiment in the garden this morning," was the detective's prompt reply.

Robin looked at him fixedly.

"But, see here," he said, "apparently it was to the deductions you formed from the result of that experiment that I owe the attentions of your colleagues who have been hanging round the house all day. And yet you now come to me and invite my assistance. Mr. Manderton, I don't get it at all!"

"Mr. Greve," replied the detective, "Miss Trevert tried to shield you. That made me suspicious. You tried to force my investigations into an entirely new path. That deepened my suspicions. I believed it to be my duty to ascertain your movements after leaving Harkings. But then I heard Jeekes make an apparently gratuitously false statement to Miss Trevert with an implication against you. That, to some extent, cleared you in my eyes. I say 'to some extent' because I will not deny that I thought I might be taking a risk in coming to you like this. You see I am frank!..."

The smile had left Greve's face and he looked rather grim.

"You're pretty deep, aren't you?" was his brief comment.

CHAPTER XX

THE CODE KING

Major Euan MacTavish was packing. A heavy and well-worn leather portmanteau, much adorned with foreign luggage labels, stood in the centre of the floor. From a litter of objects piled up on a side table the Major was transferring to it various brown-paper packages which he checked by a list in his hand.

The Major always packed for himself. He packed with the neatness and rapidity derived from long experience of travel. As a matter of fact, he could not afford a manservant any more than he could allow himself quarters more luxurious than the rather grimy bedroom in Bury Street which housed him during his transient appearances in town. The remuneration doled out by the Foreign Office to the quiet and unobtrusive gentlemen known as King's messengers is, in point of fact, out of all proportion to the prestige and glamour surrounding the silver greyhound badge, an example of which was tucked away in a pocket of the Major's blue serge jacket hanging over the back of a chair.

"Let's see," said the Major, addressing a large brown-paper covered package standing in the corner of the room, "you're the bird-cage for Lady Sylvia at The Hague. Two pounds of candles for Mrs. Harry

Deepdale at Berlin; the razor blades for Sir Archibald at Prague; the Teddy bear for Marjorie; polo-balls for the Hussars at Constantinople - there! I think that's the lot! Hullo, hullo, who the devil's that?"

With a groaning of wires a jangling bell tinkled through the hall (the Major's bedroom was on the ground floor). Sims, the aged ex-butler, who, with his wife, "did for" his lodgers in more ways than one, was out and the single servant-maid had her Sunday off. Euan MacTavish glanced at his wrist watch. It showed the hour to be ten minutes past nine. A flowered silk smoking-coat over his evening clothes and a briar pipe in his mouth, he went out into the hall and opened the front door.

It was a drenching night. The lamps from a taxi which throbbed dully in the street outside the house threw a gleaming band of light on the shining pavement. At the door stood a taxi-driver.

"There's a lady asking for Major MacTavish," he said, pointing at the cab. The Major stepped across to the cab and opened the door.

"Oh, Euan," said a girl's voice, "how lucky I am to catch you!"

"Why, Mary," exclaimed the Major, "what on earth brings you round to me on a night like this? I only came up from the country this afternoon and I'm off for Constantinople in the morning!"

"Euan," said Mary Trevert, "I want to talk to you. Where can we talk?"

The Major raised his eyebrows. He was a little man with grizzled hair and finely cut, rather sharp features.

"Well," he remarked, "there's not a soul in the house, and I've only got a bedroom here. Though we're cousins, Mary, my dear, I don't know that you ought to...."

"You're a silly old-fashioned old dear," exclaimed the girl, "and I'm coming in. No, I'll keep the cab. We shall want it!"

"All right," said the Major, helping her to alight. "I tell you what. We'll go into Harry Prankhurst's sitting-room. He's away for the week-end, anyway!"

He took Mary Trevert into a room off the hall and switched on the electric light. Then for the first time he saw how pale she looked.

"My dear," he said, "I know what an awful shock you've had...."

"You've heard about it?"

"I saw it in the Sunday papers. I was going to write to you."

"Euan," the girl began in a nervous, hasty way, "I have to go to Holland at once. There is not a moment to lose. I want you to help me get my passport viséed."

"But, my dear girl," exclaimed the Major, aghast, "you can't go to Holland like this alone. Does your mother know about it?"

The girl shook her head.

"It's no good trying to stop me, Euan," she declared. "I mean to go, anyway. As a matter of fact, Mother doesn't know. I merely left word that I had gone to the Continent for a few days. Nobody knows about Holland except you. And if you won't help me I suppose I shall have to go to Harry Tadworth at the Foreign Office. I came to you first because he's always so stuffy ..."

Euan MacTavish pushed the girl into a chair and gave her a cigarette. He lit it for her and took one himself. His pipe had vanished into his pocket.

"Of course, I'll help you," he said. "Now, tell me all about it!"

"Before ... this happened I had promised Hartley Parrish to marry him," began the girl. "The doctors say his nerves were wrong. I don't believe a word of it. He was full of the joy of life. He was very fond of me. He was always talking of what we should do when we were married. He never would have killed himself without some tremendously powerful motive. Even then I can't believe it possible ..."

She made a little nervous gesture.

"After he ... did it," she went on, "I found this letter on his desk. It came to him from Holland. I mean to see the people who wrote it and discover if they can throw any light on ... on ... the affair ..."

She had taken from her muff a letter, folded in four, written on paper of a curious dark slatey-blue colour.

"Won't you show me the letter?"

"You promise to say nothing about it to any one?"

He nodded.

"Of course."

Without a word the girl gave him the letter. With slow deliberation he unfolded it. The letter was typewritten and headed: "Elias van der Spyck & Co. General Importers, Rotterdam."

This was the letter:

> ELIAS VAN DER SPYCK & CO.
> GENERAL IMPORTERS
> ROTTERDAM Rotterdam 25th Nov.
>
> *Codes*
> A.B.C.
> Liebler's
>
> *Personal*
> Dear Mr. Parrish,
>
> Your favor of even date to hand and contents noted. The last delivery of steel was to time but we have had warning from the railway authorities that labour troubles at the docks are likely to delay future consignments. If you don't mind we should prefer to settle the question of future delivery by Nov. 27 as we have a board meeting on the 30th inst. While we fully appreciate your own difficulties with labour at home, you will

understand that this is a question which we cannot afford to adjourn *sine die.*

Yours faithfully,
pro ELIAS VAN DER SPYCK & CO.

The signature was illegible.

Euan MacTavish folded the letter again and handed it back to Mary.

"That doesn't take me any farther," he said. "What do the police think of it?"

"They haven't seen it," was the girl's reply. "I took it without them knowing. I mean to make my own investigations about this ..."

"But, my dear Mary," exclaimed the little Major in a shocked voice, "you can't do things that way! Don't you see you may be hindering the course of justice? The police may attach the greatest importance to this letter ..."

"You're quite right," retorted the girl, "they do!"

"Then why have you kept it from them?"

Mary Trevert dropped her eyes and a little band of crimson flushed into her cheeks.

"Because," she commenced, "because ... well, because they are trying to implicate a friend of mine ..."

The Major took the girl's hand.

"Mary," he said, "I've known you all your life. I've knocked about a good bit and know something of the world, I believe. Suppose you tell me all about it ..."

Mary Trevert hesitated. Then she said, her hands nervously toying with her muff:

"We believe that Robin Greve - you know whom I mean - had a conversation with Hartley just before he ... he shot himself. That very afternoon Robin had asked me to marry him, but I told him about my engagement. He said some awful things about Hartley and rushed away. Ten minutes later Hartley Parrish committed suicide. And there *was* some one talking to him in the library. Bude, the butler, heard the voices. This afternoon I went down to the library alone ... to see if I could discover anything likely to throw any light on poor Hartley's death. This was the only letter I could find. It was tucked away between two letter-trays. One tray fitted into the other, and this letter had slipped between. It seems to have been overlooked both by Mr. Parrish's secretary and the police ..."

"But I confess," argued the Major, "that I don't see how this letter, which appears to be a very ordinary business communication, implicates anybody at all. Why shouldn't the police see it?..."

"Because," said Mary, "directly after discovering it I found Bruce Wright, who used to be one of Mr. Parrish's private secretaries, hiding behind the curtains in the library. Now, Bruce Wright is a great friend of Robin Greve's, and I immediately suspected that Robin had sent him to Harkings, particularly as ..."

"As what?..."

"As he practically admitted to me, that he had come for letter written on slatey-blue official-looking paper."

The girl held up the letter from Rotterdam.

"All this," the girl continued, "made me think that this letter must have had something to do with Hartley's death ..."

"Surely an additional reason for giving it to the police!..."

Mary Trevert set her mouth in an obstinate line.

"No!" she affirmed uncompromisingly. "The police believe that, as the result of a scene between Hartley and Robin, Hartley killed himself. Until I've found out for certain whether this letter implicates Robin or not, I sha'n't give it to the police ..."

"But, if Greve really had nothing to do with this shocking tragedy, the police can very easily clear him. Surely they are the best judges of his guilt ..."

Again a touch of warm colour suffused the girl's cheeks. Euan MacTavish remarked it and looked at her wistfully.

"Well, well," he observed gently, "perhaps they're not, after all!"

The girl looked up at him.

"Euan, dear," she said impulsively, "I knew you'd understand. Robin and Hartley may have had a row, but it was nothing worse. Robin is incapable of having threatened - blackmailed - Hartley, as the police seem to imagine. I am greatly upset by it all; I can't see things clear at all; but I'm determined not to give the police a weapon like this to use against Robin until I know whether it is sharp or blunt, until I have found out what bearing, if any, this letter had on Hartley Parrish's death ..."

Euan MacTavish leant back in his chair and said nothing. He finished his cigarette, pitched the butt into the fender, and turned to Mary. He asked her to let him see the letter again. Once more he read it over. Then, handing it back to her, he said:

"It's all so simple-looking that there may well be something behind it. But, if you do go to Holland, how are you going to set about your enquiries?"

"That's where you can help me, Euan, dear," answered the girl. "I want to find somebody at Rotterdam who will help me to make some confidential enquiries about this firm. Do you know any one? An Englishman would be best, of course ..."

But Euan MacTavish was halfway to the door.

"Wait there," he commanded, "till I telephone the one man in the world who can help us."

He vanished into the hall where Mary heard him at the instrument.

"We are going round to the Albany," he said, "to see my friend, Ernest Dulkinghorn, of the War Office. He can help us if any one can. But, Mary, you must promise me one thing before we go ... you must agree to do what old Ernest tells you. You needn't be afraid. He is the most unconventional of men, capable of even approving this madcap scheme of yours!"

"I agree," said Mary, "but how you waste time, Euan! We could have been at the Albany by this time!"

In a first-floor oak-panelled suite at the Albany, overlooking the covered walk that runs from Piccadilly to Burlington Gardens, they found an excessively fair, loose-limbed man whose air of rather helpless timidity was heightened by a pair of large tortoise-shell spectacles. He appeared excessively embarrassed at the sight of MacTavish's extremely good-looking companion.

"You never told me you were bringing a lady, Euan," he said reproachfully, "or I should have attempted to have made myself more presentable."

He looked down at his old flannel suit and made an apologetic gesture which took in the table littered with books and papers and the sofa on which lay a number of heavy tomes with marked slips sticking out between the pages.

"I am working at a code," he explained.

"Ernest here," said MacTavish, turning to Mary, "is the code king. Your pals in the Intelligence tell me, Ernest, that you've never been beaten by a code ..."

The fair man laughed nervously.

"They've been pullin' your leg, Euan," he said.

"Don't you believe him, Mary," retorted her cousin. "This is the man who probably did more than any one man to beat the Boche. Whenever the brother Hun changed his code, Brother Ernest was called in and he produced a key in one, two, three!..."

"What rot you talk, Euan!" said Dulkinghorn. "Working out a code is a combination of mathematics, perseverance, and inspiration with a good slice of luck thrown in! But isn't Miss Trevert going to sit down?"

He cleared the sofa with a sweep of his arm which sent the books flying on to the floor.

"Ernest," said MacTavish, "I want you to give Miss Trevert here a letter to some reliable fellow in Rotterdam who can assist her in making a few enquiries of a very delicate nature!"

"What sort of enquiries?" asked Dulkinghorn bluntly.

"About a firm called Elias van der Spyck," replied Euan.

"Of Rotterdam?" enquired the other sharply.

"That's right! Do you know them?"

"I've heard the name. They do a big business. But hadn't Miss Trevert better tell her story herself?"

Mary told him of the death of Hartley Parrish and of the letter she had found upon his desk. She said nothing of the part played by Robin Greve.

"Hmph!" said Dulkinghorn. " You think it might be

blackmail, eh? Well, well, it might be. Have you got this letter about you? Hand it over and let's have a look at it."

His nervous manner had vanished. His face seemed to take on a much keener expression. He took the letter from Mary and read it through. Then he crossed the room to a wall cupboard which he unlocked with a key on a chain, produced a small tray on which stood a number of small bottles, some paint-brushes and pens, and several little open dishes such as are used for developing photographs. He bore the tray to the table, cleared a space on a corner by knocking a pile of books and papers on the floor, and set it down.

"Just poke the fire!" he said to Euan.

From a drawer in the table he produced a board on which he pinned down the letter with a drawing-pin at each corner. Then he dipped a paint-brush into one of the bottles and carefully painted the whole surface of the sheet with some invisible fluid.

"So!" he said, "we'll leave that to dry and see if we can find out any little secrets, eh? That little tray'll do the trick if there's any monkey business to this letter of yours, Miss Trevert. That'll do the trick, eh, what?"

He paced the room as he talked, not waiting for an answer, but running on as though he were soliloquizing. Presently he turned and swooped down on the board.

"Nothing," he ejaculated. "Now for the acids!"

With a little piece of sponge he carefully wiped the

surface of the letter and painted it again with a substance from another bottle.

"Just hold that to the fire, would you, Euan?" he said, and gave MacTavish the board. He resumed his pacing, but this time he hummed in the most unmelodious voice imaginable:

> She was bright as a butterfly, as fair as a queen,
> Was pretty little Polly Perkins, of Paddington Green.

"It's dry!"

MacTavish's voice broke in upon the pacing and the discordant song.

"Well?"

Dulkinghorn snapped out the question.

"No result!" said Euan. He handed him the board.

Dulkinghorn cast a glance at it, swiftly removed the letter, held it for an instant up to the electric light, fingered the paper for a moment, and handed the letter back to Mary.

"If it's code," he said, "it's a conventional code and that always beats the expert ... at first. Go to Rotterdam and call on my friend, Mr. William Schulz. I'll give you a letter for him and he'll place himself entirely at your disposition. Euan will take you over. Holland is on your beat, ain't it, Euan? When do you go next?"

"To-morrow," said the King's Messenger. "The boat

train leaves Liverpool Street at ten o'clock."

"You'll want a passport," said Dulkinghorn, turning to the girl. "You've got it there? Good. Leave it with me. You shall have it back properly viséed by nine o'clock to-morrow morning. Where are you stayin'? Almond's Hotel. Good. I'll send the letter for Mr. William Schulz with it!"

"But," Euan interjected mildly, after making several ineffectual efforts to stem the torrent of speech, "do you really think that Miss Trevert will be well advised to risk this trip to Holland alone? Hadn't the police better take the matter in hand?"

"Police be damned!" replied Dulkinghorn heartily. "Miss Trevert will be better than a dozen heavy-handed, heavy-footed plain-clothes men. When you get to Rotterdam, Miss Trevert, you trot along and call on William Schulz. He'll see you through."

Then, to indicate without any possibility of misunderstanding, that his work had been interrupted long enough, Dulkinghorn got up, and, opening the sitting-room door, led the way into the hall. As he stood with his hand on the latch of the front door, Mary Trevert asked him:

"Is this Mr. Schulz an Englishman?"

"I'll let you into a secret," answered Bulkinghorn; "he *was*. But he isn't now! No, no, I can't say anything more. You must work it out for yourself. But I will give you a piece of advice. The less you say about Mr. William Schulz and about your private affairs generally when you are on the other side, the better it will be for you! Good-night - and good luck!"

Euan MacTavish escorted Mary to Almond's Hotel.

"I'm very much afraid," he said to her as they walked along, "that you're butting that pretty head of yours into a wasps' nest, Mary!"

"Nonsense!" retorted the girl decisively; "I can take care of myself!"

"If I consent to let you go off like this," said Euan, "it is only on one condition ... you must tell Lady Margaret where you are going ..."

"That'll spoil everything," answered Mary, pouting; "Mother will want to come with me!"

"No, she won't," urged her cousin, "not if I tell her. She'll worry herself to death, Mary, if she doesn't know what has become of you. You'd better let me ring her up from the club and tell her you're running over to Rotterdam for a few days. Look here, I'll tell her you're going with me. She'll be perfectly happy if she thinks I'm to be with you ..."

On that Mary surrendered.

"Have it your own way," she said.

"I'll pick you up here at a quarter-past nine in the morning," said Euan as he bade the girl good-night at her hotel, "then we'll run down to the F.O. and collect my bags and go on to the station!"

"Euan," the girl asked as she gave him her hand, "who

is this man Schulz, do you think?"

The King's messenger leant over and whispered:

"Secret Service!"

"Secret Service!"

The girl repeated the words in a hushed voice.

"Then Mr. Dulkinghorn ... is he ... that too?"

Euan nodded shortly.

"One of their leadin' lights!" he answered.

"But, Euan," - the girl was very serious now, - "what has the Secret Service to do with Hartley Parrish's clients in Holland?"

The King's messenger laid a lean finger along his nose.

"Ah!" he said, "what? That's what is beginning to interest me!"

CHAPTER XXI

A WORD WITH MR. JEEKES

Life is like a kaleidoscope, that ingenious toy which was the delight of the Victorian nursery. Like the glass fragments in its slide, different in colour and shape, men's lives lie about without seeming connection; then Fate gives the instrument a shake, and behold! the fragments slide into position and form an intricate mosaic....

Mark how Fate proceeded on the wet and raw Sunday evening when Bruce Wright, at the instance of Mr. Manderton, quitted Robin Greve's chambers in the Temple, leaving his friend and the detective alone together. To tell the truth, Bruce Wright was in no mood for facing the provincial gloom of a wet Sunday evening in London, nor did he find alluring the prospect of a suburban supper-party at the quiet house where he lived with his widowed mother and sisters in South Kensington. So, in an irresolute, unsettled frame of mind, he let himself drift down the Strand unable to bring himself to go home or, indeed, to form any plan.

He crossed Trafalgar Square, a nocturne in yellow and black - lights reflected yellow in pavements shining dark with wet - and by and by found himself in Pall Mall. Here it was that Fate took a hand. At this

Valentine Williams

moment it administered a preliminary jog to the kaleidoscope and brought the fragment labelled Bruce Wright into immediate proximity with the piece entitled Albert Edward Jeekes.

As Bruce Wright came along Pall Mall, he saw Mr. Jeekes standing on the steps of his club. The little secretary appeared to be lost in thought, his chin thrust down on the crutch-handle of the umbrella he clutched to himself. So absorbed was he in his meditations that he did not observe Bruce Wright stop and regard him. It was not until our young man had touched him on the arm that he looked up with a start.

"God bless my soul!" he exclaimed, "if it isn't young Wright!"

Now the sight of Jeekes had put a great idea into the head of our young friend. He had been more chagrined than he had let it appear to Robin Greve at his failure to recover the missing letter from the library at Harkings. To obtain the letter - or, at any rate, a copy of it - from Jeekes and to hand it to Robin Greve would, thought Bruce, restore his prestige as an amateur detective, at any rate in his own eyes. Moreover, a chat with Jeekes over the whole affair seemed a Heaven-sent exit from the *impasse* of boredom into which he had drifted this wet Sunday evening.

"How are you, Mr. Jeekes?" said Bruce briskly. ("Mr." Jeekes was the form of address always accorded to the principal secretary in the Hartley Parrish establishment and Bruce resumed it instinctively.) "I was anxious to see you. I called in at the club this afternoon. Did you get my message?"

The little secretary blinked at him through his *pince-nez.*

"There have been so many messages about this shocking affair that really I forget ..."

He sighed heavily.

"Couldn't I come in and have a yarn now?"

Bruce spoke cajolingly. But Mr. Jeekes wrinkled his brow fussily.

There was so much to do; he had had a long day; if Wright would excuse him ...

"As a matter of fact," explained Bruce with an eye on his man, "I wanted to see you particularly about a letter ..."

"Some other time ... to-morrow ..."

"Written on dark-blue paper ... you know, one of those letters H.P. made all the fuss about."

Mr. Jeekes took his *pince-nez* from his nose, gave the glasses a hasty rub with his pocket-handkerchief, and replaced them. He slanted a long narrow look at the young man.

Then, "What letter do you mean?" he asked composedly.

"A letter which lay on H.P.'s desk in the library at Harkings when they found the body ..."

"There *was* a letter there then ...?"

"Haven't *you* got it?"

Jeekes shook his head.

"Come inside for a minute and tell me about this," he said.

He led Bruce into the vast smoking-room of the club. They took seats in a distant corner near the blazing fire. The room was practically deserted.

Now, Mr. Jeekes's excessive carefulness about money had been a long-standing joke amongst his assistants when Bruce Wright had belonged to Hartley Parrish's secretarial staff. Thrift had become with him more than a habit. It was a positive obsession. It revealed itself in such petty meannesses as a perpetual cadging for matches or small change and a careful abstention from any offer of hospitality. Never in the whole course of his service had Bruce Wright heard of Mr. Jeekes taking anybody out to lunch or extending any of the usual hospitalities of life. He was not a little surprised, therefore, to hear Jeekes ask him what he would take.

Bruce said he would take some coffee.

"Have a liqueur? Have a cigar?" said Jeekes, turning to Bruce from the somnolent waiter who had answered the bell.

There was a strange eagerness, a sort of over-done cordiality, in the invitation which contrasted so strongly with the secretary's habits that Robin felt dimly suspicious. He suddenly formed the idea that

Mr. Jeekes wanted to pump him. He refused the liqueur, but accepted a cigar. Jeekes waited until they had been served and the waiter had withdrawn silently into the dim vastness of the great room before he spoke.

"Now, then, young Wright," he said, "what's this about a letter? Tell me from the beginning ..."

Bruce told him of the letter from Elias van der Spyck & Co. which Robin had seen upon the desk in the library at Harkings, of his (Bruce's) journey down to Harkings that afternoon and of his failure to find the letter.

"But why do you assume that I've got it?"

There was an air of forced joviality about Mr. Jeekes as he put the question which did not in the least, as he undoubtedly intended it should, disguise his eagerness. On the contrary, it lent his rather undistinguished features an expression of cunning which can only be described as knavish. Bruce Wright, who, as will already have been seen, was a young man with all his wits about him, did not fail to remark it. The result was that he hastily revised an intention half-formed in his mind of taking Jeekes a little way into his confidence regarding Robin Greve's doubts and suspicions about Hartley Parrish's death.

But he answered the secretary's question readily enough.

"Because Miss Trevert told me you went to the library immediately you arrived at Harkings last night. I consequently assumed that you must have taken away the letter seen by Robin Greve ..."

Mr. Jeekes drew in his breath with a sucking sound. It was a little trick of his when about to speak.

"So you saw Miss Trevert at Harkings, eh?"

Bruce laughed.

"I did," he said. "We had quite a dramatic meeting, too - it was like a scene from a film!"

And, with a little good-humoured exaggeration, he gave Mr. Jeekes a description of his encounter with Mary. And lest it should seem that young Wright was allowing Mr. Jeekes to pump him, it should be stated that Bruce was well aware of one of the secretary's most notable characteristics, a common failing, be it remarked, of the small-minded, and that was an over-powering suspicion of anything resembling a leading question. In order, therefore, to gain his confidence, he willingly satisfied the other's curiosity regarding his visit to Harkings hoping thereby to extract some information as to the whereabouts of the letter on the slatey-blue paper.

"There was no letter of this description on the desk, you say, when you and Miss Trevert looked?" asked Jeekes when Bruce had finished his story.

"Nothing but circulars and bills," Bruce replied.

Mr. Jeekes leaned forward and drank off his coffee with a swift movement. Then he said carelessly:

"From what you tell me, Miss Trevert would have been

perhaps a minute alone in the room without your seeing her?"

Bruce agreed with a nod.

Adjusting his *pince-nez* on his nose the secretary rose to his feet.

"Very glad to have seen you again, Wright," he said, thrusting out a limp hand; "must run off now - mass of work to get through ..."

Then Bruce risked his leading question.

"If you haven't got this letter," he observed, "what has become of it? Obviously the police are not likely to have taken it because they know nothing of its significance ..."

"Quite, quite," answered Mr. Jeekes absently, but without replying to the young man's question.

"Why," asked Bruce boldly, "did old H.P. make such a mystery about these letters on the slatey-blue paper, Mr. Jeekes?"

The secretary wrinkled up his thin lips and sharp nose into a cunning smile.

"When you get to be my age, young Wright," he made answer, "you will understand that every man has a private side to his life. And, if you have learnt your job properly, you will also know that a private secretary's first duty is to mind his own business. About this letter now - it's the first I've heard of it. Take my advice and don't bother your head about it. *If* it exists ..."

"But it *does* exist," broke in Bruce quickly. "Mr. Greve saw it and read it himself ..."

Mr. Jeekes laughed drily.

"Don't you forget, young Wright," he said, jerking his chin towards the youngster in a confidential sort of way, "don't you forget that Mr. Greve is anxious to find a plausible motive for Mr. Parrish's suicide. People are talking, you understand! That's all I've got to say! Just you think it over ..."

Bruce Wright bristled up hotly at this.

"I don't see you have any reason to try and impugn Greve's motive for wishing to get at the bottom of this mysterious affair ..."

Mr. Jeekes affected to be engrossed in the manicuring of his nails. Very intently he rubbed the nails of one hand against the palm of the other.

"No mystery!" he said decisively with a shake of the head: "no mystery whatsoever about it, young Wright, except what the amateur detectives will try and make it out to be. Or has Mr. Greve discovered a mystery already?"

The question came out artfully. But in the quick glance which accompanied it, there was an intent watchfulness which startled Bruce accustomed as he was to the mild and unemotional ways of the little secretary.

"Not that I know of," said Bruce. "Greve is only puzzled like all of us that H.P. should have done a thing like this!"

Mr. Jeekes was perfectly impassive again.

"The nerves, young Wright! The nerves!" he said impressively. "Harley Street, not Mr. Greve, will supply the motive to this sad affair, believe me!"

With that he accompanied the young man to the door of the club and from the vestibule watched him sally forth into the rain of Pall Mall.

Then Mr. Jeekes turned to the hall porter.

"Please get me Stevenish one-three-seven," he said, "it's a trunk call. Don't let them put you off with 'No reply.' It's Harkings, and they are expecting me to ring them. I shall be in the writing room."

When, twenty minutes later, Mr. Jeekes emerged from the trunk call telephone box in the club vestibule, his mouth was drooping at the corners and his hands trembled curiously. He stood for an instant in thought tapping his foot on the marble floor of the deserted hall dimly lit by a single electric bulb burning over the hall porter's box. Then he went back to the writing-room and returned with a yellow telegram form.

"Send a boy down to Charing Cross with that at once, please," he said to the night porter.

Fate which had brought Bruce Wright face to face with Mr. Jeekes gave the kaleidoscope another jerk that night. As Bruce Wright entered the Tube Station at Dover Street to go home to South Kensington, it occurred to him that he would ring up Robin Greve at his chambers in the Temple and give him an outline of his (Bruce's) talk with Jeekes. Bruce went to the public callbox in the station, but the rhythmic "Zoom-er! Zoom-er! Zoom-er!" which announces that a number is engaged was all the satisfaction he got. The prospect of waiting about the draughty station exit did not appeal to him, so he decided to go home and telephone Robin, as originally arranged, in the morning.

Just about the time that he made this resolve, Robin in his rooms in the Temple was hanging up the receiver of his telephone with a dazed expression in his eyes. Mr. Manderton had rung him up with a piece of intelligence which fairly bewildered him. It bewildered Mr. Manderton also, as the detective was frank enough to acknowledge.

Mary Trevert had gone to Rotterdam for a few days in company with her cousin, Major Euan MacTavish. Mr. Manderton had received this astonishing information by telephone from Harkings a few minutes before.

"It bothers me properly, Mr. Greve, sir," the detective had added.

"There's only one thing for it, Manderton," Robin had said; "I'll have to go after her ..."

"The very thing I was about to suggest myself, Mr. Greve. You're unofficial-like and can be more helpful than if we detailed one of our own people from the Yard. And with the investigation in its present stage I don't reely feel justified in going off on a wild-goose chase myself. There are several important enquiries going forward now, notably as to where Mr. Parrish bought his pistol. But we certainly ought to find out what takes Miss Trevert careering off to Rotterdam in this way ..."

"It seems almost incredible," Robin had said, "but it looks to me as though Miss Trevert must have found out something about the letter ..."

"Or found it herself ..."

"By Jove! She was in the library when Bruce Wright was there. This settles it, Manderton. I must go!"

"Then," said the detective, "I'm going to entrust you with that slotted sheet of paper again. For I have an idea, Mr. Greve, that you may get a glimpse of that letter before I do. I'll send a messenger round with it at once."

Then a difficulty arose. Manderton had not got the girl's address. They had no address at Harkings. Nor did he know what train Miss Trevert had taken. She might have gone by the 9 P.M. that night. Had Mr. Greve got a passport? Yes, Robin had a passport, but it was not viséed for Holland. That meant he could not leave until the following evening. Then Robin had a "brain wave."

"There's an air service to Rotterdam!" he exclaimed. "It doesn't leave till noon. A pal of mine went across by it only last week. That will leave me time to get my passport stamped at the Dutch Consulate, to catch the air mail, and be in Rotterdam by tea-time! And, Manderton, I shall go to the Grand Hotel. That's where my friend stopped. Wire me there if there's any news ..."

Air travel is so comfortably regulated at the present day that Robin Greve, looking back at his trip by air from Croydon Aerodrome to the big landing-ground

Valentine Williams

outside Rotterdam, acknowledged that he had more excitement in his efforts to stir into action a lethargic Dutch passport official in London, so as to enable him to catch the air mail, than in the smooth and uneventful voyage across the Channel. He reached Rotterdam on a dull and muggy afternoon and lost no time in depositing his bag at the Grand Hotel. An enquiry at the office there satisfied him that Mary Trevert had not registered her name in the hotel book. Then he set out in a taxi upon a dreary round of the principal hotels.

But fate, which loves to make a sport of lovers, played him a scurvy trick. In the course of his search it brought Robin to that very hotel towards which, at the selfsame moment, Mary Trevert was driving from the station. By the time she arrived, Robin was gone and, with despair in his heart, had started on a tour of the second-class hotels, checking them by the Baedeker he had bought in the Strand that morning. It was eight o'clock by the time he had finished. He had drawn a blank.

The sight of a huge, plate-glass-fronted café reminded him that in the day's rush he had omitted to lunch. So he paid off his taxi and dined off succulent Dutch beefsteak, pounded as soft as velvet and swimming with butter and served in a bed of deliciously browned 'earth apples,' as the Holländers call potatoes. The café was stiflingly hot; there was a large and noisy orchestra in the front part and a vast billiard-saloon in the back - a place of shaded lights, clicking balls, and guttural exclamations. The heat of the place, the noise and the cries combined with the effect of his long journey in the fresh air to make him very drowsy. When he had finished dinner he was content to postpone his investigations until the morrow and go to bed. Emerging from the café he found to his relief that his hotel was but a few houses away.

As he sat at breakfast the next morning, enjoying the admirable Dutch coffee, he reviewed the situation very calmly but very thoroughly. He told himself that he had no indication as to Mary Trevert's business in Rotterdam save the supposition that she had found the van der Spyck letter and had come to Rotterdam to investigate the matter for herself. He realized that the hypothesis was thin, for, in the first place, Mary could have no inkling as to the hidden significance of the document, and, in the second place, she was undoubtedly under the impression that Hartley Parrish was driven to suicide by his (Robin's) threats.

But, in the absence of any other apparent explanation of the girl's extraordinary decision to come to Rotterdam, Robin decided he would accept the theory that she had come about the van der Spyck letter. How like Mary, after all, he mused, self-willed, fearless, independent, to rush off to Holland on her own on a quest like this! Where would her investigations lead her? To the offices of Elias van der Spyck & Co., to be sure! Robin threw his napkin down on the table, thrust back his chair, and went off to the hotel porter to locate the address of the firm.

The telephone directory showed that the offices were situated in the Oranien-Straat, about ten minutes' walk from the hotel, in the business quarter of the city round the Bourse. Robin glanced at the clock. It was twenty minutes to ten. The principals, he reflected, were not likely to be at the office before ten o'clock. It was a fine morning and he decided to walk. The hotel porter gave him a few simple directions: the gentleman could not miss the way, he said; so Robin started off, hope high in his breast of getting a step nearer to the elucidation of the mystery of the library at Harkings.

A brisk walk of about ten minutes through the roaring streets of the city brought him to a big open square from which, he had been instructed, the Oranien-Straat turned off. He was just passing a large and important-looking post-office - he remarked it because he looked up at a big clock in the window to see the time - when a man came hastily through the swing-door and stopped irresolutely on the pavement in front, glancing to right and left as a man does who is looking for a cab.

At the sight of him Robin could scarcely suppress an expression of amazement. It was Mr. Jeekes.

CHAPTER XXII

THE MAN WITH THE YELLOW FACE

In a narrow, drowsy side street at Rotterdam, bisected by a somnolent canal, stood flush with the red-brick sidewalk a small clean house. Wire blinds affixed to the windows of its ground and first floors gave it a curious blinking air as though its eyes were only half open. To the neat green front door was affixed a large brass plate inscribed with the single name: "Schulz."

A large woman, in a pink print dress with a white cloth bound about her head, was vigorously polishing the plate as, on the morning following her departure from London, Mary Trevert, Dulkinghorn's letter of introduction in her pocket, arrived in front of the residence of Mr. William Schulz. Euan MacTavish had, on the previous evening, seen her to her hotel and had then - very reluctantly, as it seemed to Mary - departed to continue his journey to The Hague, his taxi piled high with white-and-green Foreign Office bags, heavily sealed with scarlet wax.

Mary Trevert approached the woman, her letter of introduction, which Dulkinghorn, being an unusual person, had fastened down, in her hand.

"Schulz?" she said interrogatively.

"*Nicht da*," replied the woman without looking up from her rubbing.

"Has he gone out?" asked Mary in English.

"*Verstehe nicht!*" mumbled the woman.

But she put down her cleaning-rag and, breathing heavily, mustered the girl with a leisurely stare.

Mary repeated the question in German whereupon the woman brightened up considerably.

The *Herr* was not at home. The *Herr* had gone out. On business, *jawohl*. To the bank, perhaps. But the *Herr* would be back in time for *Mittagessen* at noon. There was beer soup followed by *Rindfleisch* ...

Mary hesitated an instant. She was wondering whether she should leave her letter of introduction. She decided she would leave it. So she wrote on her card: "Anxious to see you as soon as possible" and the name of her hotel, and gave it, with the letter, to the woman.

"Please see that Herr Schulz gets that directly he comes in," she said. "It is important!"

"*Gut, gut!*" said the woman, wiping her hands on her apron. She took the card and letter, and Mary, thanking her, set off to go back to her hotel.

About twenty yards from Mr. Schulz's house a narrow alley ran off. As Mary turned to regain the little footbridge across the canal to return to the noisy street which would take her back to the hotel, she caught sight of a man disappearing down this alley.

She only had a glimpse of him, but it was sufficient to startle her considerably. He was a small man wearing a tweed cap and a tweed travelling ulster of a vivid brown. It was not these details, however, which took her aback. It was the fact that in the glimpse she had had of the man's face she had seemed to recognize the features of Mr. Albert Edward Jeekes.

"What an extraordinary thing!" Mary said to herself. "It *can't* be Mr. Jeekes. But if it is not, it is some one strikingly like him!"

To get another view of the stranger she hurried to the corner of the alley. It was a mere thread of a lane, not above six yards wide, running between the houses a distance of some sixty yards to the next street. But the alley was empty. The stranger had disappeared.

Mary went a little way down the lane. A wooden fence ran down it on either side, with doors at intervals apparently giving on the back yards of the houses in the street. There was no sign of Mr. Jeekes's double, so she retraced her steps and returned to her hotel without further incident.

She had not been back more than half an hour when a waiter came in to the lounge where she was sitting.

"Miss Trevert?" he said. "Zey ask for you at ze delephone!"

He took her to a cabin under the main staircase.

"This is Miss Trevert speaking!" said Mary.

" I am speaking for Mr. Schulz, " a man's voice

answered - rather a nasal voice with a shade of foreign inflexion - "he has had your letter. He is very sorry he has been detained in the country, but would be very glad if you would lunch with him to-day at his country-house."

"I shall be very pleased," the girl replied. "Is it far?"

"Only just outside Rotterdam," the voice responded. "Mr. Schulz will send the car to the hotel to pick you up at 11.45. The driver will ask for you. Is that all right?"

"Certainly," said Mary. "Please thank Mr. Schulz and tell him I will expect the car at a quarter to twelve!"

Punctually at the appointed hour an open touring-car drove up to the hotel. Mary was waiting at the entrance. The driver was a young Dutchman in a blue serge suit. He jumped out and came up to Mary.

"Mees Trevert?" he said.

Mary nodded, whereupon he helped her into the car, then got back into the driving-seat and they drove away.

A run of about twenty minutes through trim suburbs brought them out on a long straight road, paved with bricks and lined with poplars. The day was fine with a little bright sunshine from time to time and a high wind which kept the sails of the windmills dotting the landscape turning briskly. They followed the road for a bit, then branched off down a side turning which led to a black gate. It bore the name "Villa Bergendal" in white letters. The gate opened into a short drive fringed by thick laurel bushes which presently brought them in view of an ugly square red-brick house.

The car drew up at a creeper-hung porch paved in red tiles. The chauffeur helped Mary to alight and, pushing open a glass door, ushered the girl into a square, comfortably furnished hall. Some handsome Oriental rugs were spread about: trophies of native weapons hung on the walls, and there were some fine specimens of old Dutch chests and blue Delft ware.

The chauffeur led the way across the hall to a door at the far end. As Mary followed him, something bright lying on one of the chests caught her eye. It was a vivid brown travelling ulster and on it lay a brown tweed cap.

Mary Trevert was no fool. She was, on the contrary, a remarkably quick-witted young person. The sight of that rather "loud" overcoat instantly recalled the stranger so strikingly resembling Mr. Jeekes who had disappeared down the lane as she was coming away from Mr. Schulz's house. Mr. Jeekes *was* in Rotterdam then, and had, of course, been sent by her mother to look after her. What a fool she had been to allow Euan MacTavish to persuade her to tell her mother of her plans!

Mary suddenly felt very angry. How dare Mr. Jeekes spy on her like this! She was quite capable, she told herself, of handling her own affairs, and she intended to tell the secretary so very plainly. And if, as she was beginning to believe, Mr. Schulz were acting hand in glove with Mr. Jeekes, she would let him know equally plainly that she had no intention of troubling him, but would make her own investigations independently.

With a heightened colour she followed the chauffeur and passed through the door he held open for her.

She found herself in a small, pleasant room with a bright note of colour in the royal blue carpet and window-curtains. A log-fire burned cheerfully in the fireplace before which a large red-leather Chesterfield was drawn up. On the walls hung some good old Dutch prints, and there were a couple of bookcases containing books which, by their bindings at least, seemed old and valuable.

At the farther end of the room was another door across which a curtain of royal blue was drawn. Mary had scarcely entered the room when this door opened and a man appeared.

He was carefully dressed in a well-cut suit of some dark material and wore a handsome pearl pin in his black tie. He was a dark, sallow type of man, his skin yellowed as though from long residence in the tropics. A small black moustache, carefully trained outwards from the lips, disclosed, as he smiled a greeting at his visitor, a line of broken yellow teeth. His hair, which was grizzled at the temples, was black and oily and brushed right back off the forehead. With his coarse black hair, his sallow skin, and his small beady eyes, rather like a snake's, there was something decidedly un-English about him. As Mary Trevert looked at him, somewhat taken aback by his sudden appearance, she became conscious of a vague feeling of mistrust welling up within her.

The man closed the door behind him and advanced into the room, his hand extended. Mary took it. It was dank and cold to the touch.

"A thousand apologies, my dear Miss Trevert," he said in a soft, silky voice, a trifle nasal, with a touch of Continental inflexion, "for asking you to come out here to see me. The fact is I had an important business conference here this morning and I have a second one this afternoon. It was materially impossible for me to come into Rotterdam ... But I am forgetting my manners. Let me introduce myself. I am Mr. Schulz ..."

Mary Trevert looked at him thoughtfully. Was this the friend of Ernest Dulkinghorn, the man of confidence to whom he had recommended her? A feeling of great uneasiness came over her. She listened. The house was absolutely still. From the utter silence enveloping it - for aught she knew - she and her unsavoury-looking companion might be the only persons in it. And then she realized that, on the faith of a telephone call, she had blindly come out to a house, the very address of which was utterly unknown to her.

She fought down a sudden sensation of panic that made her want to scream, to bolt from the room into the fresh air, anywhere away from those snake eyes, that soft voice, that clammy hand. She collected her thoughts, remembered that Jeekes must be somewhere in the house, as his outdoor things were in the hall. The recollection reminded her of her determination to tolerate no interference from Jeekes or her mother.

So she merely answered: "It was no trouble to come," and waited for the man to speak again.

He pulled forward the Chesterfield and made her sit down beside him.

"I had the letter of introduction," he said, "and I want

you to know that my services are entirely at your disposal. Now, what can I do for you?"

He looked at the girl intently - rather anxiously, she thought.

"That was explained in the letter," she answered, meeting his gaze unflinchingly.

"Yes, yes, of course, I know. I meant in what way do you propose to make use of my ... my local knowledge?"

"I will tell you that, Mr. Schulz," Mary Trevert said in a measured voice, "when you tell me what you think of the mission which has brought me here ..."

The snake's eyes narrowed a little.

"For a young lady to have come out alone to Holland on a mission of this description speaks volumes for your pluck and self-reliance, Miss Trevert ..."

"I asked you what you thought of my mission to Holland, Mr. Schulz," Mary interposed coldly.

It was beginning to dawn on her that Mr. Schulz did not seem to know anything about the object of her visit, but, on the contrary, was seeking to elicit this from her by a process of adroit cross-examination. She was rather puzzled, therefore, but also somewhat relieved when he said:

"I can give my opinion better after you have shown me the letter ..."

"What letter?" said the girl.

"The letter from Elias van der Spyck and Company, to be sure," retorted the other quickly.

Mary dipped her hand into her black fox muff. Then she hesitated. She could not rid herself of the suspicion that this man with the sallow face and the yellow fangs was not to be trusted. She withdrew her hand.

"This is a very delicate matter, Mr. Schulz," she said. "Our appointment was made by telephone, and I think therefore I should ask you to show me Mr. Dulking-horn's letter of introduction before I go any further, so that I may feel quite sure in my mind that I am dealing with one in whom I know Mr. Dulkinghorn to have every confidence ..."

Mr, Schulz's yellow face went a shade yellower. His mouth twisted itself into a wry smile, his thin lips fleshing his discoloured teeth. He stood up rather stiffly.

"You are a guest in my house, Miss Trevert," he said with offended dignity, "I scarcely expected you to impugn my good faith. Surely my word is sufficient ..."

He turned his back on her and took a couple of paces into the room in apparent vexation. Then he returned and stood at the back of the Chesterfield behind her. His feet made no sound on the thick carpet, but some vague instinct made Mary Trevert turn her head. She saw him standing there, twisting his hands nervously behind his back.

"Surely my word is sufficient ..." he repeated.

"In business," said Mary boldly, "one cannot be too careful."

"Besides," Mr. Schulz urged, "this was a private letter which Mr. ... Mr. Dulkinghorn certainly did not expect you to see. That makes it awkward ..."

"I think in the circumstances," said Mary, "I must insist, Mr. Schulz!"

She was now feeling horribly frightened. She strained her ears in vain for a sound. The whole house seemed wrapped in a grave-like quiet. The smile had never left Mr. Schulz's face. But it was a cruel, wolfish grin without a ray of kindliness in it. The girl felt her heart turn cold within her every time her eyes fell on the mask-like face.

Mr. Schulz shrugged shoulders.

"Since you insist ..." he remarked. "But I think it is scarcely fair on our friend Dulkinghorn. The letter is in the safe in my office next door. If you come along I will get it out and show it to you ..."

He spoke unconcernedly, but stiffly, as though to emphasize the slight put upon his dignity. One hand thrust jauntily in his jacket pocket, he stepped across the carpet to the door with the blue curtain. He opened it, then stood back for the girl to pass in before him.

"After you!" he said.

He had placed himself so close to the doorway that the

black fox about her neck brushed his face as she passed. Suddenly a warm, sickly whiff of some sweet-smelling odour came to her. She stopped on the instant, irresolute, alarmed. Then a dank hand was clapped on her face, covering nostrils and mouth with a soft cloth reeking with a horrible cloying drug. An arm with muscles like steel was passed round her waist and held her in a vice-like grip against which she struggled in vain. She felt her senses slipping, slipping ...

Valentine Williams

CHAPTER XXIII

TWO'S COMPANY ...

On the pavement opposite the post-office stood one of those high pillars which are commonly used in Continental cities for the display of theatre and concert advertisements. Robin instantly stepped behind it. It was not that he wished to avoid being seen by Jeekes as much as that he had not decided in his mind what course he had best pursue. From behind the cover of the pillar he mustered his man.

The little secretary looked strange and unfamiliar in a sporting sort of travelling ulster of a tawny brown hue and a cap of the same stuff. But there was no mistaking the watery eyes, the sharp nose, the features. He had obviously not seen Robin. His whole attention was rivetted on the street. He kept peering nervously to right and left as though expecting some one.

Suddenly he stepped forward quickly to the kerb. Then Robin saw an open car detach itself from the press of traffic in the square and, driven very fast, approach the post-office. It was a large car with a grey body; a sallow man wearing a black felt hat sat at the wheel. The car drew up at the kerb and halted within a few feet of the advertisement pillar. Robin backed hastily round it to escape observation. He had resolved to do nothing until he had ascertained who Jeekes's friend was and what business the secretary had with him.

"It's all right," Robin heard the man in the car say in English; "I telephoned the girl and she's coming. What a piece of luck, eh?"

Robin heard the click of the car door as it swung open.

"... better get along out there at once," he heard the man in the car say, "I'm sending Jan in the car for her at ..."

Then Robin stepped out unexpectedly from behind his pillar and cannoned into Mr. Jeekes, who was just entering the car.

"Good-morning," said Robin with easy assurance; "I'm delighted to hear that you've found Miss Trevert, Jeekes, for, to tell the truth, I was feeling somewhat uneasy about her ..."

The secretary's face was a study. The surprise of seeing Robin, who had dropped, it seemed to him, out of the clouds into the city of Rotterdam, deprived him of speech for an instant. He blinked his eyes, looked this way and that, and finally, with a sort of blind gesture, readjusted his *pince-nez* and glared at the intruder.

Then, without a word, he got into the car. But Robin, with a firm hand, stayed the door which Jeekes would have closed behind him.

"Excuse me," Robin remarked decidedly, "but I'm coming with you if your friend" - at this he looked at the man in the driving-seat - "has no objection ..."

Mr. Jeekes cast a frightened glance at the sallow man.

The latter said impatiently:

"We're wasting time, Jeekes. Who is this gentleman?"

"This is Mr. Greve," said the little secretary hurriedly, "a friend of Mr. Parrish and Miss Trevert. He was staying in the house at the time of the tragedy. He has, I understand, taken a prominent part in the investigations as to the motive of our poor friend's sad end ..."

Mr. Jeekes looked to Robin as he said this as though for confirmation. The man at the driving-wheel turned and gave the little secretary a quick glance. Then he mustered Robin with a slow, insolent stare. He had a yellow face and small black eyes quick and full of intelligence.

Then he bowed.

"My name is Victor," he said. "The sad news about Mr. Parrish was a great shock to me. I met him several times in London. Were you anxious to see Miss ... er ... Trevert? She has come to Rotterdam (so my friend Jeekes tells me) to look into certain important business transactions which the late Mr. Parrish had in hand at the time of his death. Did I understand you to say that you were uneasy about this lady? Is there any mystery about her journey?..."

For the moment Robin felt somewhat abashed. The question was rather a poser. Was there, in effect, any mystery about Mary's trip to Rotterdam accompanied by her cousin? She had acquainted her people at Harkings with her plans. What if, after all, everything was open and above-board, and she had merely come to Rotterdam on business? It seemed difficult to believe. Surely in such a case the solicitor, Bardy, would have been the more suitable emissary ...

"You'll forgive us, I'm sure," the yellow-faced man remarked suavely, "but we're in a great hurry. Would you mind closing that door?..."

Robin closed the door. But he got into the car first. As he had stood on the pavement in doubt, the recollection of Jeekes's inexplicable lie about the payments made by Parrish for the French lady in the Mayfair flat came back to him and deepened the suspicion in his mind. It would in any case, he told himself, do no harm to find out who this rather unsavoury-looking Rotterdam friend of Jeekes's was ...

So Robin jumped into the car and sat down on the back seat next to the secretary.

"It happens," he said, "that I am particularly anxious to see Miss Trevert. As I gather you are going to meet her, I feel sure you won't mind my accompanying you ..."

The yellow-faced man turned with an easy smile.

"Sorry," he said, "but we are having a meeting with Miss Trevert on private business and I'm afraid we cannot take you along. Jeekes here, however, could take a message to Miss Trevert and if she *wanted* to see you ..."

He broke off significantly and smiled slily at the secretary. Robin felt himself flush. So Jeekes had been telling tales out of school to Mr. Victor, had he? The young man squared his jaw. That settled it. He would stay.

"I promise not to butt in on your private business," he replied, "but I simply must see Miss Trevert before I go back to London. So, if you don't mind, I think I'll come along ..."

The yellow-faced man glanced at his wrist watch.

"I can't prevent you!" he exclaimed. Then he rapped out something in Dutch to Jeekes. The secretary leaned forward to catch the remark. The yellow-faced man threw in the clutch.

"Goed!" (good), answered Jeekes in the same language, and resumed his seat as the car glided smoothly away from the kerb into the traffic of the busy square. Robin settled himself back in the seat with an inaudible sigh of satisfaction. He did not like the look of Jeekes's companion, he told himself, and Mr. Victor, whoever he was, had certainly manifested no great desire for Robin's company. But he was going to see Mary. That was all that counted for the moment.

They threaded their way through the streets in silence. It passed through Robin's mind to start a discussion with Jeekes about the death of Hartley Parrish. But in the circumstances he conceived it might easily assume a controversial character, and he did not want to take any risk of jeopardizing his chance of meeting Mary again. And no other subject of conversation occurred to him. He did not know Jeekes at all well, knew him in fact only as a week-end guest knows the private secretary of his host, a shadowy personality, indispensable and part of the household, but scarcely more than a name ...

The car had put on speed as they left the more crowded streets and emerged into the suburbs. Now they were running over a broad straight main road lined with poplars. Robin wondered whither they were bound. He was about to put the question to the secretary when the man Victor turned his head and said over his shoulder:

"*Nu!*"

At the same moment the speed of the car sensibly diminished.

Jeekes put his arm across the young man at his side.

"That door," he said, touching his sleeve, "doesn't seem to be properly shut. Would you mind ..."

Robin pushed the door with his hand.

"It seems all right," he said.

"Permit me ..."

The secretary stretched across and pulled back the latch, releasing the door. It swung out.

"Now close it," said Mr. Jeekes.

The door was flapping to and fro with the swaying of the car over the rough road and Robin had to half rise in order to comply with the request. He was leaning forward, steadying himself with one hand grasping the back of the driving-seat, when he received a tremendous shove in the back. At the same moment the car seemed to leap forward: he made a desperate effort to regain his balance, failed, and was whirled out head foremost on to the side of the road.

Fortunately for himself he fell soft. The road ran here through a little wood of young oak and beech which came right down to the edge of the *chaussée*. The ground was deep in withered leaves which, with the rain and the water draining from the road's high camber, were soft and soggy. Robin went full length into this muss with a thud that shook every bone in his body. His left leg, catching in a bare gorse-bush, acted as a brake and stopped him from rolling farther. He sat up, his mouth full of mud and his hair full of wet leaves, and felt himself carefully over. He contemplated rather ruefully a long rent in the left leg of his trousers just across the knee.

"Jeekes!" he murmured; "he pushed me out! The dirty dog!"

Then he remembered that, with the men in the car gone, he had lost trace again of Mary Trevert. His forcible ejection from the car was evidence enough of their determination to deal with Mary without interference from outside. It looked ominous. Robin sprang to his feet and rushed to the middle of the road.

The *chaussée* was absolutely empty. About a hundred yards from where he stood in the direction in which the car had been travelling the road made a sharp bend to the right, thus curtailing his view. Robin did not hesitate. Not waiting to retrieve his hat or even to wipe the mud from his face, he started off at a brisk run along the road in the direction in which the car had disappeared. He had not gone far before he found that his heavy overcoat was seriously impeding him. He stripped it off and, folding it, hid it beneath a bush just inside the plantation. Then he ran on again.

Fresh disappointment awaited him when he rounded the bend in the road. A few hundred yards on the road turned again. There was no sign of the car. A cart piled high with manure was approaching, the driver, wearing wooden shoes and cracking at intervals a huge whip, trudging at the side.

Robin stopped him.

"Motor-car? Automobile?" he asked pointing in the direction from which the cart had come. The driver stared at him with a look of owlish stupidity.

"Automobile?" repeated Robin. "Tuff-Tuff?"

Very slowly a grin suffused the carter's grimy face. He showed a row of broken black teeth. A tiny stream of saliva escaped from the corner of his mouth and trickled over the reddish stubble on his chin. Then he continued his way, turning his head every now and then to display his idiot's grin.

"Damnation!" exclaimed Robin, starting to run again. "Not a soul to ask in this accursed desert except the village idiot! Oh! that Jeekes! I'll wring his blinking neck when I get hold of him!"

He was furious with himself for the abject way in which he had been fooled. The man Victor had given Jeekes his orders in Dutch and had purposely picked a soft spot on the roadside and slowed down the car in order that the unwelcome intruder might be ejected as safely as possible. And to think that Robin had blandly allowed Jeekes to open the door and throw him out on the road!

He was round the second bend now. The sun was shining with a quite respectable warmth and the steamy air made him desperately hot. The perspiration rolled off his face. But he never slackened his gait. Robin knew these Continental roads and their habit of running straight. He reckoned confidently on presently coming upon a long stretch where he might discern the car.

He was not deceived. After the second bend the *chaussée*, just as he anticipated, straightened out and ran clear away between an ever-narrowing double line of poplars to become a bluish blob on the horizon. But of the car nothing was to be seen.

For the second time Robin pulled up. He took serious counsel with himself. He estimated that he could see for about three miles along the road. Less than three minutes had elapsed since his misadventure, and therefore he was confident that the car should yet be in sight, unless it had left the road, for it could not have warmed up to a speed exceeding sixty miles an hour in the time. There was no sign of the car on the road, consequently it must have left it. Robin had passed no side roads between the scene of the accident and the second bend; therefore, he argued, he had the car before him still. He would go on.

When he started off for the third time, it was at a brisk walking pace. As he went he kept a sharp lookout to right and left of the road for any trace of the car. It never occurred to him that to follow on foot a swift car bound for an unknown destination was the maddest kind of wild-goose chase. He was profoundly uneasy about Mary, but at the same time immeasurably angered by the trick played upon him - angered not so much against Jeekes as against the sallow-faced man whom he recognized as its inceptor. He had no thought for anything else.

The flat Dutch landscape stretched away on either side of the road. A windmill or two, the inevitable irrigation canals with their little sluices, and an occasional tree alone broke the monotony of the scene. But away to the right Robin noticed a clump of trees which, he surmised, might conceivably enclose a house.

As he walked, he scrutinized the roadway for any track of a car. But on the hard brick *pavé* wheels left no mark. The first side road he came to was likewise paved in brick. In grave perplexity Robin came to a halt.

Then his eye fell upon a puddle. It lay on the edge of the footpath bordering the *chaussée* about five yards beyond the turning. The soft mud which skirted it showed the punched-out pattern of a studded tyre! The car had not taken this side road, at any rate. It had probably pulled over on to the footpath to pass the manure cart which Robin had met. He pushed on again valiantly.

Another hundred yards brought him to a second side road. There was no *pavé* here, but a soft sandy surface. And it bore, clearly imprinted in the mud, the fresh tracks of a car as it had turned off the road.

Breaking into a run Robin followed the track down the turning. It led him to a black gate beyond which was a twisting gravel drive fringed with high laurels. And the gravel showed the same tyre marks as the road.

He vaulted the gate lightly and ran up the drive. He was revolving in his head what his next move should be. Should he walk boldly into the house and confront Jeekes and his rascally looking companion or should he first spy out the ground and try to ascertain whether Mary had arrived? He decided on the latter course.

Accordingly, when an unexpected turn of the drive brought him in view of a white porch, he left the avenue and took cover behind the laurel bushes. Walking softly on the wet grass and keeping well down behind the laurels, he went forward parallel with the drive. It ran into a clean courtyard with a coachhouse or garage on one side and a small green door, seemingly a side entrance into the house, on the other.

There was no one in the courtyard and the house seemed perfectly quiet. From his post of observation behind the laurels, Robin observed that a tall window beside the green door commanded the view across the courtyard. He therefore retraced his steps by the way he had come. When he was past the corner of the house, he returned to the drive and keeping close to the bushes walked quietly into the courtyard. There, hugging the wall, he crept round past the closed doors of the garage until he found himself beside the tall window adjoining the green door.

The window was open a few inches at the top. From within the sound of voices reached him. Jeekes was speaking. Robin recognized his rather grating voice at once.

"... no more violence," he was saying; "first Greve and now the girl. I don't like your methods, Victor ..."

Very cautiously Robin dropped on one knee and shuffled forward in this position until his eyes were on a level with the window-sill. He found himself looking into a narrow room, well lighted by a second window at the farther end. It was apparently an office, for there was a high desk running down the centre and a large safe occupied a prominent place against the wall.

Jeekes and the man Victor stood chatting at the desk. The yellow-faced man was grinning sardonically.

"Parrish don't like your methods, I'll be bound," he retorted. "Don't you worry about the little lady, Jeekes! Bless your heart, I won't hurt her unless ..."

The loud throbbing of a car at the front of the house made Robin duck his head hastily. The car, he guessed, might be round at the garage any moment and it would not do for him to be discovered. He got clear of the window, rose to his feet, and tiptoed round the house by the way he had come. Then he crossed the drive and regained the shelter of the laurels. Crawling along until he came level with the porch, he peeped through.

Mary Trevert was just entering the house.

Valentine Williams

CHAPTER XXIV

THE METAMORPHOSIS OF MR. SCHULZ

As the girl collapsed, the yellow-faced man, with an adroit movement, whisked the handkerchief off her face and crammed it into his pocket. Then, while he supported her with one arm, with the other he thrust at the door to close it. Without paying further attention to it, he turned and, bending down, lifted the girl without an effort off her feet and carried her across the room to the Chesterfield, upon which he laid her at full length. Then he seized her muff, which dangled from her neck by a thin platinum chain.

Suddenly he heard the door behind him creak. In a flash he remembered that he had not heard the click of the lock as he had thrust the door to. He was springing erect when a firm hand gripped him by the back of the collar and pulled him away from the couch. He staggered back, striving to regain his balance, but then a savage shove flung him head foremost into the fireplace. He fell with a crash among the fire-irons. But he was on his feet again in an instant.

He saw a tall, athletic-looking young man standing at the couch. He had a remarkably square jaw; his eyes were shining and he breathed heavily. He wore a blue serge suit which was heavily besmeared with white plaster and the trousers were rent across one knee. Straight at his throat sprang the yellow-faced man.

Something struck him halfway. The young man had waited composedly for his coming, but as his assailant advanced, had shot out his left hand. There was a sharp crack and the yellow-faced man, reeling, dropped face downwards on the carpet without a sound. In his fall his foot caught a small table on which a vase of chrysanthemums stood, and the whole thing went over with a loud crash. He made a spasmodic effort to rise, hoisted himself on to his knees, swayed again, and then collapsed full length on the floor, where he lay motionless.

The sound of the fall seemed to awaken the girl. She stirred uneasily once or twice.

"What ... what is it?" she muttered, and was still again.

Bending down, the young man gathered her up in his arms and bore her out through the door with the blue curtain, through a plainly furnished sort of office with high desks and stools, and out by a side door into a paved yard. There an open car was standing. The fresh air seemed to revive the girl further. As the young man laid her on the seat, she struggled up into a sitting position and passed her hand across her forehead.

"What is the matter with me?" she said in a dazed voice; "I feel so ill!"

Then, catching sight of the young man as he peered into her face, she exclaimed:

"Robin!"

Valentine Williams

"Thank God, you're all right, Mary," said Robin. "We've not got a moment to lose. We must get away from here quick!"

He was at the bonnet cranking up the car. But the engine, chilled by the cold air, refused to start. As he was straining at the handle, a man dashed suddenly into the yard by the office door.

It was Jeekes. The little secretary was a changed man. He still wore his *pince-nez*. But his mild air had utterly forsaken him. His face was livid, the eyes bulged horribly from his head, and his whole body was trembling with emotion. In his hand he held an automatic pistol. He came so fast that he was at the car and had covered Robin with his weapon before the other had seen him come.

Mr. Jeekes left Robin no time to act. He called out in a voice that rang like a pistol shot:

"Hands up, Mr. Smartie! Quick, d'you hear? Put 'em up, damn you!"

Slowly, defiantly the young man raised his arms above his head.

Mr. Jeekes stood close to the driver's seat, having prudently put the car between himself and Robin. As he stood there, his automatic levelled at the young man, a remarkable thing happened. A black, soft surface suddenly fell over his face and was pulled back with a brisk tug. Mary Trevert, standing up in the back seat of the car, had flung her fur over the secretary's head from behind and caught him in a noose. Before Mr. Jeekes could disentangle himself, Robin was at his throat and had borne him to the ground. The pistol was knocked skilfully from his hand and fell clattering on the flags. Robin pounced down on it. Then for the first time he smiled, a sunny smile that lit up his blue eyes.

"Bravo, Mary!" he said. "That *was* an idea! Now, then, Jeekes," he ordered, "crank up that car. And be quick about it! We want to be off!"

The little secretary was a lamentable sight. He was bleeding from a cut on the forehead, his clothes were covered with dust, and his glasses had been broken in his fall. Peering helplessly about him, he walked to the bonnet of the car and sullenly grasped the handle. The smile had left Robin's face, and Mary noticed that he looked several times anxiously at the office door.

And then suddenly the engine bit. Handing the pistol to the girl, Robin warned her to keep the secretary covered and, leaping into the driving-seat, turned the car into the avenue which curved round the house.

Mr. Jeekes made no further show of fight. He remained standing in the centre of the courtyard, a ludicrous, rather pathetic, figure. As the tyres of the car gritted on the gravel of the drive, the office door was flung open and the yellow-faced man ran out, brandishing a big revolver.

"Stop!" he shouted and levelled his weapon. The car seemed to leap forward and took the sharp turn on two wheels just as the man fired. The bullet struck the wall of the house and sent up a shower of plaster. Before he could fire again the car was round the house and out of sight. But as the car whizzed round the turn an instant before the yellow-faced man fired, the girl heard a sharp cry from Jeekes:

"Don't, Victor ...!"

The rest of the sentence was lost in the roar of the engine as the car raced away down the drive.

They left the avenue in a splutter of wet gravel. The gate still stood open. They wheeled furiously into the side road and regained the *chaussée*. As yet there was no sign of pursuit. The car rocked dangerously over the broken *pavé*, so Robin, after a glance behind, steadied her down to an easier pace. Mary, who looked very pale and ill, was lying back on the back seat with her eyes closed.

They ran easily into Rotterdam as, with a terrific jangle of tunes played jerkily on the chimes, the clocks were striking two. Robin slowed down as they approached the centre of the city.

"Where are you staying, Mary?" he asked.

He had to repeat the question several times before she gave him the address. Then he found himself in a quandary. He was in a strange town and did not know a word of the language so as to be able to ask the way. However, he solved the difficulty without great trouble. He beckoned to a newspaper boy on the square outside the Bourse and, holding up a two-gulden piece, indicated by signs that he desired him as a guide. The boy comprehended readily enough and, springing on the footboard of the car, brought them safely to the hotel.

Robin left Mary and the car in charge of the boy and

went to the office and asked to see the manager. He had decided upon the story he must tell.

"Miss Trevert," he said, when the manager, a blond and suave Swiss, had presented himself, "has been to the dentist and has been rather upset by the gas. Would you get one of the maids to help her up to her room and in the meantime telephone for a doctor. If there is an English doctor in Rotterdam, I should prefer to have him!"

The manager clicked in sympathy. He despatched a lady typist and a chambermaid to help Mary out of the car.

"For a doctor," he said, "it ees fortunate. We 'ave an English doctor staying in ze hotel now - a sheep's doctor. He is in ze lounge. Eef you come, *hein?*"

The "sheep's doctor" proved to be a doctor off one of the big liners, a clean-shaven, red-faced, hearty sort of person who readily volunteered his services. As Robin was about to follow him into the lift, the manager stopped him.

"Zere was a shentleman call to see Mees Trevert," he said, "two or three time 'e been 'ere ... a Sherman shentleman. 'E leave 'er a note ... will you take it?"

Greatly puzzled, Robin Greve balanced in his hands the letter which the manager produced from a pigeon-hole. Then he tore open the envelope.

DEAR MISS TREVERT [he read], I was extremely sorry to miss you this morning. Directly I received your message I called at your hotel, but, though I have been back twice, I have not found you in. Circumstances have arisen which make it imperative that I should see you as soon as possible. This is *most urgent*. I will come back at four o'clock, as I cannot get away before. Do not leave the hotel *on any pretext* until you have seen me and Dulking-horn's letter as identification. You are in *grave danger*.

The note was signed "W. Schulz."

"H'm," was Robin's comment; "he writes like an Englishman, anyway."

He ascertained the number of Mary Trevert's room and went up to her floor in the lift. He waited in the corridor outside the room for the doctor to emerge, and lit a cigarette to while away the time. It was not until he had nearly finished his second cigarette that the doctor appeared.

The doctor hesitated on seeing Robin. Then he stepped close up to him. Robin noticed that his red face was more flushed than usual and his eyes were troubled.

"What's this cock-and-bull story about gas you've put up to the manager?" he said bluntly in a low voice. "The girl's been doped with chloroform, as well you know. You'll be good enough to come downstairs to the manager with me ..."

Robin took out his note-case and produced a card.

"That's my name," he said. "You'll see that I'm a barrister ..."

"Well?" said the doctor in a non-committal voice after he had read the card.

"I'm not surprised to hear you say that Miss Trevert has been doped," Robin remarked. "I found her here in a house on the outskirts of Rotterdam in the hands of two men, one of whom is believed to be implicated in a mysterious case of suspected murder in England. Through the part he played this morning, he has probably run his head into the noose. But he'll have it out again if we delay an instant. I told the manager that yarn about the dentist to avoid enquiries and waste of time. I have here a note from some man I don't know, addressed to Miss Trevert, warning her of a grave danger threatening her. It corroborates to some extent what I have told you. Here ... read it for yourself!"

He handed the doctor the note signed "W. Schulz."

The doctor read it through carefully.

"What I would propose to you," said Robin, "is that we two should go off at once to this Herr Schulz and find out exactly what he knows. Then we can decide what action there is to be taken ..."

He paused for the doctor's reply. The latter searched Robin's face with a glance.

"I'm your man," he said shortly. "And, by the way, my name's Collingwood ... Robert Collingwood."

"There's a car downstairs," said Robin, "and a guide to show us the way. Shall we go?"

Five minutes later, under the newsboy's expert

guidance, the car drew up in front of the small clean house with the neat green door bearing the name of "Schulz." Leaving the boy to mind the car, they rang the bell. The door was opened by the fat woman in the pink print dress.

Robin gave the woman his card. On it he had written "About Miss Trevert." Speaking in German the woman bade them rather roughly to bide where they were, and departed after closing the front door in their faces. She did not keep them waiting long, however, for in about a minute she returned. Herr Schulz would receive the gentlemen, she said.

Within, the house was spotlessly clean with that characteristic German house odour which always seems to be a compound of cleaning material and hot grease. Up a narrow staircase, furnished in plain oil-cloth with brass stair-rods, they went to a landing on the first floor. Here the woman motioned them back and, bending her head in a listening attitude, knocked.

"*Herein!*" cried a guttural German voice.

The room into which they entered would have been entitled to a place in any museum for showing the mode of life of the twentieth-century Germans. With its stuffy red rep curtains, its big green majolica stove, its heavy mahogany furniture, its oleographs of Bismarck, Roon, and Moltke, it might have been lifted bodily from a bourgeois house in the Fatherland.

A man was sitting at a mahogany roll-top desk as they entered. The air in the room was thick with the fumes of the cheap Dutch cigar he was smoking. He was a sturdily built fellow with blond hair shaven so close to the skull that at a distance he seemed to be bald.

At the sound of their entrance, he rose and faced them. When he stood erect the sturdiness of his build became accentuated, and they saw he was a man of medium height, but so muscular that he looked much shorter. A pair of large tortoise-shell spectacles straddled a big beak-like nose, and he wore a heavyish blond moustache with its points trained upwards and outwards rather after the fashion made famous in the Fatherland by William Hohenzollern. In his ill-cut suit of cheap-looking blue serge, which he wore with a pea-green tie, Robin thought he looked altogether a typical specimen of the German of the non-commissioned officer class.

"You ask for me?" he said in deep guttural accents, looking at Robin; "I am Herr Schulz!"

The German's manner was cold and formal and Robin felt a little dashed.

"My name is Greve," he began rather hurriedly. "I understand you received a visit to-day from a young English lady, a Miss Trevert ..."

The German let his eyes travel slowly from Robin to the doctor and back again. He did not offer them a chair and all three remained standing.

"Ye-es, and what if I did?"

Robin felt his temper rising.

"You wrote a note to Miss Trevert at her hotel warning her that she was in danger. I want to know why you warned her. What led you to suppose that she was threatened?"

Herr Schulz made a little gesture of the hand.

"Wass I not right to warn her?"

"Indeed, you were," Robin asserted with conviction. "She was spirited away and drugged."

The German started. A frowning pucker appeared just above the bridge of his big spectacles and he raised his head quickly,

"Drugged?" he said.

"Certainly," said Robin. "This gentleman with me is a doctor ... Dr. Robert Collingwood, of the Red Lion Line. He has examined Miss Trevert and can corroborate my statement."

"By Gad!" exclaimed Herr Schulz - and this time his English was faultless and fluent - "Shut that door behind you, Mr. Greve, and shoot the bolt - that's it just below the knob! Sit down, sit down, and while I mix you a drink, you shall tell me about this!"

CHAPTER XXV

THE READING OP THE RIDDLE

In uttering those words Herr Schulz seemed suddenly to become loose-limbed and easy. His plethoric rigidity of manner vanished, and, though he spoke with a brisk air of authority, there was a jovial ring in his voice which instantly inspired confidence. With the change the illusion supported by his appalling clothes was broken and he looked like a man dressed up for charades.

"Are you - English?" asked Robin in astonishment.

"Only in this room," was the dry reply, "and don't you or our friend, the doctor, here forget it. You'll both take whisky? Three fingers will do you good, Mr. Greve, for I see you've had a roughish time this morning. Say when!"

He spurted a siphon into three glasses.

"Before we go any farther," he went on, "perhaps I had better identify myself - to save any further misunderstandings, don't you know? Do either of you gentlemen happen to know a party called Dulkinghorn? You may have heard of him, Mr. Greve, for I can see you have been in the army ..."

Valentine Williams

"Not Ernest Dulkinghorn, of the War Office?" asked Robin.

"The identical party!"

"I never met him," said Robin. "But I was at the War Office for a bit before I was demobilized and I heard fellows speak of him. Counter-espionage, isn't he?"

"That's right," nodded Herr Schulz. "You can read his letter to me introducing Miss Trevert."

He handed a sheet of paper to Robin.

> DEAR SCHULZ [it ran], Victor Marbran's push appear to be connected with Hartley Parrish, who has just met his death under suspicious circum-stances. You will have read about it in the English papers. Miss Trevert was engaged to H.P. and has a letter from Elias van der Spyck and Company which she found on Parrish's desk after his death. I should say that the Marbran-Parrish connection would repay investigation.
>
> Yours
> E. DULKINGHORN
>
> P.S. The letter is, of course, in conventional code.
>
> P.P.S. Don't frighten the life out of the Trevert girl, you unsympathetic brute!

Robin read the letter through to the end.

"Then Mary Trevert has this letter from Rotterdam

which we have been hunting for!" he cried. "Have you seen it?"

Herr Schulz shook his head.

"Miss Trevert called here this morning," he said, "when I was out. She gave her letter to Frau Wirth, my housekeeper, with her card and address. Frau Wirth was cleaning the plate on the front door and, a moment after Miss Trevert had gone, a fellow appeared and said he was a friend of Miss Trevert who had made a mistake and left the wrong letter. My housekeeper is well trained and wouldn't give the letter up. But she made the fatal mistake of telling the fellow exactly what he wanted to know, and that was who the letter was addressed to. 'The letter is addressed to Herr Schulz,' said this excellent woman, 'and if there's any mistake he will find it out when he opens it.' And with that she told him to clear out. Which, having got all he wanted, he was glad enough to do!"

"What was this chap like?" asked Robin.

The big man shrugged his shoulders.

"I can teach my servants discretion," he replied whimsically, "but I can't teach 'em to use their eyes. Frau Wirth could remember nothing about this fellow except that he wasn't tall and wore a brown overcoat .."

"Jeekes!" cried Robin, slapping his thigh. "He must have been actually coming away from your place when I met him ..."

"And who," asked the big man, reflectively contemplating the amber fluid in his glass, "who is Jeekes?"

In reply Robin told him the story of Hartley Parrish's death, his growing certainty that the millionaire had been murdered, the mysterious letters on slatey-blue paper, and Jeekes's endeavor to burke the investigations by throwing on Robin the suspicion of having driven Parrish to suicide by threats. He told of his chance meeting with Jeekes in Rotterdam that morning, his adventure at the Villa Bergendal, his finding and rescue of Mary Trevert, and their escape.

Herr Schulz listened attentively and without interruption until Robin had reached the end of his story.

"There's one thing you haven't explained," he said, "and that's how Miss Trevert came to walk into the hands of these precious ruffians ..."

"There, perhaps, I can help you," said the doctor from behind one of Herr Schulz's rank cigars; "I have it from Miss Trevert herself. Some one impersonating you Mr. - er, ahem, - Schulz - telephoned her this morning, after she had left her letter of introduction here, asking her to come out to lunch at your country-house. She suspected nothing and went off in the car they sent for her ..."

"By George!" said the big man thoughtfully; "I suspected some game of this kind when I heard of the attempt to get at that letter of introduction. If I only could have got hold of Marbran this morning ..."

"Marbran!" said Robin thoughtfully. "When I read Dulkinghorn's letter just now I thought I had heard that name before. Of course - Victor Marbran! That was it! I remember now! He knew Hartley Parrish in the old days. Parrish once said that Marbran would do him an injury if he could. Who is Marbran, sir?"

All unconsciously he paid the tribute of 'sir' to Herr Schulz's undoubted habit of command.

"Victor Marbran," replied the big man, "is Elias van der Spyck & Co., a firm which made millions in the war by trading with the enemy. In every neutral country there were, of course, firms which specialized in importing contraband for the use of the Germans, but van der Spyck & Co. brought the evasion of the blockade to a fine art. They covered up their tracks, however, with such consummate art that we could never bring anything home to them. In fact, it was only after the armistice that we began to learn something of the immense scope of their operations. There was a master brain behind them. But it was never discovered. It strikes me, however, that we are on the right track at last ..."

"By Jove ...!" exclaimed Robin impressively. "Hartley Parrish!..."

The big man raised a hand.

"*Attentions!*" he interposed suavely. "The chain is not yet complete. I wonder what this van der Spyck letter of Miss Trevert's contained that made Victor Marbran and the secretary chap so desperately anxious to get hold of it. For you understand, don't you?" he said briskly, turning to Robin, "that they were after that and that alone. And they risked penal servitude in this country to get it ..."

Robin nodded.

"To save their necks in another," he said.

"I have the letter here," mildly remarked the doctor from his corner of the room. "Miss Trevert gave it to me!"

He produced a white envelope and drew from it a folded square of slatey-blue paper. In great excitement Robin sprang forward.

"You're a downy bird, Doctor, I must say," he remarked, "fancy keeping it up your sleeve all this time!"

He eagerly took the letter, spread it out on the table, and read it through whilst Herr Schulz looked over his shoulder.

"Code, eh?" commented the big man, shaking his head humorously. "If it beats Dulkinghorn, it beats me!"

From his note-case Robin now drew a folded square of paper identical in colour with the letter spread out before them.

"I found this on the carpet beside Parrish's body," he said. "Look, it's exactly the same paper ..."

Behind the tortoise-shell spectacles the big man's eyes narrowed down to pin-points as he caught sight of the sheet which Robin unfolded and its series of slits.

"Aha!" he cried - and his voice rang out clear through the room - "the grill, eh? Well, well, to think of that!"

He took the slotted sheet of paper from Robin's hands

and laid it over the letter so that it exactly covered it, edge to edge and corner to corner. In this way the greater part of the typewriting in the letter was covered over, and only the words appearing in the slots could be read. And thus it was that Robin Greve, Herr Schulz, and Dr. Collingwood, leaning shoulder to shoulder, read the message that came to Hartley Parrish in the library at Harkings....

ELIAS VAN DER SPYCK & CO.
GENERAL IMPORTERS
ROTTERDAM Rotterdam 25th Nov.

Codes
A.B.C.
Liebler's

Personal

Dear Mr. Parrish,

Your favour of even date to hand and contents noted. *The last* delivery of steel was to time but we have had *warning* from the railway authorities that labour troubles at the docks are likely to delay future   consignments. *If you don't* mind   we should prefer to *settle* the question of future delivery *by Nov. 27* as we have a board meeting on the 30th inst. While we fully appreciate your own difficulties with labour at home, *you* will understand that this is a question which we cannot afford to adjourn *sine die*.

Yours faithfully,
pro ELIAS VAN DER SPYCK & CO.

"'The last ... warning,'" Robin read out, "'if you don't ... settle ... by Nov. 27 ... you ... die ...!'"

He looked up. "Last Saturday," he said, "was the 27th, the day that Parrish died ..."

"The grill," remarked the big man authoritatively, "is one of the oldest dodges known to the Secret Service. It renders a conventional code absolutely undecipherable as long as it is skilfully worded, as it is in this case. You send your conventional code by one route, your key by another. I make no doubt that this was the way in which van der Spyck & Co. transacted their business with Hartley Parrish. They simply posted their conventional code letters through the post in the ordinary way, confident that there was nothing in them to catch the eye of the Censor's Department. The key might be sent in half a dozen different ways, by hand, concealed in a newspaper, in a parcel ..."

"So this," said Robin, pointing at the letter, "was what caused Hartley Parrish to make his will. It would lead one to suppose that it was what induced him to commit suicide were not the presumption so strong that he was murdered. But who killed him? Was it Jeekes or Marbran?"

Herr Schulz pitched his cigar-stump into an ash-tray.

"That," he said, "is the question which I am going to ask you gentlemen to help me answer. You will realize that legally we have not a leg to stand on. We are in a foreign country where, without first getting a warrant from London, we can take no steps whatever to run these fellows in. To get the Dutch police to move against these gentry in the matter of the assault upon

Miss Trevert would waste valuable time. And we have to move quickly - before these two lads can get away. I therefore propose that we start this instant for the Villa Bergendal and try, if we are not too late, to force Marbran or Jeekes or both of them to a confession. That done, we can hold them if possible until we can get the Dutch police to apprehend them at the instance of Miss Trevert. Then we can communicate with the English police. It's all quite illegal, of course! You have a car, I think, Mr. Greve! You will come with us, Dr. Collingwood? Good! Then let us start at once!"

Robin intervened with a proposal that they should call *en route* at his hotel to see if there were any telegrams for him.

"Manderton knows I am in Rotterdam," he explained, "and he promised to wire me the latest developments in the enquiry he is conducting."

"Miss Trevert should be fully recovered by this," put in the doctor; "apart from a little sickness she is really none the worse for her disagreeable experience. If there was anything you wanted to ask her ..."

"There is," said Robin promptly. "Her reply to one question," he explained, turning to Herr Schulz, "will give us the certainty that Parrish was murdered and did not commit suicide. It will not delay us more than five minutes to stop at her hotel in passing, We will then call in at my place. We should be at the Villa within half an hour from now ..."

"Gentlemen," said Herr Schulz as they prepared to go, "I know my Mr. Victor Marbran. You should all be armed."

Robin produced the pistol he had taken from Jeekes. Herr Schulz slipped a Browning pistol into the breast-pocket of his jacket and, producing a long-barrelled service revolver, gave it to the doctor.

"There are three of them, I gather, counting the chauffeur," commented the big man, pulling on his overcoat, "so we shall be equally matched."

Darkness had fallen upon Rotterdam and the lights from the houses made yellow streaks in the water of the canal as the car, piloted by Robin, drove the party to Mary Trevert's hotel.

They found the girl, pale and anxious, in the lounge.

"Well, now," cried the doctor breezily, "and how are you feeling? Did you take my advice and have some tea?"

"What has happened?" asked the girl; "I have been so anxious about you ..."

Her words were addressed to the doctor, but she looked at Robin.

"Mary," said Robin, "we are very near the truth now. But there is one thing you can tell us. It is very important. When you heard the shot in the library at Harkings, did you notice any other sound - before or after?"

The girl paused to think.

"There was a sort of sharp cry and a thud ..."

"I know. But was there anything else? Do try and remember. It's so important!"

The girl was silent for a moment. Then she said slowly:

"Yes, there was, now I come to think of it. Just as I tried the door - it was locked, you know - there was a sort of hiss, harsh and rather loud, from the room ..."

"A sort of hiss, eh? Something like a sneeze?"

"Yes. Only louder and ... and ... harsher!"

"Now, answer me carefully! Was this before or after the shot?"

"Oh, before! Just as I was rattling the doorhandle. The shot broke in upon it...."

Robin turned to Herr Schulz, who stood with a grave face by his side.

"The silencer, you see, sir!" he said. Then to Mary he added: "Mary, we are going off now. But we will be back within the hour and...."

"Oh, Robin," the girl broke in, "don't leave me alone! I don't feel safe in this place after this morning. I'd much rather come with you...."

"Mary, it's quite impossible...." Robin began.

But the girl had turned to a table and taken from it her hat and fur.

"I don't care!" she exclaimed wilfully; "I'm coming anyhow. I refuse to be left behind!"

She smiled at Herr Schulz as she spoke, and that gentleman's rather grim face relaxed as he looked at her.

"I'm not sure I wouldn't say the same!" he remarked.

The upshot of it was that, despite Robin's objections, Mary Trevert accompanied the party. She sat on the back seat, rather flushed and excited, between Herr Schulz and the doctor, while Robin took the wheel again. A few minutes' drive took them to the big hotel where Robin had booked a room. They all waited in the car whilst he went to the office.

He was back in a minute, an open telegram in his hand.

"I believe I've got in my pocket," he cried, "the actual weapon with which Hartley Parrish was killed!"

And he read from the telegram:

"Mastertons gunsmiths sold last July pair of Browning automatics identical with that found on Parrish to Jeekes who paid with Parrish's cheque."

The message was signed "Manderton."

At that moment a man wearing a black bowler hat and a heavy frieze overcoat came hurrying out of the hotel.

"Mr. Greve!" he cried as Robin, who was back in the driving-seat, was releasing the brake. "Did you have the wire from the Yard saying I was coming?" he asked. "Probably I beat the telegraph, though. I came by air!"

Then he tipped his hat respectfully at Herr Schulz.

"This is Detective-Inspector Manderton, of Scotland Yard, sir," said Robin.

The big man beamed a smile of friendly recognition.

"Mr. Manderton and I are old friends," he said. "How are you, Manderton? I didn't expect you to recognize me in these duds ..."

"I'd know you anywhere, sir," said the detective with unwonted cordiality.

"Have you got your warrant, Manderton?" asked Herr Schulz.

"Aye, I have, sir," replied the detective. "And I've a colleague from the Dutch police who's going along with me to effect the arrest ..."

"Jeekes, eh?"

"That's the party, sir, charged with wilful murder.... This is Commissary Boomjes, of the Rotterdam Criminal Investigation Department!"

A tall man with a short black beard had approached the car. It was decided that the whole party should proceed to the Villa Bergendal immediately. Manderton sat next to Robin and the Dutch police officer perched himself on the footboard.

"And where did you pick *him* up, I'd like to know?" whispered Manderton in Robin's ear with a backward jerk of the head, as they glided through the brightly lit streets.

"D'you mean the doctor?" asked Robin.

"No, your other friend!"

"Miss Trevert had a letter to him. Something in the Secret Service, isn't he?"

Mr. Manderton snorted.

"'Something in the Secret Service,'" he repeated disdainfully. "Well, I should say he was. If you want to know, Mr. Greve, he's the head!"

CHAPTER XXVI

THE FIGURE IN THE DOORWAY

The rain was coming down in torrents and the night was black as pitch when, leaving the lights of Rotterdam behind, the car swung out on to the main road leading to the Villa Bergendal. Thanks to a powerful headlight, Robin was able to get a good turn of speed out of her as soon as they were clear of the city. As they slowed down at the gate in the side road Herr Schulz tapped him on the shoulder.

"Better leave the car here and put the lights out," he counselled. "And Miss Trevert should stay if the doctor here would remain to look after her ..."

"You think there'll be a scrap?" whispered the doctor.

"With a man like Marbran," returned the Chief, "you never know what may happen ..."

"Zere will be no faight," commented the Dutch police officer in lugubrious accents, "my vriends, ve are too laite ..."

But the Chief insisted that Mary should stay behind and the doctor agreed to act as her escort. Then in single file the party proceeded up the drive, Robin in front, then the Dutchman, after him the Chief, and Mr. Manderton in the rear.

They walked on the grass edging the avenue. On the wet turf their feet made no sound. When they came in view of the house, they saw it was in darkness. No light shone in any window, and the only sound to be heard was the melancholy patter of the rain drops on the laurel bushes. When they saw the porch looking black before them, they left the grass and stepped gently across the drive, the gravel crunching softly beneath their feet. Robin led the way boldly under the porch and laid a hand on the doorknob. The door opened easily and the next moment the four men were in the hall.

As Robin moved to the wall to find the electric light switch, a torch was silently thrust into his hand.

"Better have this, sir," whispered Manderton. "I have my finger on the switch now, but we'd best wait to put the light up until we know where they are. Where do we go first?"

"Into the sitting-room," Robin returned.

Switching the torch on and off only as he required it, he crept silently over the heavy carpet to the door of the room in which that morning he had come upon Mary. Manderton remained at the switch in the hall whilst the other two men followed Robin through the door.

The room was in darkness. It struck chill; for the fire had gone out. The beam of the torch flitting from wall to wall showed the room to be empty.

"I don't believe there's a soul in the house," whispered the Chief to Robin.

"Ve are too laite; I have said it!" muttered the Dutchman.

"There is another room leading out of this," replied Robin, turning the torch on to the blue curtain covering the door leading into the office. "We'll have a look in there and then try upstairs. Manderton will give us warning if anybody comes down ..."

So saying he drew the curtain aside and pushed open the door. Instantly a gush of cold air blew the curtain back in his face. Before he could disentangle himself the door slammed to with a crash that shook the house.

"That's done it!" muttered the Chief.

The three men stood and listened. They heard the dripping of the rain, the soughing of the wind, but no sound of human kind came to their ears.

"The place is empty," whispered the Chief. "They've cleared ..."

"It is too laite; I have said it." The Dutchman spoke in a hoarse bass.

"We'll go in here, anyway," answered Robin, lifting up the curtain again. "They may have heard us and be hiding ..."

He opened the door, steadying it with his foot. The curtain flapped wildly round them as they crossed the threshold. The broad white beam of the electric torch swung from window to desk, from desk to safe.

"The door over there is open," exclaimed the Chief; "that's the way they've gone."

Suddenly he clutched Robin's arm.

"Steady," he whispered, "look there ... in the doorway ... there's somebody moving ... quick, the torch!"

The light flashed across the room, blazed for an instant on a window-pane, then picked out a man's form swaying in the doorway. He had his back to the room and was rocking gently to and fro with the wind which they felt cold on their faces.

"It's only a coat and trousers hanging in the door ..." began Robin.

Then, with a suddenness which pained the eyes, the room was flooded with light. The Dutch detective stepped from the electric light switch and moved to the open door.

"Too laite!" he cried, shaking his head; "have I not tell you?"

Suspended by a strip of coloured stuff, the body of Mr. Jeekes dangled from the cross-beam of the door. The corpse oscillated in the breeze, silhouetted against an oblong of black sky, turning this way and that, loose, unnatural, horrible, and, as the body, twisting gently, faced the room, it gave a glimpse of startling eyes, swollen, empurpled features, protruding tongue.

Without the least trace of emotion the black-bearded

detective picked up a rush-bottom chair and gathering up the corpse by its collar hoisted it up without an effort so that the feet rested on the chair. Then, producing a clasp-knife, he mounted the chair and, with a vigorous slash, cut the coloured strip which had been fastened to a staple projecting from the brickwork above the door on the outside of the house.

He caught the body in his arms and laid it face upwards on the matting which covered the floor. He busied himself for an instant at the neck, then rose with a twisted strip of coloured material in his hand.

"His braces," he remarked, "very common. The stool what he has stood upon and knocked avay, she lies outsaide! My vriends, ve are too laite!"

The doctor, fetched in haste by Manderton, examined the body. The man had been dead, he said, for several hours. Mary remained in the hall with Manderton while Robin and the Dutch detective went over the house. There was no trace either of Marbran or of the chauffeur. In the two bedrooms which showed signs of occupation the beds had been made up, but the wardrobes were empty.

"Marbran's made a bolt for it," said Robin, coming into the office where he had left the Chief, "and taken everything with him ..."

"I gathered as much," answered that astute gentleman, pointing at the fireplace. A pile of charred paper filled the grate. "There's nothing here, and I think we can wipe Mr. Victor Marbran off the slate. I doubt if we shall see him again. At any rate we can leave him to the tender mercies of our black-bearded friend here. As for us, I don't really see that there is anything more to detain us here ..."

"But," remarked Robin, looking at the still figure on the floor, the face now mercifully covered by the doctor's white handkerchief, "surely this is a confession of guilt. Has he left nothing behind in writing? No account of the crime?"

"Not a thing," responded the Chief, "and I've been through every drawer. Even the safe is open ... and empty!"

"But how does it happen then," asked Robin, "that Marbran has legged it while Jeekes here ..."

"Marbran left him in the lurch," the Chief broke in decisively. "I think that's clear. While you were upstairs with our Dutch friend, I went through the dead man's pockets. He had no money, Greve, except a few coppers and a little Dutch change. He had not even got a return ticket to London. Which makes me think that Master Jeekes had left old England for good."

"Another thing that puzzles me," remarked Robin, "is how Jeekes knew that Miss Trevert had a letter to you, sir? Or, for a matter of that, how he knew that she had gone to Rotterdam at all?"

"That's not hard to answer," said Mr. Manderton, who had just entered the room. "On Sunday night Jeekes rang up Harkings from his club and asked to speak to Miss Trevert. Bude told him she had gone away. Jeekes then asked to speak to Sir Horace Trevert, who told him that his sister had gone to Rotterdam. Jeekes takes the first available train in the morning, recognizes Miss Trevert on the way across, and tags her to her hotel in Rotterdam. The next morning he follows her again, shadows her to Sir ... to this gentleman's rooms, and there, as we know, contrived by a trick to see to whom she had a letter."

"But why did he not attempt to get the letter away from her as soon as she arrived? Miss Trevert never suspected Jeekes. She might have shown him the letter if he'd asked her for it ..."

The detective shook his head sagely.

"Jeekes was pretty 'cute," he said. "Before letting the girl know he was in Rotterdam, he wanted to find out what she wanted here and whom she knew. Remember, he had no means of knowing if the girl suspected him or not ..."

"So he devised this trick of impersonating Mr. Schulz on the telephone, eh?"

"Bah!" broke in the Chief; "I bet that was Marbran's idea. Look at Jeekes's face and tell me if you see in it any feature indicating the bold, ingenious will to try a bluff like that. I never knew this fellow here. But I know Marbran, a resolute, undaunted type. You can take it from me, Marbran directed - Jeekes merely carried out instructions. What do you say, Manderton?"

But the detective had retired into his shell again.

"If you will come to Harkings with me the day after tomorrow, sir, I shall hope to show you exactly how Mr. Parrish met his death ..."

"No, no, Manderton," responded the Chief; "I can't leave here for a bit. There are bigger murderers than Jeekes at liberty in Holland to-day ..."

The detective slapped his thigh.

"I'd have laid a shade of odds," he cried merrily, "that you were watching the gentleman at Amerongen , sir ..."

"Tut, tut, Manderton," said the Chief, raising his hand to silence the other; "you run on too fast, my friend! I wish," he went on, changing the subject, "I could be with you at Harkings to-morrow to witness your reconstruction of the crime, Manderton. You'll go, I suppose, Greve?"

"I certainly shall," answered the barrister, "I have had some experience of criminals, but I must say I never saw one less endowed with criminal characteristics than little Jeekes. A strange character!..."

The Chief laughed sardonically.

"Anyway," he remarked, "he had a damn good notion of the end that befitted him ..."

* * * * *

It was a still, starry night. The Flushing boat stood out of harbour on a calm sea. The high arc lamps threw a blue gleam over the deserted moles and glinted in the oily swell lapping the quays. From the fast-receding quayside the rasping of a winch echoed noisily across the silent water. On the upper deck of the mail-boat Robin Greve and Mary Trevert stood side by side at the rail. They had the deck to themselves. Above their heads on the bridge the captain stood immobile, a square black figure, the helmsman at his elbow. Otherwise, between the stars and the sea, the man and the girl were alone.

Thus they had stood ever since the mail-boat had cast off from the quay. Robin had made some banal attempt at conversation, urging (but without much sincerity) that, after her experiences of the day, the girl should go to her cabin and rest. But Mary Trevert had merely shaken her head impatiently, without speaking.

Presently he put his arm through hers. He felt against his wrist the warm softness of her travelling-coat, and it seemed to him that, though the girl made no sign, some slight answering pressure met his touch. So they leaned upon the rail for a space watching the water fall hissing from the vessel's side as the steamer, jarring and quivering, met the long steady roll from the open sea.

Then Mary Trevert spoke.

"Robin," she said gently, "I owe you an apology ..."

Robin Greve looked at her quickly. But Mary had her eyes fixed seaward in contemplation of a distant light that flared and died with persistent regularity.

"My dear," he answered, "I've only myself to blame. When you told me you were going to marry Hartley Parrish, I should have known that you had your reasons and that those reasons were good. I should have held my tongue ..."

This time the girl stole a glance at him. But now he was gazing away to the horizon where the light came and went.

"All this misunderstanding between us," he went on, "came about because of what I said in the billiard-room that afternoon ..."

The girl shook her head resolutely.

"No," she answered, "it was my fault. I'm a proud devil, Robin, and what you said about Hartley and ... and ... other women, Robin, hurt and ... and made me angry. No, no, don't apologize again. You and I are old enough friends, my dear, to tell one another the truth. You made me angry because what you said was true. I *was* selling myself, selling myself with my eyes open, too, and you've got a perfect right never to speak to me again ..."

She did not finish the sentence but broke off. Her voice died away quaveringly. Robin took her hand in his.

"Dear," he said, "don't cry! It's over and done with now ..."

Mary shook herself with an angry gesture.

"What's the good of telling me not to cry?" she protested tearfully; "I've disgraced myself in my own eyes as well as in yours. If you can't forget what I was ready to do, I never shall ..."

Very gently the young man turned the girl towards him.

"I'm not such a prig as all that," he said. "We all make mistakes. You know I understand the position you were in. Parrish is dead. I shall forget the rest ..."

Slowly the girl withdrew her hands from his grasp.

"Yes," she said wearily, "you will find it easy to forget!"

She drew her fur closer about her neck and turned her back on the sea.

"I must go down," she said. And waited for the man to stand aside. He did not move and their eyes met. Suddenly, like a child, she buried her face in her arm flung out across his chest. She began to sob bitterly.

"That afternoon ... in the billiard-room ..." she sobbed, "you will forget ... that ... too ... I suppose ..."

Robin took her face in his hands, a hot, tear-stained face, and detached it from the sheltering arm.

"My dear," he said, "I shall have to try to forget it. But I know I shan't succeed. To the end of my life I shall remember the kiss you gave me. But we are farther apart than ever now!"

There was a great sadness in his voice. It arrested the girl's attention as he dropped his hands and turned back to the rail.

"Why?" she said in a low voice, without looking up.

"Because," replied the young man steadily, "you're rich now, Mary ..."

The girl looked up quickly.

"Will men ever understand women?" she cried, a new note in her voice. She stepped forward and, putting her two hands on the young man's shoulders, swung him round to face her.

"I'm as poor as ever I was," she said, "for Hartley Parrish's money is not for me ..."

"Mary!" exclaimed the young man joyfully.

"Robin Greve," cried the girl, "do you mean to tell me you'd stand there thinking I'd accept money made like that ..."

But now she was in his arms. With a little fluttering sigh she yielded to his kiss.

"Oh, the man on the bridge!..." she murmured with her woman's instinct for the conventions.

"Come behind the boat, then!" commanded Robin.

And in the shadow of a weather-stained davit he kissed her again.

"So you'll wait for me, after all, Mary?"

"No," retorted the girl firmly. "We'll read the Riot Act to Mother and you must marry me at once!"

The wind blew cold from the North Sea. It rattled in the rigging, flapped the ensign standing out stiffly at the stern, and whirled the black smoke from the steamer's funnels out into a dark aerial wake as far as the eye could reach. With a gentle rhythmic motion the vessel rose and fell, while the stars began to pale and faint grey shadows appeared in the eastern sky. Still the man and the girl stood by the swaying lifeboat and talked the things that lovers say. Step by step they went over their thoughts for one another in each successive phase of the dark tragedy through which they had passed.

"And that van der Spyck letter," asked Robin; "how did you get hold of it? I've been wanting to ask you that ever since this afternoon ..."

"I found it in the library," replied the girl, "on the desk. It had got tucked away between two letter-trays - one fits into the other, you know."

"I wondered how Jeekes had come to miss it," said Robin. "But when was this?" he added.

"On Sunday afternoon."

"But what were you doing in the library?"

The girl became a little embarrassed.

"I knew Mr. Manderton was suspicious of you. I heard him telephoning instructions to London to have you watched. So I thought I'd go to the library to see if I could find anything which would show what they had against you exactly. And I found this letter. Then I noticed some one hiding behind the curtains, and, as I had the letter in my hand, I hid it in my dress. When I discovered that Bruce Wright was after it too, I pretended I had found nothing ..."

"But, darling, why?"

"I wanted to make sure for myself why you had sent Bruce Wright, for I guessed he had come from you, to look for this letter. So I thought I'd go to Rotterdam to investigate ..."

Robin laughed affectionately.

"Surely it would have been simpler to have given the letter to the police ..."

Mary gave him a look of indignant surprise.

"But it might have incriminated you!" she exclaimed.

At that Robin kissed her again.

"Will men *ever* understand women?" he asked, looking into her tranquil grey eyes.

CHAPTER XXVII

AN INTERRUPTION FROM BEYOND

Sudden frost had laid an icy finger on the gardens of Harkings. The smooth green lawns were all dappled with white and wore a pinched and chilly look save under the big and solemn firs where the ground, warmed by its canopy of branches and coverlet of cones, had thawed in dark patches. The gravel walks were firm and dry; and in the rosery the bare skeleton of the pergolas stood out in clear-cut silhouette against a white and woolly sky.

Overnight the frost had come. It had taken even the birds by surprise. They hopped forlornly about the paths as though wondering where they would get their breakfast. Robin Greve, idly watching them from the library window, found himself contrasting the cheerful winter landscape with the depressing conditions of the previous day. In wind and rain the master of Harkings had been laid to rest in the quiet little churchyard of Stevenish. The ceremony had been arranged in haste, as soon as the coroner's jury had viewed the body. Robin Greve, that morning arrived from Rotterdam, Bude, and Mr. Bardy the solicitor, had been the only mourners. As Robin looked out upon the wintry scene, his mind reverted to the hurried funeral with its depressing accompaniment of gleaming umbrellas, mud from the freshly turned clay, and dripping trees.

Beneath the window of the library, its shattered pane now replaced, a cluster of starlings whistled gaily, darting bright-eyed glances, full of anticipation, at the closed window.

"*He* used to give them crumbs every morning after breakfast," said Mary. "See, Robin, how they are looking up! It seems a shame to disappoint them...."

As though relieved to be quit of his dark thoughts, Robin, with a glad smile, turned to the girl. Dipping his hand into his pocket, he produced a hunk of bread and put it in her hand.

"You think of everything!" she said, smiling back at him prettily.

He pushed up the window and she crumbled the bread for the birds. He rested one hand on her shoulder.

"He thought of everything, too," was his comment, "even down to the birds. It's extraordinary! No detail was too small for him!..."

"He *was* remarkable, Robin," answered the girl soberly; "there was something magnetic about his personality that made people like him. Even now that he is dead, even in spite of what we know, I can feel his attraction still. And the whole house is impregnated with his personality. Particularly this room. Don't you feel it? I don't mind being here with you, Robin, but I shouldn't like to be here alone. I was dreadfully frightened on Sunday evening when I came here. And when I saw the curtains move ... oh! I thought my heart would stop beating! Dear, I'm glad we are giving this place up. I don't feel that I could ever be happy here ... even with you!"

"Poor devil!" said Robin. And then again he said: "Poor devil!"

"It was terrible ... to die like that!" replied Mary.

"It was terrible for him to lose *you*!" answered the young man.

She gave his hand a little, tender squeeze, but relinquished it quickly as the door opened.

Mr. Manderton was there, broad-shouldered and burly. Behind came Dr. Romain with a purple nose and eyes watering with the cold, Horace Trevert in plain clothes, Mr. Bardy, the solicitor, plump, middle-aged, and prim, with a broad, smooth-shaven face and an eye-glass on a black silk riband. In the background loomed the large form of Inspector Humphries, ruddy of cheek as of hair. Lady Margaret did not appear.

Mr. Manderton slapped his bowler hat briskly on a side table and with a little bow to Mary walked to the desk.

"Now," said Mr. Manderton with a long, shrewd look that comprehended the company, individually and collectively, and the entire room, "if Inspector Humphries will kindly close the door, we will reconstruct the crime in the light of the evidence we have collected."

He turned round to the desk and pulled back the chair ... Hartley Parrish's empty chair.

"It is just on five o'clock on Saturday evening, November 27," he began, "and growing dark outside. Mr. Parrish is sitting here" - he tapped the chair - "with all the lights in the room turned off except this one on the desk."

Here he put a large hand on the reading-lamp.

"The assumption that Mr. Parrish spent the afternoon, as he had spent the morning, over papers in connection with the business of Hornaway's in which he was interested is not correct. Mr. Archer, one of Mr. Parrish's secretaries who brought down a number of papers and letters for Mr. Parrish to sign in the morning, states that as far as Hornaway's or any other office business was concerned, Mr. Parrish was through with it by lunch. This is corroborated by the fact that no business papers of this description, with the exception of one, which I am coming to directly, were found on the desk here after Mr. Parrish's death. Nor were there any traces of burnt paper in or about the fire. These two facts were established by my colleague, Inspector Humphries."

At this everybody turned and looked at the Inspector, who blushed until the tint of his hair positively paled by comparison with that of his face.

"What Mr. Archer *did* leave with Mr. Parrish, however," Mr. Manderton resumed, looking round the group and emphasising the "did," "was his will and this letter ..." - he held up a typewritten sheet of slatey-blue paper - "which, a straightforward business communication in appearance, was in reality a threat against his life. It was with these two documents that Mr. Parrish spent the last few hours before he was found dead in this room. A few odd papers found lying on the desk have nothing to do with the case and may therefore be dismissed."

Mr. Manderton paused and then, with the deliberation which distinguished his every movement, walked round the desk to the window.

"The fire in this room," he said, turning and facing his audience, "was smoking. The butler will testify to this and state that Mr. Parrish complained about it to him with the result that the sweep was ordered for Monday morning. Owing to the smoke in the room Mr. Parrish opened the window. His finger-prints were on the inside of the window-frame and a small fragment of white paint was still adhering to one of his finger-nails.

"The window, then, was open as it is now. Mr. Parrish sat at his desk, read through his will, and wrote a letter to Miss Trevert informing her that, under the will, she was left sole legatee. This letter, with the will, was found on the desk after Mr. Parrish's death. Presumably in view of the threat against his life contained in this letter," - the detective held up the slatey-blue paper, - "Mr. Parrish had either in his pocket or, as I am more inclined to think, lying on the desk in front of him, his Browning automatic pistol. This pistol was fitted with a Maxim silencer, an invention for suppressing the report of a firearm, which was sent to Mr. Parrish by a friend in America some years ago and which he kept permanently attached to the weapon."

Mr. Manderton came to an impressive full stop and glanced round his circle of listeners. He gave his explanations easily and fluently, but in a plain, matter-of-fact tone such as a police constable employs in the witness-box. He had marshalled his facts well, and his measured advance towards his *dénouement* was not without its effect on his audience. Dr. Romain, nursing his knee on a leather settee, Horace Trevert, a tall slim figure eagerly watching the detective from his perch on the arm of the Chesterfield, and Robin and Mary, standing, very close together, behind the empty chair at the desk - each and every one was listening with rapt attention. Inspector Humphries, propping his big bulk uneasily against the wall near the door, was the only one who appeared to be oblivious of the strain.

The detective walked round the desk and seated himself in the chair.

"Mr. Parrish is seated at the desk here," he resumed, "when his attention is directed to the window."

And here Mr. Manderton raised his head and looked out towards the frost-strewn gardens.

"Maybe he hears a step, more probably he sees a face staring at him out of the dark. Very much to his surprise he recognizes Jeekes, his principal private secretary - I say to his surprise because he must have believed Jeekes, who had the week-end free, to be in London. And at that, perhaps because he thinks he has made a mistake - in any case to make sure - he gets up...."

The detective suited the action to the word. He pushed back the chair and rose to his feet. They saw he held a large automatic pistol in his hand.

" He has had this threatening letter, remember, so he

takes his pistol with him. And he reaches the window ..."

The detective was at the window now, his back to the room.

"He speaks to Jeekes, angrily, maybe - the butler heard the sound of loud voices - they have words. And then ..."

There came a knock at the library door. It was not a loud knock. It was in reality scarcely more than a gentle tap. But it fell upon a silence of Manderton's own creating, a rapt silence following a pause which preceded the climax of his narrative. So the discreet knocking resounded loud and clear through the library.

"Who is that? What is it?" rapped out Dr. Bomain irritably.

"Don't let any one disturb us, Inspector!" called out Horace Trevert to Inspector Humphries, who had opened the door.

Bude's face appeared in the doorway. He had a short altercation with the Inspector, who resolutely interposed his massive form between the butler and the room.

"What is it, Bude?" asked Robin, going to the door.

"It's a letter for Miss Trevert, sir!" said Bude.

"Well, leave it in the hall. Miss Trevert can't be disturbed at present ..."

"But ... but, sir," the butler protested. Then Robin noticed that he was trembling with excitement and that his features were all distraught.

"What's the matter with you, Bude?" Robin demanded.

Humphries had stood on one side and Robin now faced the butler.

"It's a letter from ... that Jeekes!" faltered Bude, holding out a salver. "I know his writing, sir!"

"For Miss Trevert?"

Robin gathered up the plain white envelope. It bore a Dutch stamp. The postmark was Rotterdam. He gave the letter to Mary. It was bulky and heavy.

"For you," he said, and stood beside her while she broke the seal. By this they had all gathered round her.

The envelope fluttered to the floor. Mary was unfolding a wad of sheets of writing-paper folded once across. She glanced at the topmost sheet, then handed the bundle to Robin.

"It's a confession!" she said.

From beyond the grave the little secretary had spoken and spoiled Mr. Manderton's *dénouement*.

CHAPTER XXVIII

THE DEATH OF HARTLEY PARRISH

"For Miss Trevert."

Thus, in Jeekes's round and flowing commercial hand, the document began:

> Last Statement of Albert Edward Jeekes, made at Rotterdam, this twenty-first Day of January, in the Year of Our Lord One Thousand Nine Hundred and...

Mr. Bardy, the solicitor, to whom, by common consent, the reading of the confession had been entrusted, raised his eyebrows, thereby letting his eyeglass fall, and looked round at the company.

"Pon my soul," he remarked, "for a man about to take his own life, our friend seems to have been the coolest customer imaginable. Look at it! Written in a firm hand and almost without an erasure. Very remarkable! Very remarkable, indeed!..."

"Hm!" grunted Mr. Manderton, "not so uncommon as you suppose, Mr. Bardy, sir. Hendriks, the Palmers Green poisoner, typed out his confession on cream inlaid paper before dosing himself. But let's hear what the gentleman has to tell us...."

This was the last digression. Thenceforth Mr. Bardy read out the confession to the end without interruption.

For Miss Trevert:

Madam,

I slew, but I am not a murderer: I Killed, but without deliberation.

Victor Marbran has gone and left me to meet a shameful death. But I cannot face the scaffold. As men go, I do not believe I am a coward and I am not afraid to die. But the inexorable deliberation of justice appals me. When I have written what I have to write, I shall be hangman to myself. My pistol they have taken away.

Victor Marbran has abandoned me. He had prepared everything for his flight. Even if the law can indict him as the virtual murderer of Hartley Parrish, the law will never lay hands on him. Victor Marbran neglects no detail. He will never be caught. But from the Great Unknown for which I shall presently set out, I shall stretch forth my hand and see that, here or there, he does not escape the punishment he merits for bringing down shame and disgrace upon me.

Just now he bade me stay in the office and finish burning the papers in his desk. He promised he would take me with him to a secure hiding-place which he had made ready for some such emergency as this. I believed him and, unsuspecting, stayed. And now he has slipped away. He is gone and the house is empty. I cannot follow him even did I know where he has gone. I have only a very little money left and I am tired. Very tired. I feel I cannot support the hue-and-cry they will raise. Everything is still about me. The quiet of the country is very soothing. To die like this, with darkness falling and no sound but the rustling rain, is the better way ...

Hartley Parrish was the man behind the great syndicate which systematically ran the British blockade of Germany in the war. He financed Marbran and the international riff-raff of profiteers with whom Marbran worked. Parrish supplied the funds, often the goods as well, - at any rate, until they tightened up the blockade, - while Marbran and the rest of the bunch in neutral countries did the trading with the enemy.

Parrish was a deep one. I say nothing against him. He was a kind employer to me and I played him false, for which I have been bitterly punished. To have swindled Victor Marbran - I count it as nothing against him, for that heartless, cruel man is deserving of no pity ...

Parrish was the heart and soul, brains and muscle of the syndicate. He lurked far in the background. Any and every trail which might possibly lead back to him was carefully effaced. He was secure as long as Marbran and one or two other big men in the business kept faith with him. Now and then, when the British Intelligence were too hot on the trail, Parrish and Marbran would give away one of the small fry belonging to the organization and thus stave off suspicion. They could do this in complete safety, for so perfect was their organization that the small fry only knew the small fry in the shallows and never the big fish in the deep ...

But Hartley Parrish was in Marbran's hands. They stood or fell together. Parrish knew this. But he was a born gambler and insanely self-confident. He took a chance with Marbran. It cost him his life.

All payments were made to Parrish. He was treasurer and banker of the syndicate. Money came in by all sorts of devious routes, sometimes from as far afield as South or Central America. Parrish distributed the profits. Everything was in his hands.

By the time the armistice came, the game had got too hot. All the big fish except Marbran had cleared out with their pile. But Marbran, like Parrish, was a gambler. He stuck it out and stayed on.

Parrish played fair until the war was over. The armistice, of course, put an end to the business. But some months after the armistice a sum of £150,000 was paid to Parrish through a Spanish bank in settle-ment, Marbran told me, for petrol indirectly delivered to the German Admiralty. Parrish pouched the lot. Not a penny did Marbran get.

Parrish and Marbran were old friends. They were young men together on the Rand gold-fields in the early days. In fact, I believe they went out to South Africa together as penniless London lads. But Marbran hated Parrish, though Parrish had, I believe, been his benefactor in many ways. Marbran was fiercely envious of the other because he realized that, starting with an equal chance, Parrish had left him far behind. Everything that Parrish touched prospered, while Marbran was in perpetual financial straits. He was Parrish's equal in courage, but not in judgment.

Parrish calculated that Marbran would not dare to denounce him. He had always taken the lead in their schemes and he affected to disregard Marbran altogether. So he left the latter's letters unanswered and laughed at his threats. He was quite sure that Marbran would never risk losing his pile by giving Parrish away, for they were, of course, both British subjects and both in it together ...

Marbran always distrusted Parrish, and long before the breach came, he picked on me to act the spy on my employer. I, too, was born a gambler, but, like Marbran, I lacked the lucky touch which made Parrish a millionaire. Speculation proved my ruin. I have often thanked my God on my bended knees - as I shall do again to-night before I pass over - that my insane folly has ruined no one but myself ...

Already, when Hartley Parrish engaged me, I was up to the neck in speculation. Up to that time, however, I had managed to keep my head above water, but the large salary on which Parrish started me dazzled me. I tried a flutter in oil on a much larger scale than anything I had hitherto attempted, with the result that one day I found myself with a debt of nine hundred pounds to meet and no assets to meet it with. And I was two hundred pounds in debt to Hartley Parrish's petty cash account, which I kept.

It was Victor Marbran who came to my rescue. Parrish had sent me over to Rotterdam to fetch some papers from Marbran. At this time I knew nothing of Parrish's blockade-running business. Parrish never took me into his confidence about it and the whole of the correspondence went direct to him through a number of secret channels with which I only gradually became acquainted behind his back.

I had met Marbran several times in London and also at Rotterdam. It had struck me that he had formed a liking for me. On this particular visit to Rotterdam Marbran took me out to dinner and encouraged me to speak about myself. He was very sympathetic, and this, coupled with the wine I had taken, led me to open my heart to him. Without giving myself away, I let him understand that I was in considerable financial difficulties, which I set down to the high cost of living as the result of the war.

Without a word of warning Marbran pulled out his cheque-book.

"How much do you want," he asked, "to put you straight?"

Nine hundred pounds, I told him.

He wrote the cheque at once there at the table. He would advance me the money, he said, and put me down for shares in a business in which he was interested. It was a safe thing and profits were very high. I could repay him at my leisure.

In this way I became a shareholder in Parrish's blockade-running syndicate. The return I was to make was to spy on my employer and to report to Marbran the letters which Parrish received and the names of the people whom he interviewed.

Of course, Marbran did not propose this plan at once. When I took leave of him that night, I remember, I all but broke down at the thought of his unsolicited generosity. I have had a hard life, Miss Trevert, and his seeming kindness broke me all up.
But I might have known.

I cashed Marbran's cheque and put back the two hundred pounds I had taken from the petty cash account. But I went on speculating. You see, I did not believe Marbran's story about the shares he said he would put me down for. I thought it was a charitable tale to spare my feelings. So I plunged once more in the confident hope of recovering enough to repay my debt to Marbran.

A month later Marbran sent me a cheque for one hundred pounds. He said it was the balance of fifteen hundred pounds due to me as profits on my shares less the nine hundred pounds I owed him and five hundred pounds for my shares. But my specu-lations had by this time gone wrong again, and I was heartily glad presently to receive a further cheque for two hundred pounds from Marbran. From that time on I got from Marbran sums varying between one hundred and fifty pounds and five hundred pounds a month.

When Marbran made me his shameful offer, I rejected it with indignation. But I was fast in the trap. Marbran explained to me in great detail and with the utmost candour the working of the Parrish syndicate. He let me know very plainly that I was as deeply implicated as Parrish and he. I was a shareholder; I had received and was receiving my share of the profits. In my distress and shame I threatened to expose the pair of them. Had I known the source of his money, I told him, I should never have accepted it. At that Marbran laughed contemptuously.

"You tell that yarn to the police," he sneered, "and hear what they say!"

And then I realized that I was in the net.

I make no excuses for myself. I shall make none to the Great Judge before whom in a little while I shall appear. I had not the moral force to resist Marbran. I did his bidding: I continued to take his money and I held my peace.

And then came the breach between Parrish and Marbran. I was the cause of it. But for me, his trusty spy, Marbran would have known nothing of this payment of £150,000 which Parrish received from Spain, and this tragedy would not have happened. God forgive me ...

Marbran appealed to Parrish in vain. What he wrote I never knew, for, shortly after, Parrish quietly and without any explanation took the confidential work out of my hands. I believe he suspected then who Marbran's spy was. But he said nothing to me of his suspicions at that time ...

Finally, Marbran came to London. It was on Tuesday of last week. I had been up in Sheffield on business, and on my return I found Marbran waiting for me at my rooms.

He was like a man possessed. Never before have I witnessed such an outburst of ungovernable rage. Parrish, it appears, had declined to see him. He swore that Parrish should not get the better of him if he had to kill him first. I can see Marbran now as he sat on my bed, his livid face distorted with fury.

"I'll give him a last chance," he cried, "and then, by God, let our smart Alec look out!"

This sort of talk frightened me. I knew Marbran meant mischief. He was a bad man to cross. I was desperately afraid he would waylay Parrish and bring down disaster on the three of us. I did my utmost to put the idea of violence out of his mind. I begged him to content himself with trying to frighten Parrish into paying up before trying other means.

My suggestion seemed to awaken some old memory in Marbran's mind.

"By Gad, Jeekes," he said, after a moment's

thought, "you've given me an idea. Parrish has a yellow streak. He's scared of a gun. I saw it once, years ago, in a roughhouse we got into at Krugersdorp on the Rand. Damn it, I know how to bring the yellow dog to heel, and I'll tell you how we'll do it ..."

He then unfolded his plan. He would send Parrish a last demand for a settlement, threatening him with death if he did not pay up. The warning would reach Parrish on the following Saturday. Marbran would contrive that he should receive it by the first post. As soon as possible thereafter I was to go to Parrish boldly and demand his answer.

"And you'll take a gun," Marbran said, peering at me with his cunning little eyes, "and you'll show it. And if at the sight of it you don't get the brass, then I don't know my old pal, Mister Hartley Parrish, Esquire!"

The proposal appalled me. I knew nothing of Hartley Parrish's "yellow streak." I knew him only as a hard and resolute man, swift in decision and ruthless in action. Whatever happened, I argued, Parrish would discharge me and there was every prospect of his handing me over to the police as well.

Marbran was deaf to my reasoning. I had nothing to fear, he protested. Parrish would collapse at the first sign of force. And as for my losing my job, Marbran would find me another and a better one in his office at Rotterdam.

Still I held out. The chance of losing my position, even of being sent to gaol, daunted me less, I think, than the admission to Parrish of the blackly ungrateful role I had played towards him. In the end I told Marbran to do his dirty work himself.

But I spoke without conviction. I realized that Marbran held me in a cleft stick and that he realized it, too. He wasted no further time in argument. I knew what I had to do, he said, and I would do it. Otherwise ...

He left me in an agony of mental stress. At that time, I swear to Heaven, Miss Trevert, I was determined to let Marbran do his worst rather than lend myself to this odious blackmailing trick, my own suggestion, as I bitterly remembered. But for the rest of the week his parting threat rang in my ears. Unless he heard by the following Sunday that I had confronted Parrish and called his bluff, as he put it, the British police should have word, not only of Parrish's activities in trading with the enemy, but of mine as well.

It was no idle threat. Parrish and Marbran had put men away before. I could give you the names ...

It is quite dark now. It must be an hour since Greve took you away. Soon he will be back with the police to arrest me and I must have finished by then, finished with the story, finished with life ...

Last week I worked at Parrish's city office. I told you how he kept me off his confidential work. On Saturday morning I went round to the house in St. James's Square to see whether Marbran had really sent his warning. Archer, my colleague, who was acting as confidential secretary in my stead, was there. Parrish was at Harkings, he told me. Archer was going down by car that morning with his mail. It included two "blue letters" which Archer would, according to orders, hand to Parrish unopened.

These "blue letters," as we secretaries used to call them, written on a striking bluish paper, were the means by which all communications passed between Parrish and Marbran on the syndicate's business. They were drafted in conventional code and came to Parrish from all parts of Europe and in all kinds of ways. No one saw them except himself. By his strict injunctions, they were to be opened only by himself in person.

When Archer told me that two "blue letters" had come, I knew that Marbran had kept his word. Though my mind was not made up, instinct told me I was going to play my part ...

I could not face the shame of exposure. I was brought up in a decent English home. To stand in the dock charged with prolonging the sufferings of our soldiers and sailors in order to make money was a prospect I could not even contemplate.

I thought it all out that Saturday morning as I stood at the dressing-table in my bedroom by the open drawer in which my automatic pistol lay. It was one given me by Parrish some years before at a time when he thought we might be going on a trip to Rumania ...

I slipped the pistol into my pocket. I felt like a

man in a dream. I believe I went down to Harkings by train, but I have no clear recollection of the journey. I seemed to come to my senses only when I found myself standing on the high bank of the rosery at Harkings, looking down upon the library window.

Outside in the gardens it was nearly dark, but from the window fell a stream of subdued light. The curtains had not been drawn and the window was open at the bottom. Parrish sat at the desk. Only the desk-lamp was lit, so that his face was in shadow, but his two hands, stretched out on the blotter in front of him, lay in a pool of light, and I caught the gleam of his gold signet ring.

He was not writing or working. He seemed to be thinking. I watched him in a fascinated sort of way. I had never seen him sit thus idly at his desk before ...

My brain worked quite lucidly now. As I looked at him, I suddenly realised that I had a golden opportunity for speaking to him unobserved. The gardens were absolutely deserted: the library wing was very still. If he were a man to be frightened into submission, my sudden appearance, following upon the receipt of the threatening letter, would be likely to help in achieving this result.

I walked softly down the steps to the window. I stood close up to the sill.

"Mr. Parrish," I said, "Victor Marbran has sent me for his answer."

In a flash he was on his feet.

"Who's there?" he cried out in alarm.

His voice shook, and I could see his hand tremble in the lamplight as he clutched at the desk. Then I knew that he was badly frightened, and the discovery gave me courage.

"Are you going to settle with Marbran or are you not?" I said.

At that he peered forward. All of a sudden his manner changed.

"What in hell does this mean, Jeekes?"

His voice quavered no longer. It was hard and menacing.

But I had burnt my boats behind me now.

"It means," I answered boldly, "that you've got to pay up. And you've got to pay up now!"

In a couple of quick strides he was round the desk and coming at me as I stood with my chest pressing against the window-sill. His hands were thrust in his jacket pockets. His face was red with anger.

"You dawggorn dirty little rathole spy," - he spat the words at me in a low, threatening voice, - "I guessed that lowdown skunk Marbran had been getting at some of my people!"

His voice rose in a sudden gust of passion.

"You rotten little worm! You'd try and bounce me, would you? You've come to the wrong shop for that, Mr. Spying Jeekes ..."

His manner was incredibly insulting. So was the utter contempt with which he looked at me. This man, who had trembled with fear at the unknown, recovered his self-control on finding that the menace came from the menial, the hireling, he despised. I felt the blood rush in a hot flood to my head. I lost all self-control. I screamed aloud at him.

"There's no bounce about it this time! If you don't pay up, you know what to expect!"

I had been holding my pistol out of his sight below the window-ledge, but on this I swung it up and levelled it at him.

He sprang back a pace, the colour fading on the instant from his face, his mouth twisted awry in a horrid paroxysm of fear. Even in that subdued light I could see that his cheeks were as white as paper.

But then in a flash his right hand went up. I saw the pistol he held, but before I could make a movement there was a loud, raucous hiss of air and a bullet whistled past my ear into the darkness of the gardens. How he missed me at that range I don't know, but, seeing me standing there, he came at me again with the pistol in his hand ...

And then you, Miss Trevert, cried out, "Hartley," and rattled the handle of the door. Your cry merged in a deafening report. Parrish, who was quite close to me, and advancing, stopped short with a little startled exclamation, his eyes reproachful, full of surprise. He stood there and swayed, looking at me all the time, then crashed backwards on the floor. And I found myself staring at the smoking pistol in my hand ...

It was your scream that brought me to my senses. My mind cleared instantly. I knew I must act quickly. The house would be alarmed directly, and before that happened, I must be clear of the grounds. Yet I knew that before I went I must do something to make myself safe ...

I stood at the window staring down at the dead man. His eyes were terrible. Like a suicide he looked, I thought. And then it flashed across my mind that only one shot had been heard and that our pistols were identical and fired the same ammunition. The silencer! The silencer could save me. With that removed, the suicide theory might pass muster: at any rate, it would delay other investigations and give me a start ...

In a matter of a second or two I believe I thought of everything. I did not overlook the danger of leaving finger-prints or foot-marks about. I had not taken off my gloves, and my boots were perfectly dry. In climbing into the room I was most careful to see that I did not mark the window-sill or scratch the paintwork ...

I stood beside the body and I caught the dead

man's hand. It was fat and soft and still warm. The touch of it made me reel with horror. I turned my face away from his so as not to see his eyes again....

I got the silencer. Parrish had shown it to me and I knew how to detach it....

I went back through the window as carefully as I had come in. And I pushed the window down. Parrish would have done that, I thought, if he had meant to commit suicide. And then my nerve went. The window frightened me. The blank glass with the silent room beyond; - it reminded me of Parrish's sightless gaze. I turned and ran....

I did not mean to kill. As there is a God in ...

On that unfinished sentence the confessionended.

*   *   *   *   *

Mr. Bardy put the bundle of manuscript down on the desk and, dropping his eyeglass from his eye, caught it deftly and began to polish it vigorously with his pocket handkerchief. As no one spoke, he said:

"That's all. It ends there!"

He looked round the circle of earnest faces. Then Horace Trevert crossed to the desk.

"Robin," he said, and held out his hand, "I want to apologize. I ... we ... behaved very badly ..."

Robin grasped the boy's hand.

"Not a word about that, Horace, old boy," he said. "Besides, Mary is putting all that right, you know!"

"She told me," replied Horace; "and, Robin, I'm tremendously glad!"

"Mr. Greve!"

Robin turned to find Mr. Manderton, large and impressive, at his elbow.

"Might I have a word with you?"

Robin followed the detective across the room to the window.

Mr. Manderton seemed a trifle embarrassed.

"Er - Mr. Greve," he said, clearing his throat rather nervously, "I should like to - er, - offer you my congratulations on the remarkably accurate view you took of this case. I should have been able to prove to you, I believe, but for this curious interruption, that your view and mine practically coincided. It has been a pleasure to work with you, sir!"

He cast a hasty glance over his shoulder at the other occupants of the room, who were gathered round the desk.

"I'm not a society man, Mr. Greve," he added, "and I have a lot of work on my hands regarding the case. So I think I'll run off now ..."

He broke off, gave Robin a large hand, and, looking neither to right nor to left, made a hurried exit from the room, taking Inspector Humphries with him.

"Now that we are just among ourselves" - the solicitor was speaking - "I think I may seize the opportunity of saying a word about Mr. Parrish's will. Miss Trevert, as you know, is made principal legatee, but I understand from her that she does not propose to accept the inheritance. I will not comment on this decision of hers, which does her moral sense, at any rate, infinite credit, but I should observe that Mr. Parrish has left directions for the payment of an allowance - I may say, a most handsome allowance - to Lady Margaret Trevert during her ladyship's lifetime. This is a provision over which Miss Trevert's decision, of course, can have no influence. I would only remark that, according to Mr. Parrish's instructions, this allowance will be paid from the dividends on a percentage of his holdings in Hornaway's under the new scheme. I have not yet had an opportunity of looking further into Mr. Parrish's affairs in the light of the information which Mr. Greve obtained in Rotterdam, but I have reason to believe that he kept his interest in Hornaway's and his - ahem! - other activities entirely separate. If this can be definitely established to my own satisfaction and to yours, my dear Miss Trevert, I see no reason why you should not modify your decision at least in respect of Mr. Parrish's interest in Hornaway's."

Mary Trevert looked at Robin and then at the solicitor.

"No!" she said; "not a penny as far as I am concerned. With Mother the case is different. I told her last night of my decision in the matter. She disapproves of it. That is why she is not here to-day. But my mind is made up."

Mr. Bardy adjusted his eyeglass in his eye and gazed at the girl. His face wore an expression of pain mingled with compassion.

"I will see Lady Margaret after lunch," he said rather stiffly.

Then the door opened and Bude appeared.

"Luncheon is served, Miss!"

He stood there, a portly, dignified figure in sober black, solemn of visage, sonorous of voice, a living example of the triumph of established tradition over the most savage buffetings of Fate. His enunciation was, if anything, more mellow, his demeanour more pontifical than of yore.

Bude was once more in the service of a County Family.

Choose from Thousands of 1stWorldLibrary Classics By

Adolphus WilliamWard
Aesop
Agatha Christie
Alexander Aaronsohn
Alexander Kielland
Alexandre Dumas
Alfred Gatty
Alfred Ollivant
Alice Duer Miller
Alice Turner Curtis
Alice Dunbar
Ambrose Bierce
Amelia E. Barr
Andrew Lang
Andrew McFarland Davis
Anna Sewell
Annie Besant
Annie Hamilton Donnell
Annie Payson Call
Anton Chekhov
Arnold Bennett
Arthur Conan Doyle
Arthur Ransome
Atticus
B. M. Bower
Basil King
Bayard Taylor
Ben Macomber
Booth Tarkington
Bram Stoker
C. Collodi
C. E. Orr
C. M. Ingleby
Carolyn Wells
Catherine Parr Traill
Charles A. Eastman
Charles Dickens
Charles Dudley Warner
Charles Farrar Browne
Charles Ives
Charles Kingsley
Charles Lathrop Pack
Charles Whibley
Charles Willing Beale
Charlotte M. Braeme
Charlotte M.Yonge
Clair W. Hayes
Clarence Day Jr.
Clarence E. Mulford

Clemence Housman
Confucius
Cornelis DeWitt Wilcox
Cyril Burleigh
D. H. Lawrence
Daniel Defoe
David Garnett
Don Carlos Janes
Donald Keyhole
Dorothy Kilner
Dougan Clark
E. Nesbit
E.P.Roe
E. Phillips Oppenheim
Edgar Allan Poe
Edgar Rice Burroughs
Edith Wharton
Edward J. O'Biren
John Cournos
Edwin L. Arnold
Eleanor Atkins
Elizabeth Cleghorn
Gaskell
Elizabeth Von Arnim
Ellem Key
Emily Dickinson
Erasmus W. Jones
Ernie Howard Pie
Ethel Turner
Ethel Watts Mumford
Eugenie Foa
Eugene Wood
Evelyn Everett-Green
Everard Cotes
F. J. Cross
Federick Austin Ogg
Ferdinand Ossendowski
Francis Bacon
Francis Darwin
Frances Hodgson Burnett
Frank Gee Patchin
Frank Harris
Frank Jewett Mather
Frank L. Packard
Frederick Trevor Hill
Frederick Winslow Taylor
Friedrich Kerst
Friedrich Nietzsche
Fyodor Dostoyevsky

Gabrielle E. Jackson
Garrett P. Serviss
Gaston Leroux
George Ade
Geroge Bernard Shaw
George Ebers
George Eliot
George MacDonald
George Orwell
George Tucker
George W. Cable
George Wharton James
Gertrude Atherton
Grace E. King
Grant Allen
Guillermo A. Sherwell
Gulielma Zollinger
Gustav Flaubert
H. A. Cody
H. B. Irving
H. G. Wells
H. H. Munro
H. Irving Hancock
H. Rider Haggard
H. W. C. Davis
Hamilton Wright Mabie
Hans Christian Andersen
Harold Avery
Harold McGrath
Harriet Beecher Stowe
Harry Houidini
Helent Hunt Jackson
Helen Nicolay
Hendy David Thoreau
Henrik Ibsen
Henry Adams
Henry Ford
Henry Frost
Henry James
Henry Jones Ford
Henry Seton Merriman
Henry Wadsworth
Longfellow
Henry W Longfellow
Herbert A. Giles
Herbert N. Casson
Herman Hesse
Homer
Honore De Balzac

Horace Walpole
Horatio Alger, Jr.
Howard Pyle
Howard R. Garis
Hugh Lofting
Hugh Walpole
Humphry Ward
Ian Maclaren
Israel Abrahams
J.G.Austin
J. Henri Fabre
J. M. Barrie
J. Macdonald Oxley
J. S. Knowles
J. Storer Clouston
Jack London
Jacob Abbott
James Allen
James Lane Allen
James Andrews
James Baldwin
James DeMille
James Joyce
James Oliver Curwood
James Oppenheim
James Otis
Jane Austen
Jens Peter Jacobsen
Jerome K. Jerome
John Burroughs
John F. Kennedy
John Gay
John Glasworthy
John Habberton
John Joy Bell
John Milton
John Philip Sousa
Jonathan Swift
Joseph Carey
Joseph Conrad
Joseph Jacobs
Julian Hawthrone
Julies Vernes
Justin Huntly McCarthy
Kakuzo Okakura
Kenneth Grahame
Kate Langley Bosher
L. A. Abbot
L. T. Meade
L. Frank Baum
Laura Lee Hope

Laurence Housman
Leo Tolstoy
Leonid Andreyev
Lewis Carroll
Lilian Bell
Lloyd Osbourne
Louis Tracy
Louisa May Alcott
Lucy Fitch Perkins
Lucy Maud Montgomery
Lydia Miller Middleton
Lyndon Orr
M. H. Adams
Margaret E. Sangster
Margaret Vandercook
Maria Edgeworth
Maria Thompson Daviess
Mariano Azuela
Marion Polk Angellotti
Mark Overton
Mark Twain
Mary Austin
Mary Cole
Mary Rowlandson
Mary Wollstonecraft
Shelley
Max Beerbohm
Myra Kelly
Nathaniel Hawthrone
O. F. Walton
Oscar Wilde
Owen Johnson
P.G.Wodehouse
Paul and Mable Thorn
Paul G. Tomlinson
Paul Severing
Peter B. Kyne
Plato
R. Derby Holmes
R. L. Stevenson
Rabindranath Tagore
Rahul Alvares
Ralph Waldo Emmerson
Rene Descartes
Rex E. Beach
Richard Harding Davis
Richard Jefferies
Robert Barr
Robert Frost
Robert Gordon Anderson
Robert L. Drake

Robert Lansing
Robert Michael Ballantyne
Robert W. Chambers
Rosa Nouchette Carey
Ross Kay
Rudyard Kipling
Samuel B. Allison
Samuel Hopkins Adams
Sarah Bernhardt
Selma Lagerlof
Sherwood Anderson
Sigmund Freud
Standish O'Grady
Stanley Weyman
Stella Benson
Stephen Crane
Stewart Edward White
Stijn Streuvels
Swami Abhedananda
Swami Parmananda
T. S. Ackland
The Princess Der Ling
Thomas A. Janvier
Thomas A Kempis
Thomas Anderton
Thomas Bailey Aldrich
Thomas Bulfinch
Thomas De Quincey
Thomas H. Huxley
Thomas Hardy
Thomas More
Thornton W. Burgess
U. S. Grant
Valentine Williams
Victor Appleton
Virginia Woolf
Walter Scott
Washington Irving
Wilbur Lawton
Wilkie Collins
Willa Cather
Willard F. Baker
William Makepeace
Thackeray
William W. Walter
Winston Churchill
Yei Theodora Ozaki
Young E. Allison
Zane Grey

www.ingramcontent.com/pod-product-compliance
Lightning Source LLC
Chambersburg PA
CBHW021309250626
47155CB00002B/444